Jessica Cameron

CORPUS

This book is dedicated to my mum, who enjoyed the paranormal, spiritual side of life and binge watching crime shows. Missed more than words can describe, and forever loved.

Prologue

Death. It is at best a hard subject for many and off limits for some. Many of the world's population ignore it and pretend that the inevitable ever approaching end will not reach them or those they love if they avoid acknowledging it, as though that will make it not exist. Death is something you will experience in all paths of life and it will affect every individual at some point, with no prior warning or choice in the matter. Well, sometimes people get the warning that their death is imminent but in those cases every individual behaves differently but typically in one of three ways.

Some appreciate the heads up and live the last of their days doing things they'd always wanted to do but put off, whilst others spend the last of their time mourning what they will miss instead of trying to make the most of the time left. The last way is simply living in denial, as though the looming expiry date they had been given was never uttered, and life could continue its original uneventful course.

As is to be expected, the majority of the world's population find death in any form to be a scary prospect. To face ones demise is surely terrifying but it is your perspective of death that will either trap or free your soul. The invisible tether that binds us here to the earth cannot be broken if the soul is unable or unwilling to accept that the time has come to move on.

What many fear with dying is the very event itself, not what comes after. Does it hurt? How long for? Do you know it is happening? Do you consciously feel your lungs inhaling their last ragged breath, hear your heart pumping its last weakened beat or your brain sending off its final signals to tell your body it doesn't need to do anything more, the end is here? Does your life flash before your eyes and if so do you accept death in its entirety, or do you fight for the life you had and death has to haul you away kicking and screaming? Or maybe, just maybe, sometimes it is just like falling asleep. Most don't even know death is coming for them and can't prepare for it, its shadowy form lurking around the next corner eager to take them in its icy grip for eternity whether they feel ready or not.

Some can't handle death and its closely guarded secrets, but there are others with the opposite mind-set, they welcome it – even long for it. The unknown facets of death offering little to no fear value for them. They are thankful for it as it is a respite from the pain of living, their mental or physical burdens having become too much. They may even beg for the end, the idea of leaving loved ones behind and bereft not enough to make them want to stay a minute longer. People can now pay to be released from life's embrace, in facilities that allow you to choose to leave this plane using a dose of an antiemetic drug followed by a liquid overdose of pentobarbital.

Death can be a curse, and a gift. It's all down to perspective, but it is one thing that can be given, and not taken. Not like life. Once the gift of death has been delivered there are no go backs, no refunds. Every day thousands of people die, but also thousands are brought into this world and the balance of life on earth is restored. When death occurs it is argued that the soul contained within the vessel we call a body is then freed into the universe. Some souls go to 'the other side' whilst others linger on, stuck in limbo sometimes not even sure themselves why they've not gone anywhere. Whether the cause is not accepting death, or not fulfilling ones' purpose, we will never know for sure.

This is what happened to Martha Tawn's son. His death came about in an abrupt manner, without warning, and left his family and friends wishing for the return of their loved one. What follows is the story of what became of

Steven Tawn's soul, and the lengths a mother will go to keep her child with her.

Chapter One

Steven Tawn was not quite your average man for a few reasons but not all of them were obvious at first glance. He was adept at many things and yet chose to avoid those skill sets that came so easily to him, and instead embarked on a very different path to that which the most of his family and childhood friends had taken. His dislike for having anyone try to direct him or hold an expectation of him caused him to make a string of rebellious choices in life. He was twenty-four, well-built and had a select group of associates. He had no job and no desire to get one as his steady - if risky - stream of income already lined his low-slung denim pockets. Steven found it easy to fit in seamlessly with certain groups of people in his area who sought hand-outs just for being alive in this world, whilst they themselves also garnered income from illicit means.

He came from a large family, close-knit and always together for family holidays and events. He was particularly close to his mum, she had raised him by herself after his father decided parenting wasn't for him and skipped town without so much as a glance back. That suited them fine as he didn't know how it felt to have a father and so didn't miss it. Society would probably later down the road imply that not having a father figure in his life combined with him and his mum occasionally falling on hard times will have led on to his questionable choices in life. But his mother had always done her upmost to keep him safe and on the straight and narrow.

In spite of her best efforts he led a life full of petty crime and fighting in the streets, his street reputation having more significance to him than anything else. He had started smoking and hanging around in the wrong crowds at a young age, having been scouted by the older boys who loitered on the street corner near the school. It all escalated from there and he was vetted to become a dealer for someone whose name he didn't even know at the start. He had to learn how to blend in whilst toeing the line between being respected and feared. Above all else he learned to protect his reputation as an unyielding man, someone not to be messed around.

Not many made it to where he was, they ended up dead or out of the game. For the most part people readily accepted his position because the few who thought they could mess with him, had often paid a hefty price. But this reputation and his own cockiness was his own downfall as one day, whilst selling a packet of the 'dopest' weed, he chose to stand his ground with the wrong person. Young lad led astray by elders, smoking pot and starting to deal to cover the costs of a growing habit and get extra cash. Then getting stuck owing money to the wrong people and not being able to get out of the debt because they'd smoke the profits time and time again, thinking they could make it up in the next batch. A never ending loop of being under the hand of those who ranked above them in the streets. There was also the addictive yet false godlike feeling the sellers would get from having a string of 'good' luck by not getting caught or beaten, then as a direct result cockily crossing or pushing the wrong person and then enduring the inescapable bout of bad luck, something that could come in many forms and severities.

Steven Tawn ended up being one of the unfortunates after a long run with luck, he became the main character in the commonly told sad story involving another premature death in a troubled area. For him it was all thanks to a man looking for a cheap fix who didn't get the deal that he wanted, even using his own position in the streets to try and push him. He became aggressive towards Steven, and naturally Steven had refused to back down and look the weaker person in front of his peers. What he couldn't have known was the man had concealed a blade up his sleeve, and had no qualms about brandishing and using it. It cut effortlessly into Steven's femoral artery and he died within minutes, before the ambulance had even been called – let alone arrived to help.

His so-called friends had scattered out of sight, realising they shouldn't talk to officers whilst their pockets were laden with illicit goods and donning pupils as wide as their irises. The perpetrator was gone before Steven had hit the ground, having suddenly registered in his foggy mind that he had acted hastily where a messy brawl could have probably sufficed. As ever the realisation that a different reaction would have been better is always in hindsight, people always think of a better way to have dealt with something after the fact, because in the moment they're fuelled by adrenaline and act on their first impulses without any thought as to the consequences that will be incurred. Now there was more blood spilt on the streets and another statistic sprawled on the pavement getting colder as his blood pooled out onto the speckled slabs underneath him.

When the police finally arrived on the scene there wasn't much sympathy offered, it was another run of the mill stabbing associated with dealers. Yet more paperwork that they had to fill out far too often. They had become hardened to the fact that this was another life lost, someone dying too young at the hands of another in a troubled area, a person who would never go home and see their family again or utter another word. No one could now say if this was a man who had lost his way, or was born for this path as there was no redemption for him now. Or was there?

Chapter Two

Everything was surreal and his senses were overloaded. There was a distant crackling noise somewhere and his vision struggled to stay in focus. Steven blinked rapidly, crunching his weighted eyelids closed in a bid to aid his impaired vision, it seemed to work and he could make out more of what was around him. Quickly realising he was standing, he looked down at what appeared to be a gurney and frowned whilst confusion rippled through him in tingly waves. He tried to remember where he was and why he was looking down at this lumpy hospital bed. He felt intensely cold, the iciness was set deep inside his bones, even a steaming hot bath wouldn't alleviate the chill.

He was aware of an unsettling sensation of being lost, and aside from the obvious he wasn't sure why he had that feeling. He didn't know where he was or how he even got here, he had no recollection of anything. Had he been out partying? No, he would at least remember going out, unless him and Shells had hit it hard beforehand. He assessed his surroundings, he was in a large square room painted an off white colour. He was pretty sure that the gurney in front of him had a dead person on it looked a lot like a body. Or maybe someone was playing a prank and they were just waiting for the best moment to leap out and surprise him, which wasn't so funny. If that was what this was he would make them pay, people knew not to mess him around, he hadn't earned the nickname Brute for no reason.

He considered looking under the sheet to see if it was a body, but despite his hardened nature, a light fear of death and potentially seeing a dead body in all its glory set his teeth on edge. It was different when you saw someone get hit on the streets, it was quick, and you dashed. If there was a dead person under that sheet he would be voluntarily facing off with the deceased, and who knew how long they'd have been gone and what changes they'll have gone through. He needed to get out of here, wherever here was.

Steven turned to face the door on his right, and winced at the row of a further three gurneys lined up the other side of the room, all with white sheets covering very human body shaped lumps – he didn't spot those when he initially glanced around. This place was giving him the creeps, and he was now sure it wasn't some prank, he must have somehow got himself in a room of dead people on one of his benders. He made to open the door, hand poised ready to turn the brass handle, and he cried out in surprise when his hand passed straight through it as though it wasn't there.

"What the hell?!" he shouted out.

Maybe this was a dream, he couldn't remember going to sleep, couldn't remember coming here. Couldn't remember anything really, only that he had been out dealing at some point and then nothing. Blankness. He strained his mind and couldn't come up with anything. He tried the door again but once more his hand slipped straight through with no resistance, he stared in fascination as his hand went through solid wood. Either this was a dream or he was really high and this was some elaborate trip. He could feel the wood grain scraping over his skin painlessly, the grooves reminded him of holding his fingers lightly on a turning record. He assessed his hands. Clapped them together. They kind of worked, they made an impact but no audible sound. He waved his arm aggressively towards the wall, and then the leg of the gurney, then the silver sink in the corner. He went straight through everything like it was nothing, everything except himself lacked substance. Despite the rapidly increasing alarm he found himself enjoying the strange sensation of being able to move through solid objects. A childlike glee bubbled up inside him and he had to remember to keep his cool, he still hadn't worked out what on earth was going on here.

Steven abruptly stopped, an instinct deep within him telling him to halt and pay attention. He always tried to listen to that inner voice, it had gotten him out of sticky situations a fair few times. He tilted his head while looking to the door, unsure of what he could hear and realised that the distant crackling noise from before had faded away to almost nothing now. What he could hear now was that someone was click clacking with intent towards this room, and he was glad, because he had some questions that needed answering. One of which was why he had suddenly lost the ability to touch things, just as he thought about that he realised something and directed his sudden guffaw inwards – it was all a projection! That was why he couldn't physically touch or smell things, this was a seriously elaborate plan to achieve what? Pranking him? Unnerving him? He stood tall and puffed his chest out to show the person coming in that they hadn't fazed him with this puerile game they were playing. He waited with baited breath as the footsteps got closer and closer, watching the door handle to see when it moved and he would potentially have to spring into action. He realised there were multiple sets of footsteps and he began to flex his hands in preparation, not sure how many people were on the approach but there were at least two.

    The handle turned with a click and the door swung inwards without pause, to gain the advantage of surprise Steven leapt to one side into the view of the door ready to startle the incoming people. His actions faltered though when he realised who was there, it was a nurse he had never seen before but that wasn't the person who surprised him, it was his mum. There was something wrong and he took three quick steps forwards to take her hands in his and speak with her but horror crashed through him when his dishevelled looking mother stepped forwards at the same time and passed straight through his outstretched arms. The reality unfolding before him was unthinkable and Steven refused to accept what was becoming more and more obvious. It had been a minor tingling thought a few minutes ago but he had dismissed it, because it didn't seem right to him. Didn't feel like it could be true, he wasn't done yet. He couldn't be beaten, he was Brute. This must all be some kind of strange projection, or a nightmare, it just had to be.

"Mum!" his voice not making a sound.

He could feel his whole form crackling with the strength of the emotions coursing through him. He stared on helplessly, the tsunami of emotions getting too much for him to handle as he watched his mum approach the gurney he had been stood in front of when he gained consciousness. The reality was becoming too close, too real. He couldn't handle what he knew was about to happen,

"No, no, NO!" he shouted, but neither the nurse or his mum reacted to his increasingly frantic cries.

The nurse held her hand up in a gesture to make his mum wait, and she quickly and unceremoniously pulled part of the sheet back to reveal a blue tinged foot with a tag wrapped around the big toe. The nurse examined it quickly and nodded discreetly to herself. His mum was standing there barely containing herself, wringing her hands and chewing the insides of her cheeks to shreds. She always did that when something was upsetting her.

"Mum! It's ok! I'm here!" he croaked, knowing by now she couldn't hear him but unable to hold back.

All his bravado he usually carried with him was long gone. He stared at her, wondering what he should do, as he watched the nurse pull the sheet back from the face of the person on the gurney. He didn't want to look at all but the morbidity of it pulled him even closer and he found himself stood next to his mum, looking down at his own pallid features. His eyes were closed though, thankfully. Empty eyes were something he avoided looking at, and he had a feeling that seeing his own may be just too much right now whilst he was trying to process everything. His mum was silently crying, rubbing her thumb over his cheek and whispering she loved him the 'mostest' – something he had always said to her since he was a kid. The grief hung heavy in the air and the nurse excused herself for a moment to give his mum some privacy. Steven wondered what had happened and why he was stuck here watching all of this. He had heard that when you die, if you have unfinished business you cannot move on. He wondered if this was what was happening, if this was all actually happening. He still retained a little hope that he would come around on a scruffy beanbag soon on the other side of a hard trip.

"I will find the man who did this to you and we will make him pay my son, mark my words." She said quietly, the tears drying on her cheeks and her face taking on a determined and angry expression.

So, someone did this to him. He wondered who, he had been doing his job well, and wasn't stepping on anyone else's turf so it wasn't likely to be that. Maybe a deal gone wrong? Then the memory hit him with such force he had to focus to make sense of it. It was Yeti! His real name was Jake, an oversized, bad tempered thug. He lived in a studio flat with smashed out windows, which he never fixed because he didn't feel the cold. Steven could remember it now with full clarity. He shoved down the sadness and anger that bubbled when he realised this was really happening.

Yeti had come to get a bag, and wanted to get half off the asking price because of who he was. Obviously Steven wasn't going to take that and Yeti didn't like the answer no. He could now recall the glint of the flick-blade as Yeti yanked it out of his sleeve and whipped it open in a fluid motion and thrust it forward into his thigh before he could react. The sudden shock of pain had sent him to the ground and the next thing he knew, well, he was here. He must have bled out. He hoped his mates took Yeti out. Maybe they hadn't. He had to find out as he had a feeling that was why he was still here and not kicking back somewhere else enjoying the afterlife he'd seen in the movies. Rage bubbled through him. This wasn't fair. It wasn't supposed to be like this. How could he be dead? He was twenty-four! His mother stood before him heartbroken, the loss of her child dulling her very being despite simmering with all the overwhelming emotions. The fury boiled up inside of him to the point it felt like a physical mass and he couldn't contain it. He felt it gathering in his core and the pressure was immense, something gave and to his surprise it burst forth from his chest in a wave and the sheet that covered him was swept up and away in the gust. His mum spun on her heel in surprise and frowned. She looked at to her sons inert body, the heavily bloodstained jeans that they hadn't even bothered to remove yet, then back to where Steven stood holding his breath.

"Steven?" she whispered, barely audible.

Steven opened his mouth to answer but nothing came out, instead he reached forwards and stroked his mum's cheek and to his surprise she tilted her head as though she felt it. She allowed herself a quick lip tremble and whimper before standing tall again and speaking clearly.

"I knew you wouldn't leave me. I just knew you'd be here. You're a strong lad, we can fix this together my boy, you'll see. Just trust in your mum, she knows what she is doing."

He didn't know what to think nor say. He was a bit taken aback at the lack of reaction his mum gave at interacting with him as a ghost. Either she believed it wholeheartedly and was taking it in her stride, was in shock and didn't really register what just happened, or assumed the stress was too much and her mind was playing tricks. She had mentioned to him in the past that she had to tell the voices to leave her alone and they did, most of the time. The door knocked and opened, the nurse poked her head in apologetically,

"The police are here to talk to you Mrs Tawn, they're waiting for you outside." She spotted the sheet laying behind Steven Tawn's body and tutted, "I should have said, please refrain from removing the sheets entirely. It isn't necessary for the identification."

This earned a harsh look from Martha Tawn and the nurse realised her lack of tact and backed out of the room again, holding the door open for her to follow. With one glance back at the empty vessel that was once her son, Martha stepped out with the nurse, followed closely by Steven. Only problem was, as he got to the other side of the doorframe, everything faded from his vision and went black.

Chapter Three

Martha stood in front of the two police officers, both of whom looked bored and restless. She already sensed she didn't need to waste her breath on them as they were just here to jot down the basic information and leave this statistic in a dusty file somewhere never to be reopened. She had over the years interacted with many officers who had been trying to find a speck of arrest worthy information on Steven and she never gave them anything, she never did. No matter what she thought of what her son had gotten himself into she would always protect him. He was her baby and he had been through enough growing up in hard times with her. Sure they'd always had family around, but it wasn't the same and she knew it. But she did now need to break the awful news of her son passing to said family and they'd be devastated. Despite his street reputation he was still her boy. In his family home he kept a different persona, that was the one they all loved and would now sorely miss. She swore to herself that she would make whoever took him from her pay, no matter the cost to herself.

"Ma'am? Can you confirm your name and relation to the … eh … victim?" One of the officers was saying.

His reluctance to call him a victim despite the fact he died at the hands of a blade wielding murderer infuriated her but she just stared him down and answered dully,

"Martha Tawn. Mother."

"And the person you just viewed was in fact your son, Steven Tawn?" he pressed, Martha looked at his name badge before answering.

"Yes, officer Bridges. Tell me, how old are you?" she asked, and took some pleasure in watching both officers exchange a confused glance.

"Thank you. I am twenty-seven, Mrs Tawn." He replied tersely, she was surprised he answered without hesitation.

"Well, my son was just twenty-four. Three years younger than you are now. He was a loving man, with a loving family. Don't assume he isn't a victim because of other things in his life. Tell me, if that person in there laying cold and motionless was your brother or your father would you still scoff at the idea they were a victim just because of other circumstances? No matter what, my son was still stabbed and he died defenceless and alone in a gutter, and has now been stuffed in a back room of a hospital with other lost souls who have been cast aside."

Officer Bridges stared at the floor, embarrassment flushed his face at being taught such a lesson by the mother of a victim. He looked up eventually and met her eye,

"Apologies Ma'am, I didn't mean to infer that Steven Tawn was not a victim, it was a slip of the tongue. It was insensitive and you are correct." His co-worker nodded dutifully at this and stepped in,

"Do you know the events that preceded your sons untimely demise?" officer Gord asked.

"No, he left home around midday after lunch with me, told me he was off to meet some people. Next thing I have is a phone call asking me to come and identify my son." Martha's voice broke as she said this, again the reality of the situation hit her and she struggled to maintain her composure.

"Do you know who could be responsible for this?" he asked her.

Martha shook her head in response, knowing that if she spoke her voice would be barely above a whisper. She didn't know anything yet, but that would change soon, she would make sure of it.

"Ok. We are sorry for your loss. If you do think of anything at all, please contact the station and ask for officer Gord or Bridges as we will be dealing with this case. As I'm sure you can appreciate, due to the nature of the case we would appreciate it if you allowed us to do our jobs in finding the culprit and avoid putting yourself in dangers way." He said.

Martha nodded slowly, feeling words would be too painful and unnecessary at this point. She still had to go home and inform the others that their cousin/nephew/grandchild was dead. Dread filled her and joined the heavy grief that sat in her core, her heart and stomach felt as though they were laden with slowly setting concrete. She thought back on being in the room with Steven and knew without a shadow of a doubt that he had been in there with her. She needed to aid him to contact her properly and knew it would take some time, then she could get the answers she needed to exact the justice he deserved. The officers patted themselves down and bid farewell, then promptly left Martha standing alone in the side room of the waiting area in the hospital.

As the door closed the sob that had been barely suppressed burst out of her, after the phone call she had still maintained hope that it was a mistake and this wasn't happening. Not to her son. Her family. Her. But it was, this was the reality. Standing alone for the first time since the news her poise crumbled, her façade of togetherness fell away as swiftly as a leaf being swept off by the wind. She allowed herself to cry for a while as she knew full well that bottling it all up would only result in disaster. Once she felt drained, she stood to leave and again felt someone was in the room with her. She looked around but couldn't see anything, and knew it didn't make sense to try and reach Steven yet, not properly anyway. Neither of them were ready for that but she took comfort from the fact she felt his presence again and made her way out of the hospital, and back to her home.

****

Steven had stood behind his mum, watching her cry. He wasn't sure what had happened or how he had arrived in this room with her. It was like he blinked and teleported somewhere new. He assumed his mum had had her interview already with the police, as they weren't here and she was just gathering herself up ready to leave. He saw her looking for him, and he felt his sadness and anger build again for the whole situation. He wanted to be able to speak to her. He tried, he even started shouting but Martha just stood and walked right past him, oblivious to his attempts. Frustration coursed through him then everything faded out and started turning dark, although he tried to blink it away so he could follow his mum home, it enveloped and took him away again.

Chapter Four

Instead of coming back into a room like he had the first two times Steven found himself on a racing journey which he could only think to describe as a wild trip. Imagery and sounds blurred together and became one smudgy mess and abruptly tore apart to show him a scene from his childhood where he was playing with his cousins, then the image contorted and ripped into shreds. There was blackness for less than a second then a new scene came of him as a really small boy, crying at a chipped wooden door and his mum crouched beside him comforting him, he barely recognised her with black hair and a tight perm. Blackness. His mum sweating in the kitchen of their maisonette trying to cook dinner whilst he ran circles around her crashing his wooden train into her thighs. Blackness. A family gathering where his nanna Jess was berating his mother who simply hung her head in defeat. Blackness. His mum in what seemed to be present time sitting with everyone in their front room, he couldn't hear what she was saying over the loud crackling that filled his ears but his instinct told him she was breaking the news of his death. Blackness. His mum finding him with a joint hanging out of his window and screaming at him, her spittle spraying in slow motion towards him as he put his hand up to defend himself from the verbal onslaught. Blackness. Tidge, the boy who gave him his first joint exposing his yellowed teeth in a grimace as he told Steven he owed him now and had to sell this bag or else. Blackness. Hammering his fist into some nameless guy who'd pissed him off. Blackness. Tidge being pounded into the pavement by Runner, who became his new boss. Blackness. His family in present time all hanging their heads with tear streaked faces, two of his younger cousins being comforted by nanna Jess, whilst his mum sat alone, watching it all with a tormented expression. Blackness.

Steven waited for something new to come, like his present day life, his murder, what was happening now. But nothing came. The inkiness was overwhelming and he tried to move or make a sound, but nothing was happening. He felt something tingling in his forearms and focused on them, wishing them into being. Something moved, he felt it, it was the most physical sensation he had experienced since standing over his own dead body. He pushed harder, and suddenly with a loud banging noise both of his hands shot forwards and into something hard. Steven gasped. Maybe this whole thing had really been a bad trip like he initially thought.

    He realised he was laying down and fought back the panic that started to build up. Throwing his arms up once more he smashed into whatever was above him again, only this time his right hand went through it with a cracking splintering noise, it was deafening in the silence. He shouted out in triumph, but it fell flat when he realised he now couldn't pull his right arm back. The panic threatened to overtake him and he forced it away knowing it wouldn't help anything. He regathered himself and ignored his right arm for now and pushed up hard with his left hoping to break whatever was trapping him. It gave almost instantly but trapped his other arm too. It was strange as he couldn't feel any pressure or pain he was just unable to retract his arms. As soon as he registered the lack of sensation he felt something shift and just like that he was able to move again. He instantly sat upright in the darkness only marginally surprised that his head didn't hit the same obstacle his arms had. He was already realising with a sore heart that this wasn't real again, and instead of trying to work out what was what he decided to just tackle each moment head on. He carried on pushing upwards using invisible footholds and handholds to progress and lift his seemingly weightless body upwards, all whilst wondering what was happening and why.

    Steven became aware of a strange taste, it was acrid. He tried to move his tongue around to test the flavour further but discovered he didn't seem to have a tongue to give that command to and ignored the eerie feeling that the thought conjured. Though it was difficult to tell he was sure he could see something light above him and gave one final heave to launch himself up, with a strange swooshing sensation he found himself out in daylight. He cast his gaze around and saw the retreating backs of a group of people, all dressed in black and walking away through a graveyard brimming with mossy headstones interspersed with the odd bright new one here and there. The realisation of where he was and why hit him with a sickening thud, and he became grateful for the fact he had been unable to see around him before. He had been in his own grave, and the cracking wood was him smashing through his own coffin. The significance of that he wasn't sure, but it made him shiver to think he had just laid in a wooden box with his own rotting corpse.

He spotted his mother and willed himself forwards, finding the whole sensation of weightlessness disconcerting. He wasn't sure if he had felt it this strongly back in the hospital room, but out here it was overwhelming, he found he had to really focus on moving forwards now. He made it to her side and kept pace with her, as she dabbed her eyes and patted the arm of her niece, which was looped through her own. Someone he didn't recognise approached her,

"Oh Martha, we know there aren't any words we can say to take the pain away. But know he is always with you, in your heart."

Martha nodded, and replied with a croaky voice,

"I don't question that for a minute." She replied with a quiet tone.

The person tilted her head at her sympathetically and moved on whilst Martha made her way to the car park to go to the wake. His cousin Lily stayed by her side, and her mother Alicia walked nearby with a tear-streaked face, holding her son Tom's hand. Anger suddenly resurfaced for Steven, and he realised he had forgotten to be mad for a moment, having been caught up in the confusion of everything and allowing himself to feel self-pity. Pathetic. What was he going to achieve feeling like that? He needed his rage to get revenge. His mother had reached Alicia's car and stood by it glumly, waiting for the others to catch up and get in.

"You know I loved him like a son too." Alicia said as she got level with Martha.

Martha looked at her with cold eyes, the anger at her sister's words too much to ignore,

"Like a son? If you loved him like a son you would have helped us when you had more than us, I never expected you to but goodness I beg you do not say a stupid thing like that. It doesn't make me feel you understand the pain of losing a child more, it makes me think you're insensitive. You have four children, and only two of them came here today to support our family."

Tom and Lily looked at one another then back to their aunt and mum. Alicia looked at them both sadly and thought for a moment before replying,

"You're right. I'm sorry. I didn't really think about what I was saying. I guess I thought it would be comforting but I can see it wasn't. Please don't bring Seth and Ross into this, they couldn't get day release, they tried. We are all hurting, Mattie, I didn't mean to make it worse." And just like that the tension was broken again, Martha started to cry at this, her sister hadn't called her Mattie in years as there had been so much bickering and hurt that they just couldn't put behind them.

She pulled her in for an embrace and the kids joined them, all taking some much needed comfort from one another. What they couldn't see was Steven standing by, watching everyone and everything. He had felt some joy when he heard his mum be called Mattie, it made him recall being young and all his family and neighbours gathered around in one of their gardens having a barbecue. There would be a constant murmuring of noise where the twenty or so people would be chatting to each other, in some cases talking louder and louder because the neighbouring conversation drowned out their own. He could remember the smell of slightly burnt sausages and his nanna Jess nodding approvingly as the plate of steaming food was passed to her to put on the table, she would always say,

"Best when they've got the crispiness, you know they're cooked all the way through!"

This rule applied to a lot of her cooking, she always flavoured it well though so no one ever really minded that extra crunch in her home cooked meals. Steven could remember playing 'take down bulldog' with Alicia's first children Seth and Ross. They were around his age and made perfect playmates. Not so much as adults though, they went their own way as they grew older and pulled away from the family. It was another sore point between his mum and aunt Alicia. Alicia had often told Martha where she thought her failings as a mother were because of Steven's choices in life and Martha hadn't held back in reciprocating when Alicia's own two ended up on similar paths, but both skipped the 'lucky' phase and got caught with a hefty amount of weed early on in their street careers. They no longer spoke to anyone other than their parents Alicia and John, and nanna Jess on occasion. Steven was suddenly brought out of his reverie by the sound of slamming doors, and tyres crunching over gravel. He watched on as the cars pulled out one by one, until he was just left by himself, alone in the carpark of the place his body would now lay idle forever.

Chapter Five

Steven found himself on the streets near his home, watching the paving slabs drift away underneath and behind him and he found if he lost focus enough, they merged and became seamless making them appear like an endless grey streaky blur. He had nothing on his mind except angry circling thoughts that were only fuelled further by his funeral.

Numbness was threatening to override all other emotions and he was batting it away lazily without much heart, everything that had happened felt surreal and hard to accept making disassociation appealing. He felt aimless whilst completely sure of what he needed to achieve, he just wasn't sure what steps to take to get want he wanted. He had to work out a way to contact his mum again, she would know what to do. No matter what, even if it angered or upset her she was always ready to try and help him find a solution to any given situation – something he had always been grateful for given the amount of peers he encountered in his line of work whose family had disowned them. Even in death, he was confident that she would pull through for him and have his back, helping him do whatever it took to make things even again. It seemed clear to him that his so called mates didn't have what it took.

He didn't see any of them at his funeral, despite having been late to the party himself there should have been one or two who cared enough to hang back and pay respects. He admitted to himself that it stung that he hadn't seen Shells there. At just twenty-four he had his whole life ahead of him and hadn't even peaked yet. Rage bubbled again at the injustice. He should have been given a choice, not taken out by some jumped up jackass playing with big boy toys. Yeti played him dirty and Steven was damn sure he wouldn't let him get away with it. If his boys didn't do anything, then it was obviously down to him.

Steven pulled himself out of his stream of thoughts and paid attention to his surroundings, everything had changed and he had no idea where he was. He looked down to his legs to see that although he couldn't feel them, they were moving as though he was walking. Well, he was *walking* like he was walking – except his feet didn't seem to be touching the floor. He cocked his head and watched with some curiosity and then made the conscious effort to stop his legs from making the walking motion, just as soon as he thought about it they ceased and he carried on moving forwards in a glide. He carried on watching this for a short time and found himself looking up now and then to make sure he wasn't going to bump into anything or anyone, only to belatedly realise each time that this was no longer a thing he needed to concern himself with. He had no physical body any more. The view of his unmoving legs carrying him through the streets started to unnerve him, and he looked away whilst telling his legs to move like they did in life. He checked them to make sure the instruction was carried out and instantly felt comforted to see the familiar motion and visual.

As he moved along in his blur a barrage of varying emotions started to tumble through him, coming to the surface and forcing him to start processing them. The strongest emotion he noted was anger, although it was like an unadulterated rage. Fairly so, he thought, he had his life taken away from him. Another intense emotion bubbling beneath the surface seemed to be sadness, but he wasn't sure. Steven wasn't one to get sad. Any time he had felt sad in the past he channelled it elsewhere to be more useful. What use would he have been to the street, himself or his family if he just wallowed when things got hard. No use, was the only answer he could see. And yet here he was, the razor sharp edge of the blade of sadness was slowly but surely cutting into his non-existent chest. He marvelled at how even though he didn't have the physical body any more, everything he was feeling and doing was still felt and located in the places they would have been in life as though he was still controlling a body. He tried to shake it off but the emotion persisted, forcing him to accept its presence and deal with it. He closed his eyes and waited for a moment only to feel something prising his eyelids open. He looked and there was nothing there so he closed them again with a growl. There was the pressure again, pulling his eyes open.

"Fine!" He bellowed, the barely contained rage resurfacing to drown the sadness.

As he shouted the scene before him seemed to speed up, the road signs became unreadable as they flew by in a blur. Then it all stopped abruptly and he found himself looking at what seemed to a young boy of around twelve years old with his nan. They were tearing up chunks of bread into little squares and throwing it lazily into the murky pond in front of them, home to four hungry ducks scrabbling to get to the soggy feast first. He wondered why he was seeing this and what the significance was, then he noticed the boy looking over his shoulder shiftily, to a group of older boys in baggy hoodies and tracksuit bottoms leaning against the trunk of an enormous tree. He could practically smell the smoke that was trickling out of the nostrils of one of the lads. They were watching the young boy with his nan, Steven knew how this played out. That boy would now come back later to find these boys and they would give him a taste, then he'd be hooked. That was how easy it was. He felt a small tug of that sadness again which he thought was interesting.

He suddenly got pulled backwards and everything whizzed by nauseatingly fast, until it all settled and he found himself outside the front of an unremarkable run down building. He scanned the area for clues as to why he was here, everything was covered by a dark fog, except one window high above him. As he saw it he was propelled upwards and found himself on the ledge. Inside the window was a young woman, cradling an infant. She was cooing and rocking the baby, and nuzzling its soft little head. Steven wondered why he was seeing this, although he figured he could very well guess. A man came out to join the woman and wrapped his arms around her waist, propped his chin on her shoulder and looked down at the sleepy baby, with an expression more tender than any man should ever wear as far as Steven was concerned. But even as he thought it, he felt his sadness jab him in the chest again. He hadn't even begun to consider having a family and experiencing that burden. On reflection, he wouldn't have been against it, he would have done better than his own good for nothing father. A burst of anger at this thought process tore through him suddenly and unexpectedly, it erupted from him in an invisible mass of force and he heard the window shift in its pane.

   He fell backwards before he could see the couple's reaction and blackness enveloped him for a moment, upon opening his eyes again he found himself inside a dark room. He knew this place. Even though it was dim and hard to see he knew it without doubt, it was his old bedroom. Despite having moved out a few years ago and renting a small flat, his mums house was still his 'home', the flat was just a location to sleep and store. He could hear something over by where the bed was and he tried to focus his vision in the darkness. It was his mum. She was curled up in his shark print bedsheets cuddling a bear he had been enamoured with as a boy. He felt guilty, she must have been waiting for him to give another sign that he was here with her and he failed her. He tamped down the renewed anger this drew from his core, he wanted to try and store that as twice now his rage had caused a reaction in the physical world he didn't want that to happen right now, he could see his mum needed quiet and calm for the moment.

Chapter Six

Martha didn't know how long she had lain there; her sorrow sodden thoughts were so heavy that she was physically exhausted from carrying them. The comfort she had sought from Steven's room wasn't as relieving as she had hoped. The funeral had been arduous, something she could never have envisioned having to go through and she wouldn't wish it on anyone. She knew she had one small positive, she knew she would be able to contact him but that didn't make the reality of the loss much easier to process. She had already felt him near her multiple times, she just needed to create the space for him to reach her with ease. A plan had already formulated in her mind, she knew she couldn't live out the rest of her days without her boy in her life and necessary actions had to be taken. All that needed to be done was some cautious scouting and a whole lot of research.

She was sure he had joined her in the room at some point in the night, but in spite of the fact she was thinking forwards and working out a plan, the grief was still taking its toll and it left her in a weakened state. She couldn't even lift her head it felt so weighted. Martha was acutely aware that Steven would be in a horrid state of limbo but took solace from the knowledge that despite his questionable choices in life, she knew he had a good head upon his shoulders and was likely processing it all. For this moment she needed to allow herself the time she needed to try and begin to filter the astronomical amount of emotions that had been swamping her since the news of her son's death. At some point in the whirring thoughts and idleness sleep finally took her in its gentle hold to give her some much needed respite.

***

He realised he had no concept of time, he seemed to be at the mercy of the timelines whether it be past, present or future, he was being taken to see all sorts of things and where he was now he assumed was present time – yet had no idea how long it had been since his death nor even how long he sat here looking at his mum. Maybe time itself only applied to living beings whose physical body degraded as it passed, because as far as he could work it out, being dead and whatever he was now – be it a spirit or a ghost or something else – he couldn't see how time passing could make him 'age' or deteriorate as he had no substance.

What he could work out was that his mother's day was about to start as the sun was just starting to light up the bottom of his bedroom curtains, orange streaks slowly pushing their way into the room through the gaps created by the curtains creases. Martha was always up with the light, a fact she would always proudly share, not one to let anyone think she didn't make good use of her time. She had barely moved the whole time he was here, at one point he had to focus on her back and make sure it was moving as her breathing was so shallow. Sure enough and true to form, she started to stir as the light trickled in and crept across the dusty floor and looked around her, bleary eyed. He watched with turbulent emotions as his mum quickly lost her final layer of sleep fog and registered real life again and began to crumble. She caught herself though, physically shaking herself out of the dark funk that threatened to consume her.

"Not today, Mattie. Not today!" she muttered to herself.

Steven wanted to reach out to her and let her know he was there and offer some sort of comfort to his grieving mother. The frustration at being here in the room with her but not being able to communicate at will was getting too much for him again and he felt his already intense emotions bubble up like a volcano on the brink of eruption. He caught the feeling, remembering that this was how he had shown his presence before, and pushed it further allowing the rage to grow and like before a force suddenly exploded from him in a gust and the curtains billowed as though a wind had torn through them. His mum looked up in surprise with her mouth agape, then smiled broadly. It took less than two seconds for Martha to know what had happened. She already knew it couldn't be because of the window, that hadn't been opened in years because the wood had swollen too much and lodged itself solidly in the frame.

"Steven! I knew it, I thought I sensed you here with me during the night. My boy I'm sorry if you saw my moments of weakness, I'm okay really. I started to doubt myself, thinking I had made up you being there in the hospital with me. Thought maybe the grief had made me wish you had achieved what so few manage to. Well done boy, you're doing so well. It isn't easy grounding yourself once you've passed on and it seems you've done it, without guidance, no less!" she exclaimed, the pride taking the edge off her sad tone.

He looked at her feeling the glow of happiness at this mothers' words of praise. Even as a grown man whose entire life was based on being strong and feared by his peers, his softer side still resided within. Not being able to reply to her quickly dampened that glow, and frustration became the main emotion again.

"I assume you've not had any guidance, anyway. I know you cannot answer me right now, and I can't even be certain you're in the room with me but I believe you are. I can feel your presence. A mother always knows; the bond we have doesn't require physical bodies for me to see you. How I wish you were in physical form, though." She said, the last few words cracked as she struggled to continue speaking whilst the sadness threatened to take over. "We will work on this, I will find a way for you to speak with me, so you can tell me who did this, they will pay. Mark my words Steven, they'll pay for what they've done to you. I need some time to gather some things, it has been so long since I have used my skills they need to be honed again. For now, allow yourself to go where you are taken and trust that you'll be brought back to me when the time is right. Pay attention, you will only be shown things of relevance."

As she finished her sentence Steven felt something wrap around his entire being and wrench him off into the darkness again, and he wondered where he was being taken this time, his last view before it all faded away was his mother's stricken face, trying to be brave and positive.

Chapter Seven

The room reeked of damp and one could imagine the mould particles floating straight up into their airways. It was enough of a mental image to create the desire to hold your breath for an indefinite amount of time. What was strange though was the fact that Steven *could* smell. He hadn't noticed before but in all the other places he didn't seem to smell anything, perhaps all his senses had just been overloaded, or maybe he was imagining it because it was the smell you'd expect in a place like this. The room was gloomy and looked as though a film was over the scene preventing him from focusing on what was there. He could see the blurry outlines of three figures, two sat at a small table and one stood in front of them with their hands resting on the surface. He couldn't hear what they were saying and Steven shook his head to unblock his ears, then channelled his focus on the shadowy people in front of him, and suddenly as though the volume had been turned up, their voices became audible.

"Do you understand what a stupid thing you've done? You're lucky you're still breathing." the person standing up said.

"Come on man, he was a class A prick. Who cares?" scoffed one of the men sitting. The standing man didn't appreciate that. He punched down on the table and both men jumped in alarm.

"He was one of our best runners, but more importantly we now have eyes on us because of your foolishness. Those same eyes have loose lips and when this shit gets out they'll wonder why we have you on payroll as well as the guy you took out. We will lose respect and business, because of a lowlife like you. You know what that means right?" he gestured with frustration at the two men who now sat quietly, neither of them answering. It was a rhetorical question and they knew it. "When we lose respect, people think we can't control our runners and we lose business. Competing dealers will try to take our corners and we lose business. We lose business? What happens then?" he asked, again, rhetorically.

One of the men at the table didn't pick up on the fact he wasn't meant to reply,

"We lose money?" he said, keeping his voice level.

The standing man inclined his head at him for a moment before swiftly pulling a gun from his pocket and with no hesitation shot the man between the eyes.

"Why the fuck did he answer me? Did I ask a question?" he said, staring down the last man sitting, who was studiously looking anywhere but next to him where his friends head had smashed down on the table with a cavity the size of a tennis ball on the back of it. The man shook his head quickly, not trusting himself to speak.

"What the hell you on about. I did ask a question. You really are dumb as shit, you know that?" the guy at the table nodded dully, not certain whether he was about to meet the same fate but not willing to risk pissing him off more in case there was a chance he would walk out of here. "We have runners all over the place. Pull anymore dumb ass moves like you did with Brute, I'll leave pieces of you all around town for people to find, a Yeti puzzle. How about that? Understood?" Yeti nodded rapidly at this, realising now wasn't his time to be dispatched but it was a close call. "Clean this shit up, you owe us. I want him gone within the hour as the boss is coming. If there is even a speck of that piece of shit on the table, it'll be your head next." And with that he swept away out of the room through a door off to the left.

Steven watched on in fascination as the strange film he was seeing the room through dissipated and he could now see clearly. The previously silhouetted figure of Yeti now stood staring at the door with resentment before looking round to his friend sprawled across the table, it brought Steven pleasure to see Yeti retch just from looking at his deceased friend. Had he not have been the one responsible for ending Steven's life he may have felt some pity for him but as far as Steven was concerned, he wanted to see Yeti suffer for his unforgivable actions. This man was the reason he was stuck here and not in whatever afterlife he should have been in by now. If the murder wasn't enough, the hindrance to his ability to move on sealed the deal on Steven's hatred towards him. He watched with contempt as Yeti visibly tried to gather himself for the task that lay ahead of him,

"Why the hell did you answer? Idiot!" Yeti said forcefully to his friends' corpse.

He shook his head to himself and started looking around the room, presumably for something to wrap the body up in. Steven's anger went up a notch, being so close to the man who took his life over a bag of weed and watching him pity himself over having to clean up the mess caused by his actions fuelled the rage. He felt it ball up in his chest and consciously evicted it with as much force as he could muster and watched with grim satisfaction as Yeti received the brunt of it. The force made him stumble from his position rummaging through the boxes next to the table and he crashed into the leg face first. The impact knocked the table about a foot and Yeti's dead friend folded down in a bloody mess onto him and an ungodly shriek emitted from Yeti as he scurried away backwards staring in horror at the blood stains on his legs and hands. He looked around him with fear emblazoned across his features and that was the last thing Steven had the pleasure of witnessing before he was pulled away into the darkness once more.

Chapter Eight

Martha was in the local library studiously avoiding any kind of contact with the fellow visitors that day. She used to have quite a decent quantity of reading material for what she sought but after some less than ideal situations she had sold them off at a local car boot event. Her journey with that side of 'life' had started when she was much younger, she had always had the natural ability to see and hear things, one day she shared with her parents these experiences she had been having and they told her each time it was all in her head. For a long time she wondered if she was a little unhinged, because she still saw the occasional figure of a person at the end of her bed, or caught the silhouette of someone walking through a room she knew was empty. It didn't even need to be a physical representation of a person, she would see orbs too and although visually that was all they were she would *sense* what they were, one that drifted past her often was one she was certain was a young playful girl. She could envision her with dark locks of hair and an off-white summer dress despite never having seen her. It was only when she was a bit older and saw things on the television of other people who had similar experiences and she finally felt she wasn't alone.

She never held resentment for her parents and accepted that they simply didn't understand and so could never have been a source of comfort or knowledge for her. The problem she ended up encountering was trying to reconnect with those abilities that had once come so naturally to her, the years of doubt and being told it was in her head made her repress them and ignore them. She spent hours watching shows, reading books and meditating hoping it would come back to her and soon enough it did. It was a little more draining than she remembered it being but then again, she was having to work at it more.

Before long one of the girls from her school asked if she had ever used an Ouija board as they were notorious for being a great way to contact those who were no longer living. It turned out this girl, Susie, had one stashed in her attic because her grandmother had once upon a time dabbled in those matters too. Once her grandmother had passed away her mum had decided it made her too uneasy and stored it up there with her other possessions in a trunk, and forgot about them. Susie and Martha formed a quick and solid friendship and one day they decided to get the Ouija board out and experiment. They took it to all sorts of random places and more often than not nothing happened. But the buzz they felt when that planchette moved was second to none. They were in direct contact with the other side and although this wasn't completely new to Martha, it was exciting to give the spirits a voice. Susie on the other hand didn't have any experiences with the supernatural and the whole experience was both terrifying and exhilarating for her. They had done their research beforehand to make sure they had some element of control over how the conversations could go, because there were some less than appealing reports of misuse and the wrong spirits coming through.

The board as is it is recognised today had been designed by a businessman called Charles Kennard and was initially marketed as a toy in the 1890's for all to play with, one that could give answers to most questions with uncanny accuracy. They say that once the prototype was created Charles asked the board what it should be named and the planchette promptly spelled out the word 'Ouija' – he enquired what that meant and the response spelt 'good luck'. It was only later with the introduction of movies and books involving the Ouija board that people began to question whether channelling ghosts was in fact not always such a harmless activity after all. Both Susie and Martha agreed to never do anything with the Ouija board without the other.

"Excuse me miss?" Martha was pulled out of her deep thoughts abruptly and looked around, a short stocky lady was standing there with a book in each hand, shuffling from foot to foot with an awkward expression on her face.

"Can I help you?" Martha asked, trying to keep her tone in check. This woman couldn't know what she was going through and Martha was not about to subject her to her hurt and anger.

"I, er, yes please. I just needed to get to that shelf. I was waiting but you haven't moved for a while. Are you ok?" she stuttered back.

"I'm fine. Sorry, I just drifted off for a moment. I'll move." And without glancing back at the little lady she moved away from the shelves and looked for the rented games and puzzles section, but not without feeling the enquiring eyes of the lady she had quickly left behind upon her back.

****

She soon found what she had hoped to see and she felt pangs of fear and sadness mingling with anticipation whilst reading the side of the box. Martha hadn't expected to find an Ouija board so quickly, but as most people feared them they donated or threw them away, so she knew she'd come across one sooner or later – she took the fact she found one in the first place she looked as a good sign. This one looked well-loved judging by the aesthetic of the box. Perfect, this board had already been used as a channel, somehow this made her feel more at ease. She allowed herself a quick moment of thinking about the old days and then blinked it away, ready to face the present and future head on and do what needed to be done to speak with her son again. What she wouldn't give to hear his voice again. He hadn't been gone that long and when he was alive she sometimes didn't hear from him for a week or two sometimes, but the knowledge that his voice was so far away now made it worse.

She tucked the box under her arm and made for the occult section to see what she could find. With a hefty sigh she saw there wasn't anything of use to her, although she was intrigued by the witchy books that lined the shelf they would only serve as a distraction at this time. She would have to go off of memory it seemed. Which wasn't a bad thing, she needed to have more faith in her abilities. With that she went to the desk to check out, ignoring the curious looks from the spectacled elderly lady who stamped the card. She nodded her thanks and departed without further interaction. She found just being out of the house again exhausting and realised she just wasn't ready to face the world yet, grief was holding her firmly in its grasp and she knew she needed to get things moving as soon as possible to alleviate its hold over her.

Chapter Nine

Steven was at his mums' house again and she was sat at the kitchen table staring at a dirty looking box. He moved closer to see what had her so transfixed; it had to be interesting if it distracted her from the seventies-style black and white chequered vinyl tablecloth he had always hated. It was such an eyesore and clashed with the old-fashioned chunky forget-me-not blue tiles that covered the wall directly above the counters. He read the label on the box, Ouija board? His surprise was short-lived when he realised it made clear sense. Even though his mum had mentioned dabbling in the past with contacting the other side she always shut the conversation down just as soon as he started asking questions, but he'd seen enough to know of the Ouija board and its purpose. She looked up and gazed around the room, her eyes red rimmed and face downturned.

"Steven? Are you there?" she asked, voice hoarse.

"Yes mum, I am." He replied instantly, but the words were lost as he was without a voice.

Despite not hearing him he could see she knew he was there, she shook her head to herself lightly and opened the Ouija box, pulled out the board and planchette then set them down neatly on the table.

"Steven, you need to focus your energy on moving the planchette. Let's try." She took a deep breath, clearly struggling to proceed.

He had expected it to be emotional but this was something else, she seemed scared and he wondered if it had anything to do with the reason she always changed the topic when discussing her past experiences with this stuff. He tried to place his hand on the planchette to move it but his hand went straight through the board and table and frustration instantly bubbled up.

"Steven? You won't be able to physically move it, it will be your energy that does, look at the planchette closely, clear your mind and focus on nothing but moving it to where you want it to go. Picture a tether connecting your mind to the object. When you can, move it to the word yes for me."

Steven gathered himself once more, centring his attention on the planchette and allowing everything to become a blur around it. To his surprise the dark piece of wood trembled ever so gently on the board. He looked to see if his mum had noticed this and she was smiling broadly whilst staring intently at the board. Pride welled up inside him and he tried to direct the planchette but now it had stopped moving, and he didn't understand why.

Instant fury coursed through him and he let it out in a huff sending the board and planchette soaring across the room and smashing into the cupboard, the Ouija board snapped in two on impact. His mum gasped and leapt up from the table, dashing across the floor to collect the pieces.

"It's ok Steven, it is frustrating I know. Hold on let me just get some tape to fix this up good as new again."

Guilt raced through him, he should've kept his cool because now his already distraught mum was having to clean up after him even in death. She had found the tape in the clutter draw and was busily putting the board together, her tongue poking out the side of her mouth in concentration. She placed it carefully back on the table with the planchette on top. It looked more than a little sorry for itself now but it would still serve its purpose, and she would now have it forever unless the library didn't bother checking the condition on return. Not that she cared, she only cared about one thing right now. Her son.

"Let's try it again, when you're ready." His mum said.

Steven regathered himself, determined to do it this time. He allowed everything in the room except that little heart shaped piece of wood to go blurry, and once he had locked in he thought about mini expulsions of energy and directing them. He kept calm this time when it trembled slightly, then finally moved, he pushed it towards the top left and stopped when the circle perfectly contained the word yes. Only then did he allow himself to look back to his mum who sat with teary eyes nodding to herself.

"Well done my boy. You may not realise just how hard that is to do so early on. Is there anything you want to tell me?"

Steven made the planchette tremble and then settle so it stayed on yes.

"Do you feel ready to talk?"

This was his opportunity, he pushed it neatly and precisely to the letter Y. He found the focus required to be quite draining but was determined. He carried on for three more letters and his mum looked confused.

"Yeti?" she mumbled, mostly to herself.

Steven realised she wouldn't know who that was, and decided to spell out another word.

"M.U.R.D.E.R."

He felt his fury at Yeti rise again as he watched his mum break down in tears. She knew he had been killed and now she knew the guys name, her hurt was almost too much to bear. He felt completely depleted as though he had used up his quota of energy. He saw the word goodbye at the bottom of the board and forced the planchette onto it, and his mum smiled sadly and nodded.

"Yes, that must have been exhausting for you. Go and reenergise yourself. I will be waiting."

As though her permission was all he needed, he felt himself being pulled away into nothingness. Martha sat with her thoughts for some time, knowing that Steven would likely be recharging now for a day or so. She needed to find out how she could work out who this Yeti character was, and formulate a plan to bring him to justice – whether that justice came from the police force or elsewhere would be another matter. For now, she felt relieved that she had successfully made contact with her son and they could now start to plan.

Chapter Ten

It was the next day and Martha waited with baited breath for her sister to reply to her question. She knew her request was a hard one for Alicia to process and consider, she may have felt the same if was the other way around. They both sat drinking coffee at the small round oak table in Alicia's conservatory, and although Martha was eager to reconnect with her sister she was here with an ulterior motive. She was being as open as she could with Alicia, without giving anything important away.

Although she had always tried to be understanding, Alicia was always dubious about Martha's willingness to address the more spiritual elements – a feeling that turned into dislike after her last dealings many years ago. Martha had actually promised everyone she would not dabble any more after tragedy had struck. She had intended to stand by that promise but how could anyone expect her to in this situation, when the only way she could have contact with her own son would be to do that exact thing that they all asked her to not do. She had found that her need and desire to stay connected to her son overrode that promise and her fear, by a long way.

"I don't know Mattie, you know they don't want anything to do with anyone. I guess they would like to pay their respects in person though." Alicia was saying whilst chewing on the inside of her cheek.

"I know and I do respect that. I just feel it would be a comfort to me to see them after losing Steven. I haven't seen them for such a long time, and I miss them, they're my nephews after all." Martha pushed.

"You're right, I'll contact them and get the go-ahead. I can't see them turning down their auntie Mattie." Alicia said with a sigh.

"Thank you Al, it means the world to me. I know it is a hard ask and you know I wouldn't ask if I didn't think it would help me tremendously with the healing process."

Alicia nodded sympathetically at her, and put her hand out for Martha's empty cup.

"Here, I'll stick the kettle on and get us another coffee going whilst I call the prison."

Martha smiled and handed the cup over whilst giving her thanks. It didn't feel good knowing she was manipulating her sister but needs must and she wasn't lying, she really did want to see her nephews as she hadn't seen them since the day of their incarceration. She watched her sister's retreating back and mulled over the unexpected thought that perhaps it would have been better if she had caved to the officers who'd spent so long trying to catch her and her son out. If Steven was in prison he wouldn't have been killed by Yeti, he would have been safe behind bars. She quickly dismissed that thought process though, there was no way she would ever be ok with being the one responsible for her son being incarcerated.

"All sorted Mattie, you can go and see them during visiting hours whenever you are ready. I spoke to Seth, he said he was sorry about Steven." Martha jumped, she hadn't even heard or seen Alicia coming back in. She didn't even realise she had been gone long enough to make the phone call and make coffees. She took the steaming cup that was being offered to her.

"Thank you Al, I'll probably go tomorrow. Bit tired today." She replied. Alicia nodded sympathetically, then looked at the large clock on her wall and grimaced.

"Time to go get Tim and Lily. Do you want to come with me?"

Martha couldn't think of anything worse right now, going on a school run and being surrounded by a youthful innocent representation of what she had just had taken from her. She shook her head and gulped down the scalding coffee.

"No. I don't think so, I'll see you later or tomorrow." she stood up, brushed herself down and gave Alicia a hug goodbye.

She was pleasantly surprised to feel Alicia stiffen in surprise, then loosen up and return the embrace. They separated and left the bungalow together, neither interested in small talk, and each went their own way to their next task of the day.

****

Martha trod the familiar uneven and discoloured concrete pathway on the route back to her house but had no intention of returning home just yet. She was off to do some general scouting of the area. They weren't exactly well off and the region was full of characters from all walks of life, but she was looking for just one type. She headed past the turning that would have taken her into her courtyard and carried straight on to the local park. She bit back the wistful feeling as she cast her eyes over the creaky swing set that Steven had loved so much as a kid, and the rusty bench behind it that she spent so many hours sitting on chatting to other parents, whilst watching their kids be carefree and joyful. How many of those kids grew up to be carefree, or joyful? Not many, she would have thought, if any. Not in these times. Seemed every youth was picked up and led astray no matter how they were raised.

There was often some kind of loner here, an outcast who didn't have a group they fit in. She could see a huddled mass on the slope behind the metal slide and didn't need to approach them to see it was an elderly man sipping from his paper bag. Not what she needed at all. She sighed, somehow disappointed that what she was looking for wasn't immediately there. She would keep moving along and perhaps she would spot the person she was looking for when she stopped trying, in fairness she wasn't completely certain who she was looking for, she just had a vague idea in her mind. She hadn't voiced her plan to Steven yet, but she was quite sure he would be on board. She would speak with him about it all when he was back and ready for more communication, for now she needed to work on keeping her spiritual channels open without allowing anything unwanted in. Her self-proclaimed job title was now to be Steven's soul guide, and she would not – could not – mess this up. For the first time in a very long time he needed her just as much as she needed him and she was not prepared to fail him. This path was her calling, always had been. It hurt her to have this reminder in the form of her own deceased child but it was like the fates were forcing her hand into dealing with the other side again. Who was she to ignore fate?

Chapter Eleven

Steven blinked away the foggy film obscuring his vision and took stock of his surroundings. he was in a large concrete room with a multitude of scratched wooden tables dotted around. Some of them were occupied by hunched figures and it didn't take him long to realise that it was a prison visitation room. The humming sound of multiple hushed conversations was somewhat comforting after an unknown amount of time spent in nothingness. He had no idea how long he had been gone for but was aware of the feeling of being revitalised – something he never would have thought could be possible to say about a non-physical entity. He actually felt more energetic than when he would have from a pre workout shake before hitting the gym.

He heard something click behind him and turned to see the source of the noise and a feeling of relief came over him when he saw his mum walk through the door directed by a middle-aged man with a bulging stomach. He didn't seem to be aware of his physique and bumped Martha with his tummy as he turned, causing Martha to wince and move out the way with a polite smile and apology as though it were her fault. He looked her over to see how she was doing and he was glad to see she looked better than when he saw her last, with more colour on her cheeks and eyes marginally less dulled. Steven wondered what she was doing here in prison. Had he been gone a really long time and she had done it all and found Yeti? That wouldn't make sense for her to be in a visiting area though.

He didn't have to wonder much longer as the clicking sound of a door on the other side of the room caught his attention and he saw with great surprise his cousins Seth and Ross being led in by a stern faced woman. His mum walked towards them with some reservations, likely waiting to see how they reacted to her. He guessed they knew she was coming, they would have been told of her arrival and visitation request.

"Seth, Ross. It is so good to see you again." Martha said, her tone cracking a little, belying the undercurrents of emotions constantly threatening to sweep her away on a self-pitying tide.

Both Seth and Ross nodded at her stoically before Seth shook his head lightly to himself and stepped forwards to embrace his aunt. Ross didn't follow suit but this was in keeping with his character, he had never been one for displays of emotion instead he grunted out,

"I'm sorry about Steven, and that we wouldn't get day release for the funeral."

Martha waved her hands in dismissal at them both,

"I know it wasn't your fault. I am here now and seeing you both. Let's take a seat, shall we?"

They all sat, the marks covering the tables surface a crude tapestry of the emotions felt by the previous occupants over the years. They started out by talking about how Seth and Ross had been, when they expected to be released and Martha even went so far as to ask them if they would be willing to see her again once they were out, they hesitated for a moment before agreeing. Steven was watching over the whole interaction with some level of confusion, from the way they were speaking he assumed it still wasn't that long since his funeral, so why had his mum decided now to come and visit his cousins? Was it some way to deal with her grief?

He wanted to understand but in reality it frustrated him because he didn't understand and she knew he was here waiting for her instructions. She didn't need to grieve any more when he was right here, he just wasn't physical any more. He felt his annoyance bubble up and had to fight to keep himself present and focus on what was being said. His mum had stopped talking and was looking around the room with a lightly knitted brow.

"Are you ok?" Ross grunted.

Martha just nodded back at him. Steven wondered if she sensed him there and if that was why she had stopped the conversation.

"Seth, Ross. I have something to ask you and I hope you understand why. I won't say a word to anyone I just need closure." she said.

She reached her hands out, holding her palms face upwards towards her nephews. Ross looked sceptical and Seth just looked on waiting for the question with a poker face.

"I know my boy didn't make the wisest decisions, none of us have really, but I do need to know what happened. I cannot rest, my heart is broken and I fear Steven won't be able to pass on to the spiritual world if it is left unsaid. Do you know who did this to him?"

Ross looked around the room, nervously rubbing his thumbnail into the groove of one of the many deep scores on the tables. Once he was sure no one was listening in he nodded discreetly to Seth who took the lead.

"We've heard a few things. But it isn't worth you getting mixed up in all this aunt Mattie, what do you expect to be able to do?"

"I don't expect to do anything with the information, I just want to know so I can rest again. Please tell me you understand." She implored.

Steven was off to the side bristling with anticipation and pride for his clever mum, it was all becoming clearer now.

"Brute, – sorry -," he shrugged apologetically, "Steven was quite well known and obviously word has moved about that he was killed in the streets." Martha held her hand up to pause him,

"Brute?" she asked in shock.

"Yeah, sorry. We all get names on the street, Steven was Brute. I don't need to elaborate do I?" Ross said drily.

"No. Please don't." Martha said, disapproval clear in her expression.

She looked around the room without looking at anyone in particular and in that moment Steven knew she was trying to show him how she felt about this nickname of his. Seth continued,

"He was taken out by a new runner, he has been around a while but only recently got on payroll. We only know him by the name Yeti. My guess is he will have been taken out himself by now, by the upper folk. That or he'd be made to run the streets for free. Maybe he will be forced to take Steven's slot but that would leave his open. Who knows?"

"The upper folk?" Martha asked, head tilted in confusion.

"Yeah. We don't know their names unless we're on the inside. Which technically we are, but the wrong type of inside." Seth allowed himself to laugh quietly at his own joke. Ross shook his head in disdain.

"Tell me something, now that being in prison has taken you out of the 'game', will you stay out?" Martha asked, staring them down one by one.

"It's a lifestyle. How else do you expect people to get by around here?" Ross asked, a sharp edge to his tone.

Seth on the other hand looked at her with a curious expression upon his face. Martha could see the differences between the brothers were still the same. Ross was always the standoffish one getting into all sorts of trouble, and his brother Seth was always there for him even at cost to himself. She wondered idly if Seth would ever break that habit and make a life for himself as he had always shown so much promise. Not that Ross hadn't, but Seth had always had dreams.

"Who am I to ask? Look what happened to my boy. I'm sorry to pry." Martha said, struggling to keep the sadness from her tone. "Anyway, I think that is enough for today. I miss you boys, as does your mother. I'll try and get back soon if you'll allow me to."

They all said their goodbyes and Martha left with a feeling of accomplishment, armed with more information and a step closer to one of her goals. Steven was left in the visiting room, processing what he had just watched, when once more he found himself being pulled in a new direction.

Chapter Twelve

Click clack, click clack, click clack. The man's low-heeled loafers beat a steady rhythm on the white tiled floor as he made his way down the brightly lit hallway towards the exit. He hastened towards the polished silver handle, eager to be out of his office and on his way home where he could shut out the world and all the people in it. As far as he was concerned the moment that clock turned five o'clock he no longer had to be extroverted and smiley with anyone who crossed his path. He was well aware of the receptionist's glare upon his back as he left and frankly he didn't care, he didn't really care about much except being alone and at peace. He hated his job, being a dentist who specialised in children's dentistry didn't exactly pay much around here but he didn't interview well and this was his lot unless he found the money to launch a private practice elsewhere. All his patients did today was squirm and scream, the little runts who actually sat still were ass kissers, only after a lolly and a sticker.

He took a strange level of pleasure in telling the proud parent present that their little cherub had a cavity or needed plaque removing because they didn't care well enough for their child's dental wellbeing. They never argued, just looked at the floor with guilt. It wasn't like he wished ill upon any of them, he just needed to spruce his day up a bit and break the monotony of doing the same thing all day every day. Frankly, some people just had bad luck with their teeth but he wasn't there to comfort them so didn't bother with that nugget of information. He placed his hand on the handle and allowed himself to exhale as it clicked down, the sound of catch releasing music to his ears. He stepped out into the dwindling daylight and began his trudging walk home to his flat.

***

Once home he settled down into his blue and green chequered armchair and picked up his day old newspaper, which was already propped open on the puzzles page. He gazed down upon it with disdain, feeling uninspired to even try and answer any of the clues. With a huff he threw it back towards the side table and grunted in annoyance when it overshot and went sprawling across the floor.

"Dammit!" he muttered and hauled himself out of the chair to pick it up.

He knew he was making a meal of the physical exertion; he was slim but strong. He just didn't want to have to do anything more today, even if it was as small a task as cleaning up after himself. The fact it was a small task was actually more annoying to him, if he needed to do something he wanted it to be worthwhile with some sort of reward. This is where having someone in your life would come in handy, but he didn't need the rest of the nonsense that went alongside it. He would rather live a life alone than have to cater to anyone else's needs, even a pets' need to be fed and petted regularly was too much.

He had no family to speak of, he grew up jumping between orphanages and foster homes, never finding the forever family that so many of his fellow orphans did. It just wasn't meant to be, he had realised early on he was just an isolated fellow and it didn't upset him one bit. Except now, when he had to pick up the newspaper off the floor and sort dinner. He decided he was unlikely to bother doing the puzzle any time soon and instead of putting the pages back together in order he crumpled them all into a ball to carry out to the recycling bin alongside the empty milk bottle he forgot to take out this morning.

****

He was in his own world of self-serving thoughts when he was abruptly pulled away from them,

"Evening Tim." Came a voice, it sounded tired.

He turned to look and see who it was that knew his name, mostly so he could dismiss them and go back inside. It was Martha, the lady who lived down the road. For reasons he wasn't sure of, Tim didn't want to be rude to her right now, she looked downcast and there was no fun in that.

"Evening Martha." He replied, he started to turn to the bin again when she spoke once more.

"Tim?" she said questioningly.

He looked at her, and was surprised to see her looking at him so intently. Was she coming on to him? She must be around fifty but she was in quite good shape and had a pretty face, there was a little bit of a jowl but nothing he couldn't overlook. Her body was trim and she obviously took care of herself. He might not like people, but he did have needs.

"Yes, Martha?" he said, making sure to loosen his frame a little and be less intense with his demeanour.

She was looking at him with assessing eyes, and where there had been a downturned expression a moment ago he was sure he could see her visibly perking up with each passing moment. He could be onto a winner here, he might not even have to make dinner, he smiled lightly to himself.

"Tim." She said, almost breathless. Then she gathered herself and spoke clearly, "I need to talk with someone and I don't have anyone around here. I know we don't know each other but my family don't really understand my needs. Have you got an ear you could lend me?"

Tim decided that sounded as close to and invite for 'coffee' as it got and nodded at her slowly, making sure to hold her gaze. He watched her falter for a moment and her eyes shuttered. Perhaps she didn't expect him to take her up on such an obvious offer. He repressed the urge to laugh triumphantly at having seen her game plan right from the off.

"When?" he murmured.

"Now?" she uttered back, imitating his behaviour.

He was now taken aback by the directness but he liked it. She could be a fast learner. Problem was he was still grubby from work and hadn't expected to be entertaining.

"Give me ten? I need to sort something quickly." He asked, and threw in a small side smile.

"Sure, meet me at mine Tim. I'll put the kettle on." And with that she smiled at him, eyes dancing and drawing him in.

He merely nodded back at her and watched as she walked away, certain that the sway in her hips was only for his eyes in that moment.

Chapter Thirteen

Martha opened the front door and entered her home with measured movements, absolutely convinced that if she didn't control everything including her slightly laboured breathing she may implode. She couldn't believe she hadn't thought of Tim whilst scouting the streets the other day. The person who would fit the job was just a few houses down, and in great condition! She knew he was stand offish, lived alone without pets, worked down the road at the dentist and she was pretty sure he didn't have a family to speak of. She needed to fish for more information. Martha felt a pang of guilt when she reflected on the fact that she had noticed his mistaken reading of her body language and used it to her advantage, but needs must. She had to think of her boy and this was all going to work out perfectly if she played her cards right. She flicked the switch on her kettle and felt her stomach turning with nerves, it was all so nauseating. She busied herself with straightening the assortment of pots and pans that hung on the back wall of the kitchen above the stovetop. The door still hadn't knocked by the time she was done with that so she pulled her metal polisher out of the cupboard and starting wiping down the already gleaming surface of her oven.

A gentle rapping noise at the door allowed her to step away from her fussing and she stashed the bottle and pad away with relief. She stepped quickly through the open plan area and pulled the door open to greet Tim with a small smile on her face. Martha hoped that her body language didn't give away her nerves.

"Martha." He said curtly, with a light nod. She was surprised to see such a twinkle in his eyes, he always struck her as a particularly dark character.

"Tim, thanks for coming. Tea or coffee?"

"Tea for me thanks. Strong and bitter."

"Make yourself comfortable, I'll bring them through." Martha replied, gesturing to the sofas in the corner of the cosy living area.

She watched him closely as he nodded and dutifully went over and sat on the two seater. Martha went back to the kitchen and poured the teas, brewing them for a while whilst she gathered her thoughts. After a few minutes she realised that leaving the bags in any longer would be too much and removed them hastily then returned to Tim. It was clear he was making an effort to be amiable because he thought there was an ulterior motive, he wasn't wrong, mostly. The expectation was just a touch wrong. Martha shook her head to herself, then scouted her surroundings to see if she could feel Steven nearby. She had felt his presence in the prison but not since.

"If it is too strong let me know, I'll remake it. My mind got away from me." She said, handing him the mug. Her hand brushed his as he took it and he looked her dead in the eye, measuring her up again. She didn't balk and simply returned the gaze with a softened look. Tim chortled lightly, and nodded almost unperceptively.

"I like it strong." He said, making sure to push his suggestive tone towards her. She smiled back at him, fully aware that she needed to start pushing him now or he would lose interest.

"Tim, I said to you outside that my family doesn't understand what I need to talk about, to an extent that is true." She watched as his demeanour change substantially, a genuine surprise registering on his features that she actually wanted talk to him about something. She ignored this and continued. "Do you know Steven?"

He looked at her, confused about where this was going. This wasn't what he signed up for.

"Your son? What about him? A trouble maker, right?" he said, having realised that he may have misread the whole situation and regretting it. He didn't notice Martha flinch at Steven being referred to as a trouble maker.

"Yes, my son. He died a couple of weeks ago." She could see the shock register on his face for a moment, and he looked to her.

"I'm sorry to hear that. I guess it was unexpected?" Tim asked.

"Yes. He was only twenty-four and fighting fit, he was murdered." She said bitterly.

Tim clearly didn't know how to react to this information and scanned the floral rug underfoot for any kind of distraction. "I can't really talk about it with my family and I guess I just needed to tell someone, anyone. I don't have many people round here I can turn to. Do you know what I mean?" she was looking at him with glistening brown eyes, her very being begging him to reassure her. His usually detached nature buckled and he spoke,

"I do. I don't have any family or friends at all. But I also don't have this kind of thing to talk about as a result of that. I don't like people and it causes me no sadness that I have no-one to reach out to. That said, it doesn't mean I'm unaware, I get that humans need to offload." He stopped himself, that was the most he had said to someone outside of work in years. He didn't like it. Martha sensed his hesitation.

"Thank you Tim. That means a lot to me that you just shared with me at all. Shows me I am not alone in feeling like I can't talk to anyone. It is lonely." She put one of her hands gently upon his knee.

She watched the confusion ripple across Tim's face for an instant before he recovered himself.

"You're welcome." He replied, trying to keep himself in check.

He couldn't work out if he was annoyed at what felt like having been being played, or flattered by her attention and desire to confide in him. He wasn't sure what it was but he found himself drawn to this lady perched across the sofa from him, and that in itself unnerved him. He had spent a lifetime being self-serving and hating the general population of the world, never finding anyone who didn't frustrate him within minutes of opening their mouths. Until this moment, it seemed. He decided to be forthcoming with this new feeling to see how she reacted, it would have been even more uncharacteristic for him to stymie away his thoughts.

"I am finding myself quite drawn to you. I think you should know that."

Martha's eyebrows shot up into her fringe covered forehead for a moment, before settling back down to their original positions. Despite knowing she was pushing for the connection with him, she was surprised he had been swayed so quickly. She had thought he may be a bit more of a challenge based on what she had seen of him and general aura.

"Thank you, for being so open with me Tim." She patted his leg again, cementing the words into his mind with the action.

She idly thought about how manipulating people was similar to training a pet. In this case she was treating him to human connection and physical touch – something that he wouldn't have realised he needed on a surface level but her strong intuition had told her he craved in his core. He will have now subconsciously linked connecting with her with that reward and she planned to keep pushing it to get the information she needed, and ultimately reach her goal.

Chapter Fourteen

Martha sat nursing a lukewarm cup of tea later that evening whilst mulling over the day's events. She hadn't sensed Steven's presence around her yet but this didn't faze her and she thought about the prison visit, she had been surprised to feel him there, having anticipated him being away for at least two days. She moved her thoughts to Tim next, he had been pleasantly receptive to her and she had expended far less energy in the first point of connection than she thought she would have to. This part of the plan looked like it would flow smoothly and easily especially given his circumstances, he didn't have any family or friends and no social life or love life. The only place his existence was noted was at his work. With the lack of close friends, a transition would be relatively easy to achieve whilst the workplace element could be dealt with using little effort. The added perk was that he lived on the same street, it was almost too good to be true. Despite her sore heart and heavy spirit Martha felt like luck was on her side. She could hardly wait until she saw Steven to fill him in. As she allowed her thoughts to land on her sons whereabouts again she felt the unmistakable shift in the air around her and instinctively looked around, despite knowing she was unlikely to see anything.

"Steven? Is that you, are you back?" she asked the question gently.

The hairs on her neck prickled suddenly and her instinct warned her it wasn't him. She chewed her lip and rubbed her thumb nervously on the side of her cup, trying to distract herself by wishing the tea could be piping hot again. She regretted speaking and acknowledging the presence without taking time to read the energy first, that was a rookie error. Acting like she hadn't spoken and pretending her heart wasn't thudding painfully in her chest she rose up to reheat her tea, she moved over to her microwave with calm collected movements, opened the door and put the mug in. Just as soon as she took her fingers away from the handle the mug lifted a millimetre and smashed into the back of the microwave and chunks of porcelain and liquid exploded outwards.

Martha shrieked in surprise and jumped back, her front now drenched with lukewarm tea. She felt a rapid surge of gratitude that her visitor decided to show off before she had reheated it otherwise that would have been much worse. She heard a light knocking sound the other side of the room over by the coffee table, the sound was coming from the small shelf under it, her visitor wanted to talk. The box for the Ouija board was shifting towards the edge of the shelf, close to falling off the stack of home-keeping magazines she had stashed under there. Martha focused on keeping her steps strong and the tremor out of her hands. She got to the table, bent down and retrieved the box, the presence in the room was so powerful she expected to look to her side and see it in form or at least the air vibrating.

"OK, give me a moment." She said, directing her words to where she felt the being was.

She went back over to the kitchen table and quickly took the taped up board out of the box and placed the planchette on it. She didn't have to wait long for it to start to move. Whoever this was, was particularly strong and had a lot of control, the movements were smooth and direct. She watched as the circle in the planchette first showed the letter S, then it neatly moved over to U, back to S, then paused. Martha exhaled heavily, realising where this was going. Sure enough, the planchette drifted over to I, then E. It came to a stop and Martha felt her eyes tear up and her heart ache from years of missing her best friend.

"Is it really you?" she asked, voice cracking.

"YES" came the instant response.

"I want to talk to you properly. Are you strong enough?" She asked even though she knew the answer.

Martha carried so much guilt in her heart for all that had transpired all those years ago, and her intuition told her that Susie wasn't a malicious form – something that she had feared would become of her because of the nature of her passing. She shouldn't have ever doubted her though, Susie was her best friend and if the shoe had been on the other foot Martha wouldn't have blamed her for what happened either. The planchette shivered on YES again, and Martha nodded, she needed to prepare herself for this. She stood up from the table and glanced at the smashed mug pieces on the floor, then shook her head to herself. One of her biggest issues in life was being easily distracted. The task at hand was a clear one, she had a date with a very old friend and didn't want to miss it. She grabbed her bag off the counter and made for the door quickly, she didn't have any candles and she would need some. She glanced at the clock and saw it was past 8pm so her only option was the small one-stop shop around the corner which she didn't mind this as it was faster than a drive to the superstores anyway.

  Without a look back Martha made her way out the house, and jogged the couple of minutes down the street and took a left onto the main stretch. She came to the next left and entered the shop that sat directly on the corner. She usually came in here if she only needed a couple of bits, it was one of those handy shops that stocked a really random assortment. She went down the aisle with fabric softeners and washing up liquid, and right there next to the bin bags she saw the candles and long life matches. She racked her memory, ideally she would be using violet candles as they increased her psychic abilities and in turn the length of time she could host before exhaustion but they only had white. This would have to do, if she remembered correctly she had some cinnamon or frankincense incense sticks in her stash at home and these could serve the same purpose as the violet candle. She grabbed three chunky white candles and some matches and headed straight to the till, eager to get home.

She felt the tingling of excitement mixed with fear and she fought back the guilt that was trying to creep in over not focusing solely on Steven. She knew in her heart that she needed to do this and Susie was clearly a strong entity, which actually made her perfect for Martha's first steps back into the world of hosting a séance. Her last one was with also Susie but she had been alive back then. Shaking off the dark thoughts she handed the money to the cashier and hurried home.

***

Back at home she felt at ease in Susie's presence, she had a feeling similar to when one sat enshrouded in a weighted blanket. She lay a blanket on the floor in the middle of the living room, placed the candles on a wooden board, lit some frankincense incense sticks and laid out the Ouija board for just in case she wasn't able to channel Susie properly. Without any more hesitation she nodded to herself and closed her eyes slowly, drew in a deep breath and began to speak clearly and concisely:

"I pray for protection from any being who would do me harm. I ask my protectors to allow only good spirits into my presence this night. I reach out to Susie Knight, please join me when you are ready."

Martha kept her eyes closed and rested her hands with her palms facing upwards on her crossed legs. It wasn't long until she started to see some beginnings of shapes behind her eyelids and she kept her breath steady and shallow making sure to be a welcoming host for Susie. All of a sudden a whooshing sensation swept through her and chilled her to the core. A small smile tugged at her lips and she spoke once more,

"Susie, it has been so long. I thought you would have moved into the spirit realm long ago."

"I would have hoped to have too, but something is holding me back my friend. You have been closed off to me since I departed my physical form. Why?" the voice of her old friend sounded distant and it wasn't because of the volume at which she spoke. At this point she had been on the other side of life for over thirty years.

"I was afraid. I wasn't cautious the last time and assumed that I knew better, neglecting to perform a protective incantation which would have taken a mere half a minute. I welcomed a spectra into our midst and in doing so gave them the power to latch on to you. I had to promise my family I wouldn't contact the other side again after you died, and I accepted because it was my fault, I wasn't careful and it cost you everything."

Martha let it gush out of her and she was breathless by the time she stopped. It felt good to verbalise how she felt about it and acknowledge her guilt to the one it mattered most to. She wondered if the connection had been broken, as silence was the only response for nearly a minute, she waited patiently for Susie to speak once more,

"It's silly to blame yourself for anything that happened. I entered that séance with you knowing there was something in the room with us, it wasn't just up to you to remember the protective incantations. I knew I was putting myself at risk and had assumed nothing could happen to us. We cannot change the past and it doesn't make sense to torture ourselves over such things. He was such an evil spirit I don't think a protective incantation would have done much to stop him in the end, he tortured me for what felt like months and I wasn't his first. I knew I couldn't rid myself of him so I made my decision. I didn't know you'd blamed yourself all these years. I wish you had tried to connect with me and talk to me about it, although I understand why you didn't." Susie said softly, her voice echoing through Martha's head.

Her head bowed as she listened to Susie's words, to hear from Susie herself that she didn't blame her lifted a weight she had carried for more than half her lifetime.

"Mattie?"

"Yes Susie?"

"Something is happening Mattie, oh my! It's finally happening, well now we know. After all this time I was here waiting for you, and it was worth it. It's beautiful Mattie, you should see it someday."

Tears burned in the corners of Martha's eyes as she listened to her old friend. It seemed cruel that after four decades she finally got to hear her voice again and she was now being taken away once more. She knew what was happening, the tether that had bound Susie to this plane was finally broken.

"I love you Susie. Thank you for waiting for me."

"Goodbye, my friend." Came Susie's response, the echo so long and distant now Martha knew they were the last words she would hear and her grief felt renewed. This combined with the pain that rested in her heart from losing Steven made her feel like she could hardly breath for a moment.

She ended the séance and opened her eyes, gasping when she was greeted with the ghostly face of Susie smiling at her, eternally youthful at nineteen years old. Susie met her eyes then nodded and faded away, leaving Martha slumped on the floor trying to process the renewed pain which was hardly lessened by the alleviation of the guilt she had carried for so long.

Chapter Fifteen

Loud rhythmic smashing noises was all he could hear and Steven looked around trying to work out where it was coming from. The area he was in was hazy and smoke filled so he couldn't make anything out.

"This oughta do it man. Ain't nobody done anything for Brute since he was hit and Yeti has been around his spot like nothing happened. How'd he manage to keep his brains in his thick skull huh?" the ranting came from a burly looking guy, his features were obscured by the ski mask he wore but Steven would recognise that voice and stature anywhere, it was Shells.

He still couldn't make out many details and he moved himself closer to the commotion, there was a hooded figure repeatedly smashing a crowbar down onto the bonnet of a car, impaling the thin metal over and over again. The guy wielding the crowbar had a huge joint hanging from his lips and he paused every few seconds to take a hefty toke and released thick new plumes into the air around him.

"You got the fuel?" he panted up to Shells, who quickly lifted a faded red jerry can up to show him. "Good."

"Hey Grid. Just a thought. Maybe we shouldn't burn it yet, how will Yeti see his car has been hit if we burn it? We should do that another day right? Show him someone is after him."

Grid? He was surprised to see him there with Shells considering the last time they'd hung out Brute had laid into him for being loose-lipped and chatting about things that didn't concern him, or them. The air was still heavy with smoke but Steven wanted to see where he was so he moved back a bit and took in the surrounding area. They were in a big underground garage by the looks of it, he assumed it was attached to the flats occupied by Yeti. There weren't many other cars in here but he could see a couple of dusty looking surveillance cameras in the corners. Not that they were ever on in places like this, people were paid to disconnect the wires and look the other way.

"You might be right, we should come back and hit him again later. Really screw with him."

"Cool to see you on side like this man." Came Shells muffled voice.

"He was one of the good ones, kept it real. Don't see that a lot no more. We didn't always get on but he did put me back in line and I'd probably be dead by now if he hadn't. Least I can do, bonus is Yeti is a class A prick and I want to see him go down." Grid replied.

Steven was surprised by this and felt pride boom inside of him. Shells was nodding his agreement at him, Steven was sure that if his face hadn't been obscured by a ski mask he would be able to see that sloped smile on his friends face.

"You know it. Let's get out of here before someone catches us." Shells said and they stubbed out their smokes, gathered the crowbar and fuel canister up and dashed to the ramp leading out onto the main street.

As they left the air cleared quickly and Steven couldn't help but be impressed at how much smoke two people had created. His surprise at the evaporating cloud was short-lived, replaced quickly by satisfaction at the state of Yeti's pride and joy. It wasn't every day you saw a BMW 3 series with blacked-out windows sporting more puncture wounds than your average punk. He glanced over to see the retreating backs of Shells and Grid and wondered why he was still here when clearly nothing was happening anymore. He made to move out of the garage towards the ramp but something fixed him in place and the more he fought it the more he felt the invisible ties that bound him tighten, he struggled with the concept of being restrained whilst not having physical form.

He was learning more and more about just how little the vessel in which he spent his short physical life mattered, it was all about the energy contained within it – his soul. He could move things, feel things, even smell them at times and the more he considered the magic of it the more powerful he felt. He submitted to the pressure holding him in place and it eased off instantly, reminding him of being a toddler yanking his mum's hand to go a certain direction whilst she steadily held her ground and didn't budge. Everything started to fizzle in front of him and he blinked rapidly to clear the view but all that happened was everything began to sway after each blink. He came in and out as though he was losing consciousness, when suddenly with a thud everything cleared and he was in the same place but it was substantially darker now, and someone was approaching the beaten up BMW.

He gazed upon the fast approaching figure and his excitement mounted, it was Yeti. So that was why he was held back, he chastised himself for not remembering that everywhere he had gone so far had held some purpose, even drifting along the streets early on was for him to process. Yeti got level with his car, his dishevelled appearance made worse by the heavy bags under his well-dilated eyes and gaunt cheeks. Good, thought Steven, Yeti deserved all the unrest and problems that he had coming his way, it made him feel a little better about being killed over a crappy bag of weed to see him suffering.

"What the…" Yeti murmured to himself, before frantically looking around the garage to see if he had company, "who's there? Show yourself!" he shouted out, it simply echoed back at him and he looked enraged.

He looked down at the bonnet and Steven revelled in glee watching his enemy's demeanour crumble before his eyes, here came that infamous temper. He smashed his fists down on the already irreparable bonnet and caught both his hands on the punctured metal. He roared out in uncontrollable rage and kicked the number plate before smashing both his now torn hands onto the windscreen crushing it inwards. He huffed out a few breaths and stood back, then looked around the room and his breathing evened out, he even let a grim smile cross his features. He dug into his pocket and pulled out his phone, smearing dark blood on his jeans but not seeming to notice nor care. Steven wondered who he was going to call, when Yeti abruptly turned on his heel and stalked towards the closest security camera and got up close to it. He read something on the side and tapped it into his keypad and hit dial, it rang for a few minutes all whilst Yeti paced back and forth barely controlling his temper. He suddenly stopped in his tracks and tilted his head, the recipient of the call had clearly just picked up.

"Hi. I'm calling about some of your cameras, I need the footage. Now."

Steven tried to listen to the other side but couldn't hear, it was just broken babbling sounds. He kept trying to go near the phone but Yeti was fidgeting and moving from spot to spot in an angry pace. He focused on the handset and tried to channel his hearing to it directly and felt an uneasy sensation come over his entire being, and suddenly he couldn't see anything. There were some tinny sounds that wove in and out of an offensive pitch and Steven tried to work out what had happened when a clear female voice penetrated through all the other noises.

"I understand what you're saying sir, but it looks like the cameras for Fox House flats are not in use currently."

"What do you mean? There are two cameras I can see near me. Two! What the fuck is the point in them if you do not use them?" came Yeti's reply, his voice rippling with his barely controlled rage.

"I can see they were deactivated around two months ago, at the request of the building owner. You'll have to speak with him if you wish to discuss this further."

"Why would he disable the cameras on his building? Someone has smashed my car up and I need to know who did it!"

"I'm sorry sir, I don't know what I can say to you. The cameras are not set to record."

"Don't say sorry to me you stupid cow, that doesn't fix it does it?!" and with that the line went dead and Steven could hear the tinny noise again.

The blackness was heavy and Steven imagined pushing out with some force and that uneasy sensation came over him again and he found himself in the light once more, looking upon a very angry Yeti. He must have somehow moved himself inside the phone, or was he around it? He couldn't tell. Yeti was scrolling now and nodded to himself before hitting the dial button once more. The wounds on his hands had started to clot already, and he idly scratched the one holding the phone to his ear whilst he waited. He seemed noticeably more calm now.

"Gem? Hey babe. Look, somethings come up and I can't get to the party tonight. You're going to have to take one for the team and deal on your own. You good?" he spoke clearly, not belying his current emotional state at all. "I know, I know. But I trust you, we can make up anything we lose by hitting another house party tomorrow. Don't worry. Come back hot and ready you hear?" He leered into the handset and terminated the call.

With that he gave one last look at his car, one of the only things in life he had any care for and riled himself up, then walked with purpose to the door that Steven assumed gave direct entry to the flats. Finally, after a few minutes of wondering if he needed to move on or if he would be taken somewhere the setting faded away from him.

Chapter Sixteen

Everything was moving at an alarming speed and Steven found himself struggling to focus on anything, the surroundings zipped past him but he wasn't moving forward, he was moving up. The view kept warping and huge metal frames and wooden panels kept appearing then just as quickly blurring back into the mess of muted colours flying past him. This felt like it went on for a long while before he found himself stationary in a large well-furnished living area, there was a commotion happening somewhere nearby and Steven looked around to see where he was.

There was a photo on the wall above the sofa of a weathered guy with his arms around two teenagers, presumably his kids based on their similar features. Steven didn't recognise him at all so why was he here? He picked up on the sound of scuffling and followed it through a narrow doorway the other side of the room, he was in a dimly lit hallway and there were two rooms to choose from. He could see one of them was a bathroom through the open door, and the sound wasn't coming from there. He turned his attention to the second option, just past the first door and as he approached it the sounds became louder,

"You screwed with the wrong guy! Do you know who I work for? Who I am?" Yeti was angrily hissing into the ear of the man he had pinned to the four poster bed that filled most of the small room.

It was the older guy from the picture in the living room, he was whimpering back at Yeti trying to tell him he didn't know who he worked for.

"Well that's your mistake then isn't it!" Yeti lost his control and shouted into his face, bringing his blood-crusted fist down onto the mans chest which was rising and falling at an alarming rate. He choked and spluttered at the force. "Why the hell did you turn off the cameras?"

"You told me to! You said you had business here and didn't want – and I quote – nosey pricks in your business. You told me my life depended on it!" The guy on the bed spluttered.

"Bullshit!" Yeti roared.

"It's true! About two months ago, you said you had a new job and needed privacy. I didn't want to know, you said you'd add tips to the rent so that worked fine for me. I haven't even chased you for the rent you haven't paid since then, forget about the tips!"

Steven had to give credit to the guy, despite facing off with an overly angry, clearly high and well-built Yeti he was still fighting his own corner. Yeti was looking a little confused.

"I did start my new work about two months ago…" he murmured.

Steven wished he could say something, tell Yeti he couldn't remember it because he was probably too busy getting lit off the gear he was meant to shift to remember important things like who he had threatened and why. He was surprised anyone put any faith in him or had any respect for him.

He felt his own rage bubbling up again, thinking about how this pathetic excuse of a person had the nerve to end his life. He decided to let loose and take pity on what seemed to be the owner of the building. He felt his core heating up, the energy amassing into one big invisible ball and with a single thought he forced it outwards and watched as it smashed full force into Yeti, sending him crashing into the guy on the bed and then over, cracking his head on the wooden headboard.

"What the hell!" Yeti shrieked in horror. He scrambled backwards away from the bewildered landlord, "Was that you?!"

"Obviously not!" came the landlords laboured reply.

Yeti let out a frustrated roar, leapt forwards and started pummelling the landlord in the face, the man tried to ward off the punches by holding his hands up but it proved futile. Yeti didn't stop until the man under him stopped twitching, the blood on his hands a grisly mixture of his own and the landlords. He moved away from him and spat at him in disgust. Steven was watching the whole thing, a grim sensation gripping him. Yeti's unpredictability had won again, Steven had thought he would leave after being thrown into a wall by an invisible force, he might have to up his game if he was going to make any kind of impact on him.

He realised Yeti lived in a semi-permanent state of being high and would likely forget about these events or assume he was tripping. Steven scanned the room for inspiration and his gaze landed on a small ornament of a dog, one of those old-fashioned china ones that lived in the nooks and crannies in grandparents' homes. He thought back to the planchette and Ouija board and tunnelled his focus into that small dog, after clearing his head Steven found himself feeling a connection to the object and honed in on the sensation. It quivered for a moment much like the planchette had, but this time felt a little different. Although he had no body and therefore no hands to feel the weight of anything anymore, he could feel the displaced weight about his being which he knew instinctively was his energy being exerted to raise the china dog off the side. He hovered it around Yeti's head for a moment trying to get his attention which only took around two seconds. The bewilderment that came across his previously furious expression was worthy of a photo and Steven had to work hard to maintain his focus. Now he had Yeti's attention he channelled the last dwindling spare energy he had left and launched the ornament into his agape face, feeling some semblance of joy when it crunched into his nose. It made a satisfying squelching noise and instantly exploded with sprays of blood. Yeti yelped in shock and covered his face whilst backing away out of the room, staring at the surprisingly unbroken china dog that lay on the threadbare rug.

They used to take much more care in making products back in the day, everything was so flimsy and broke easily nowadays. Steven wanted to torment him more but his exertions had completely drained him and he found himself fading in and out of the room, much like after he had done the Ouija board reading with his mum. His vision completely faded out whilst looking upon a simultaneously enraged and unnerved Yeti holding his nose, frantically looking around the room, searching for something that made sense – the only being present that could have been an outlet for the emotional bomb ticking inside him was steadily getting colder, dead on the bed.

Chapter Seventeen

Tim sat staring at the lady in front of him, her loose wavy hair mostly light brown with a few white hairs, the ends giving away the fact it had once been darker but age had lightened the overall hue. She looked back at him inquisitively and he couldn't work out why or how this woman was managing to draw him in so effortlessly. Once he left her place last time he felt something lift away from him enough that he remembered he had no interest in forming any kind of friendship or connection with anyone, let alone someone twenty years his senior but somehow here he was here once more.

He had been sat at home in his baggy lounge pants mulling over the monotony of life and all its beings, when the phone started jangling its incessantly annoying tune, reminding him he needed to put it on silent. He wanted to ignore the ringing handset as he usually would, but something compelled him to pick up. He heard her honeyed voice as soon as he put the phone to his ear and before he knew it he was agreeing to walk around to hers and let her 'sound off' at him. He was acutely aware of how out of character it was for him to even talk to someone without having to restrain himself from tearing them limb from limb in a verbal assault, and yet couldn't say no to this woman who before a few days ago he had only seen in passing and shared a handful of words with.

"Sorry, what did you say?"

"I asked if you wanted a drink? Or something to eat? It's the least I can do for you after you've come all the way around here after work." Martha replied.

"I would enjoy a tea." He replied, and watched as she got up and sashayed to the kitchen area to make their drinks.

He thought back to the other day when she walked away from him and he had been so convinced she had walked in a certain manner to entice him. Either that was the way she walked or she was again trying to keep his attention. In case it was the latter he made a point of looking away so if she glanced back she could see he wasn't completely drawn in by her.

He focused on the rug below him, allowing his eyes to skim over the old fashioned floral design that bordered it, then once he had followed the outermost pattern all the way round he moved in to the next rectangle of patterns. He repeated this until he heard Martha's footsteps approaching him again and he looked up and as he did he noticed a concerned look upon her face.

"Is everything ok?" he asked, extending his hand to take one of the steaming mugs from her.

"Sure. I think so. I don't know." She murmured.

"Right. So you went from sure to I don't know pretty quickly there. Sit down, talk. That was what you wanted, wasn't it?" Tim asked pointedly.

Martha's face twitched for a moment, taken aback but she couldn't argue, that was why she asked him round.

"It was, it is. I think this grieving process is very much a rollercoaster. Some moments I feel fine and I'm functioning great, then I'm hit with a wallop of guilt that I'm not actively mourning Steven, like I should spend the rest of my days in the corner of his old bedroom wishing he could return. I don't want to do that and he wouldn't want me to, he was never one to show much emotion and if he could he would likely tell me to stop wallowing right now and do something for myself. I feel stuck between two places without any control over where I am at any time." Martha finished with a long exhalation, feeling better for voicing her feelings.

"I understand. I think. Maybe not through personal experience as my early childhood memories are vague and I've never formed a lasting attachment with anyone. But when I was younger I felt loss too. A loss of opportunity to have those relationships, not that I have wanted to pursue any relations with anyone – but on a very rare occasion I realise it'd be nice to have someone that could fit into my life somewhere."

Again, Tim was taken aback by how openly he was speaking with this woman, saying things he didn't even think about himself. He knew the words were true though, it was like she was opening something in him and he wasn't sure if he liked it.

"You shouldn't feel guilt at feeling alright sometimes though. Like you say, Steven would want you to be okay, I don't know if you believe in the afterlife but I bet he is looking down on you with pride. You strike me as a strong woman Martha Tawn."

He felt a warmth in the pit of his stomach as he looked at her and spoke words of encouragement. Martha's eyes sparkled as he talked and it reassured him.

"The afterlife you say? What do you think of it? Tell me more." Martha pushed.

A small frown knitted his brow, he paused before responding,

"I don't know what I think of it. No-one knows anything about it or if it even exists do they?"

"I wouldn't say that. What about those who have been brought back from the brink of death and regaled their tales? There are quite a few consistencies in the stories about their experiences." Martha replied.

"True. I can't say I've read into it at all but there could be the reasoning that the hormone that is released when you're close to death simply incurs hallucinations of a sort."

"But how could so many hallucinate the same things? Unconnected people, people from all over the world that had no way of knowing what anyone else had experienced?" she argued.

"Ok. Fair point. I don't have an answer to that. I don't believe that there is simply nothing when we pass on, I don't even think that through fear of death, I just believe that we have to go somewhere and there are so many ghost stories it'd be nice to know we stick around for a bit." Tim replied.

"Me too, I believe in ghosts and I've seen some, if you'd believe it." She dropped the information tentatively, not sure if it was too early to give this information away. She was pleasantly surprised at how well he took it. After raising his eyebrows, and looking into her eyes for a moment Tim realised he fully believed her. Maybe not fully believing in the actual seeing of ghostly beings but he definitely bought that she believed she had.

"Really? Tell me about one, I'm curious."

"Ok. One of the most memorable times I saw a ghost was when I had not long moved into my first flat. I was having trouble sleeping, it took me a long time to adjust to living on my own, so I went to the kitchen to make myself a glass of water and I could see something shadowed in the corner by the broom cupboard. I can't say how, but I knew it was a ghost. I remember taking a deep breath and just staring at that spot showing it that I was aware of its presence and ok with it. It then broke away from the corner and took two or three steps towards me before fading into nothing. There were no details, just a shadowy silhouette."

"Didn't that scare you?" Tim asked.

"No, if you're open minded you can pick up on the intentions of an ethereal being. I saw him a couple of times whilst I lived there and he never bothered me much. He wasn't a bad ghost, just stuck in the plane between the spirit world and earth." Martha realised she was maybe going a bit too much into it but Tim was lapping it up.

"That's quite something." Was all Tim said. He was enthralled by this conversation. Again for reasons unknown to him, something that before held no appeal was now piquing his interest. "What about now? Do you see them often?"

"No. I realised I had something of a gift – or curse – with no real idea what I was doing so I ignored all the things I saw and heard until my ability disappeared. It can be foolish to open connections with those who have passed on because those open connections can create pathways for less desirable energies to travel." She replied tersely.

"Did that ever happen to you?" his tone was cautious, sensing difficult ground but unable to resist asking.

"Yes." The way she said it made it clear that this was not a conversation she was willing to have now. He wondered also if she would be able to see her son too, then dismissed the thought when he recalled she had said she had given up her ability. He was so curious about it all but sensed he shouldn't try to push more on it just yet. "Don't forget your tea Tim." She said pointedly with a nod to his cup. He was about to reply when the door started knocking, Martha jumped and looked around in confusion. "Excuse me." She said and jumped up to answer the door. She pulled it open just as it started to knock again with an impatient rapping, it was Alicia.

"Hi! I wasn't expecting you, are you ok?" Martha said whilst keeping the door partially closed. Alicia cocked her head and frowned.

"Since when do you 'expect me'? What are you doing?" she asked.

"Nothing, just having tea. Now isn't a good time." came Martha's reply.

"How is it not a good time. You're one of the people I can absolutely guarantee would be able to accommodate someone for a cup of coffee last minute. Again, what are you doing?" she pushed. Martha sighed and stepped closer to her sister, keeping her voice low, "I have company."

"Someone I'm not supposed to know about?" Alicia pried, confusion and vague amusement at Martha's behaviour twisting her lips upwards.

"No, nothing like that. I wasn't going to say anything but I didn't want to put more pressure on you and I haven't been handling the grief very well, so I went to the doctors and they've assigned me a grief counsellor for a couple of sessions. This is my first one." She replied.

"Oh Mattie. I'm sorry. You should have said, you are never putting too much pressure on me but I do understand the need to outsource to someone unconnected. I just came by to check in on you and ask if you wanted to come to the prison tomorrow to see Seth and Ross with me?" Alicia said, feeling bad for pushing.

"I don't know, can you come by before you go and ask again? I'm really having to take each day as it comes at the moment."

"Sure, sure. I understand. Look, go back to your session. If you need to, call me or pop round later." She said, giving Martha a quick squeeze and a meaningful look in the eyes and then she turned on her heel and walked back down the path towards her home. Martha breathed out a sigh then stepped back in, pulling the door closed behind her. Tim was just sat holding his now empty mug.

"Everything alright?" he asked, not belying his curiosity as to why she lied to her visitor about him. She obviously wasn't aware that he was keen of hearing thanks to years of having to listen out for footsteps in the night when he'd spent some time on the streets, and earwigging on murmured conversations by his various carers. Martha had taken care to speak in a lower tone when talking to her unexpected visitor but the effort was wasted in this instance.

"Yes, all ok. Nothing important. Just my sister popping in to check on me." Martha replied, not meeting his gaze.

"Did you want me to leave?" Tim asked, half hoping she would say yes so he didn't have to deal with this strange pull he had to this woman anymore.

"No, not at all. Do you want a refill?" she replied, gesturing at his cup. Tim shook his head in response. "Very well. Alicia wanted to know if I wanted to go to the prison tomorrow to see her sons with her." She explained. He couldn't hide his surprise at that.

"Prison?"

"Yes. Both found in possession of drugs." Came her short reply, foreseeing the question and answering before he bothered.

"That must have been hard for you all to know that was in your family. I know your son was a trouble maker but I assume not in that way because you'd have mentioned it, right?" Tim replied, despite his incredibly rocky upbringing he had never turned to any kind of drugs or drink. In fact, he was studiously against it having realised many years ago he preferred to stay sober.

"Yes. It came as a surprise." Replied Martha simply, once more not meeting his eye and looking uncomfortable for a moment before she resumed her neutral expression, "So you seem to have an interest in the afterlife, going by your questions earlier at least. Have you ever had any experiences?"

Tim didn't bother to address the sudden switch in direction for conversation,

"I don't think so. I've had times where I'm sure there is something with me but I have never seen or heard anything to show me there is an actual ghost."

"Would you ever be interested in interacting with someone who had passed on?" Martha asked, pushing harder now.

"I don't know anyone who has died that I care enough to speak to again, so I am not sure, why?" Tim replied, starting to feel wary. Martha picked up on this.

"No reason, just one of those random questions that popped into my head. I know people have this curiosity about the dead and what happens. I guess because I've seen and heard things from a young age it doesn't create that small band of unease in my tummy, you know?"

"Unease?"

"Yes, or unsureness maybe. It is the unknown until you experience it no matter what you read, hear or see on television."

"I suppose." Tim replied, feeling like he was being sold something and had no idea what or why.

"How is work?" came the unexpected question from Martha. He frowned before answering.

"I hate it, and the people. I actually quite enjoy the dentistry side of things but the rest of the daily scene that greets me when I step foot through that damn door every day drains the very soul from my body." he said bluntly.

"Sounds awful. Must be hard having a role in something you're passionate about only for the enjoyment to be nullified by everything else. Is there anything you can do about it?"

"No. I want to own a private practice but don't have the funds, I'd like to choose my clientele and staff, if you met my receptionist you'd understand why."

Tim said with a bitter edge. Martha nodded sympathetically. He watched her again, seeing her reactions to his true feelings about these things and realised she hadn't reacted at all badly which was unheard of. He realised then that maybe all this time he just needed someone who could listen and not judge, and not pressure him with anything. He decided Martha fit the bill of someone he could readily accept in his life as an acquaintance – something he never thought he would feel or think about anyone.

Chapter Eighteen

He found himself in his old bedroom and wondered why he was in here as it was vacant, he looked around for a clue and realised he could hear a low conversation happening somewhere outside the room. He couldn't make out much and his instinct told him he was here to pay attention, so he focused harder on trying to listen. No luck. He felt frustration bubble and tamped it down.

He wasn't sure how long he had been gone for again but was quickly learning that big expulsions of energy meant he had to go and recharge in the void. Not that it meant anything to him as he had no sense of time passing. It was like he simply ceased to be, until he was ready to exist in some format again. He wanted to go the other side of the door so he could see what was happening, but he hadn't practiced anything or moved through objects since he first came around after death. He inhaled deeply, then berated himself for such a stupid move. He didn't have lungs.

Somehow he kept forgetting that he wasn't in a physical form anymore and kept walking, breathing and blinking as though he had the relevant parts to do all those things with. To be fair when he looked down at himself he could see his body in a strange translucent way, he thought about when he told his legs to stop moving and they had obliged readily, this gave him an idea. Now he looked down and assessed them again and thought about them being nothing, and just like that his legs dissolved into thin air and he was just his upper body. He swung what would have been his leg towards the door and nothing happened. He went through the same process with the rest of his body and just as easily as the legs, it vanished.

Steven found himself pleased at this discovery and found it laughable that his only hindrance had turned out to be himself, and with full confidence drifted towards the door, through it, and then out the other side.

The only thing of note from that was a woody taste, but the taste was an all over sensation as opposed to something you'd taste in your mouth, a bit like when he had had to climb out of his own grave and could taste substances he'd rather not think about.

"I fully believe that if you can somehow source the funding you should take the leap Tim. How can you not think that it was about time you chased your own dream, you deserve your own happiness."

His mum was talking to a tall lean guy sat on the sofa, his hand clasped between her own. Steven tried to assess the situation but failed to make sense of it, missing so many things by being elsewhere meant he didn't know what was going on, especially with his mum it seemed.

"You know, you're right! I damn well should. I've paid my dues, I shouldn't have to deal with snotty kids and snobby parents day in day out when all they have to do is a little hygienic practice a couple times a day. It's embarrassing really! They say all sorts, they even claim that their kids *do* brush and floss but the evidence doesn't lie Martha!" he replied passionately.

Steven recognised him from somewhere but he was sure he hadn't seen him around his mum. His mum didn't really have any friends and kept everyone except family (mostly) at arm's length. She was nodding back at her guest, showing her appreciation of what he was saying.

"You're right, it must be difficult. I couldn't do it. When my Steven was little he was so good at caring for his teeth he didn't have a single filling. I always made sure to teach him the importance of oral hygiene."

Steven felt surprised to see his mum lie so fluidly, he hated brushing his teeth as a kid and she was lucky if he did it once a day. She was clearly trying to get this guy on side for something. She seemed to notice his presence suddenly and if he didn't know her so well he would have missed her subtle change in demeanour.

"That doesn't surprise me. He was lucky to have you, not many parents take such care with their kids and it is always the kids who pay for it in the long run. Hard to pity them though when they've been raised to be little swines."

Martha was unable to hide her reaction to this and winced. He saw it and carried on quickly,

"I'm sorry. We should perhaps stop talking about him for a moment?"

"No, I should be able to refer to him without breaking down. Thank you though."

"Strong lady. I realise that despite you telling me you wanted me to come over so you could talk I've done most of the talking. I promise I'm not normally like this." Tim said a little apologetically.

"Sometimes it helps just to listen too. Don't worry, you've done more than enough." Martha replied. Tim nodded, then glanced at the clock on the wall opposite him,

"You've given me a lot to think about Martha, thank you. I hope I have been of some service to you too. I must go, I have work tomorrow and if I don't rest properly I won't handle the people who cross my path half as well as I ought to."

And with that he stood up, placed the teacup on the kitchen side and made for the door, allowing Martha to close it behind him as he stepped through with a nod goodbye. Martha rested her head against the door with her eyes closed for a moment, trying to gather herself enough to keep going on to the next step. Steven noticed this and realised that everything she was doing was for him in some way and he shouldn't have questioned it.

For some time Martha remained there and Steven could have easily mistaken her for sleeping, she looked so peaceful and unmoving. She finally inhaled deeply and looked around the room,

"Steven. Thank you for waiting for me, I had to rest for a moment to replenish some energy. I don't know how much you heard of that, but if you're up for direct contact with me I'll explain everything. I'll put the board out too, in case you need it."

Her voice was weary, but she looked a little more animated as she stepped away from the door and headed over to the table to pull out the Ouija board. Martha was taking control and he knew to simply do as instructed at this moment.

He was enjoying the sensation of being bodiless, not that his ghost body carried any sensations per se, but he realised that having hands and legs when he couldn't use them was unnecessary – the idea of having them now felt like it would be a refusal to accept the reality of his passing. His mum moved swiftly, placing the white candles down, lighting a frankincense incense and placing the fragile Ouija board gently in front of them. She sat cross legged in front of everything and visibly readied herself before speaking,

"I reach out this evening to the spirit of Steven Tawn. Please join me when you are ready."

Steven didn't know what to do, this wasn't the same as before where he moved the planchette. He moved closer and looked over the objects to see if anything became glaringly obvious but nothing stood out, his mum was already in a state of meditation with her eyes closed and palms facing upwards. He had seen something similar to this in movies. She was clearly expecting a different interaction this time as how could she possibly see where he moved the planchette to with her eyes closed? He moved it over to the word no, making sure to make it shake and rattle in place for a moment to gain his mums attention. It worked, she opened her eyes slowly and looked down at the board with the realisation dawning on her that Steven didn't know what do to.

"You need to contact with me directly son, my channel is open for you to connect with me. You will be able to speak with me direct without the use of the board, it will sap your energy but it is more effective for communication." she smiled, not sure quite where in the room he was but maternal instinct telling her the reassuring smile of a loving mother would help him in this moment. It worked, Steven felt ready to try. He focused on his mum this time, and much like with the phone he channelled all his energy into connecting with her direct. The uneasy sensation swamped his being and darkness enshrouded him.

"Mum?" he said, hearing his own voice echo back at him eerily.

That was unexpected, he hadn't actually heard himself since he died, all the shouts and utterings he had tried had all been silent and his imagination simply let him hear what he should have sounded like. Now though that was definitely his voice, a little distant sounding and raspy but it was his.

"Steven! I wasn't sure I'd ever hear your voice again. You've come so far in such a short time since your passing, you're a powerful entity already. Something I wish I'd never have had to witness in my time on this earth but I'm so proud of you nonetheless. You're doing more than most can do at this point." Her tone was teary, but strong.

"It's not that bad." He grunted back. He felt her smile, even though he couldn't see her.

"You must be wondering what is going on. I've been gathering information and my plan is coming together, I've even found a potential vessel for you to use."

"A vessel?" Steven interrupted, confused.

"Yes, a vessel. A body you can take over. Don't you worry about that part I'm sorting it all out for you and will let you know when I am good and ready. I'm just working everything out so there will be no loose ends. It also keeps my mind occupied, I miss you so much but you still need time to strengthen yourself before we attempt anything or you risk doing irreparable damage to your soul."

"Taking someone's body and doing damage to my soul? What would that mean?" Steven asked, feeling uncomfortable about the idea.

He had a sudden barrage of questions about everything but felt like she would tell him more when she was ready, she sounded manic as it was.

"You wouldn't ever be able to leave this plane if you do too much damage your soul, you'll be eternally tethered to the earth and become what is commonly known as an earthbound ghost or a poltergeist."

"That doesn't sound like something I'd want." He replied tersely.

"No I know. I spoke with your cousins the other day which I'm sure you saw. They told me about Yeti, they've confirmed what I needed to hear which is important for when I give the police his name. Do you know his real name?"

"Jake something. I don't know his surname; we never used our real names in the street."

Steven's energy broiled just thinking about Yeti, but he had some level of comfort knowing he'd had the opportunity to torment him multiple times now.

"Right, do you know where he lives? I can try and point them that way."

"Yeah, he lives over on Jewel Street in the corner flats. There'll be police there soon anyway, he just killed his landlord." He said bluntly.

He felt the shock in his mums' reaction at this, as she tried to process the news.

"How do you know this, where you there?" she asked quietly.

Steven started to answer but something stopped him, it felt like his connection to his mum was being strained. He fought to retain the contact but the darkness was lifting around the edge of his vision and he realised it was futile, he could hear a maniacal laughing somewhere nearby and felt the prickles of fear from his mum.

"Mum?" he tried to call out but it sounded so distant he doubted she could hear him.

"Steven! Oh god no, please Steven hold on don't break the connection! Wait!" she sounded panicked, each word heavy with fear. "All entities who are not Steven Tawn are not welcome in this session. Please leave." She shouted, trying to keep authority in her voice.

Steven couldn't hold it anymore and was wrenched away. The light smashed into his vision and it took a moment to balance out again, his mum was still sat on the floor. The candles were lit and flickering wildly whilst her fingers twitched rapidly. There was a translucent dark mass looming over her and Steven did all he could think to do, he gave himself a body again and started waving his hands wildly at the mass. Nothing happened except the laughing he had heard a minute ago started up again and a voice rang out,

"Don't bother young thing, I've been around much longer than you and you can't compete with my strength." it taunted. "Silly little boy like you shouldn't get caught up in a big man's world. Don't think I didn't see you throw that china doggy at your hairy boyfriend, very impressive for a young soul, but it will never be enough."

"What are you?" Steven asked, putting as much brawn into his words as he could. He still couldn't hear his voice outside of his head but it didn't seem to matter to this being, he could hear him just fine.

"I'm someone you would wish not to know. Thanks for opening the gateway to your mother, she was so eager to talk to you she forgot to protect herself. Now I shall see how I can go about convincing her to join little Susie." He sneered.

"Susie was my mums friend. What do you know about her?" Steven asked.

"Well, you'll have to ask dear mother that question, won't you. She was only talking to her the other day you see. Bet she didn't tell you. Anyway, you bore me. Keep on being subpar, perhaps we will speak again."

Suddenly the air lifted and his mum slumped forwards, exhausted. She looked around the room quickly and straightened her back,

"I close this session and pray to my protectors to prevent any more entities making contact." Then she looked down at the floor with an expression of defeat. "I'll talk to you later Steven, please give me some time." And just like that he was dismissed, and pulled away into darkness.

Chapter Nineteen

She had so many things to do but very little motivation to do them. She knew why, and it didn't boil down to just any one reason but some were more prevalent than others. One of the biggest reasons was the fact she had once more let herself and another down in a terrible way. In her haste to make the connection with Steven she had jumped straight into the séance without protecting herself. The last time this happened ended up costing Susie her life and she had now carelessly repeated the mistake, the fears that had sat dormant in her for decades came to fruition – the obsessive evil spirit that had tormented her friend had returned.

It only took two séances, a thought that caused shame to flood through her. He was such a powerful entity that she wasn't sure she could fight him alone but she was going to try - otherwise she would have to seek someone to cleanse her, something she only learned after everything that happened with Susie. Susie had never told her the extent of the torment she had been enduring prior to ending her life, if Martha had known she would have done everything in her power to fix it. Now this evil entity had managed to attach itself to her she was now fully open to any interaction he chose to bestow on her, Martha shuddered at the thought. She needed to hurry up and try to complete a successful cleansing ritual before he drained too much of her energy.

She looked around and checked that the room was as dimmed as it could be for this time of day, happy that it was she sat herself down and crossed her legs aware of his presence, like her intentions had summoned him. He didn't do anything and she knew he was waiting to see what she was going to do. Martha closed her eyes and took three deep breaths,

"I ask the powers that protect me to remove the energy that has wrongfully attached itself to me. I have my auric field open and I expel that which is not desired."

She chanted loudly, drawing strength from her core, repeating it three times feeling her words strengthen each time. Eyes tightly closed she allowed the room around her to fade away and disappear. She envisioned her aura to be clean and white and pushed the image of the darkened figure that shadowed it from the centre outwards, aiming get it to the edge and banish it, slowly it began to move with some resistance. Suddenly her auric field flickered like a dying flame and faded from white to dirty grey and the figure she had been pushing away forced itself back into the centre, Martha could feel the dismay enveloping her. It spoke with a deceptively charming tone,

"Oh Mattie dear, you didn't think I was going to go so soon did you? Don't you know how this works? I need your energy to keep me going, I'm not going anywhere."

"Who even are you?" she asked, swallowing her panic. "Why me?"

"Who am I? Well, I'm an old friend!" he taunted. "I am the one who is going to ensure your wellbeing, if you're a good girl that is. Little Susie was very naughty indeed, kept trying to tell me to go away. I sang her to sleep so many nights you know, songs of the past. Sure the lyrics were sometimes a little less than cheery but the melody was to die for! She never appreciated the effort you know?"

"I'm guessing that is rhetorical." Martha sneered. A sudden shooting pain pierced through her head and she reeled back in shock.

"Now now Mattie. Be nice." He said in a singsong voice.

"What is your name?" Martha asked again, breathing deeply.

"Does it matter? You're getting on a bit now Mattie you'll likely forget it in a few minutes."

"Try me." Martha said, trying to keep civil, the pain in her head was certainly thanks to her unwanted guest and preferably avoided.

"Fine. Have it your way, you can earn my name. You do as I say and I will give you letters of my name."

"What would you have me do?" Martha asked tentatively, she was surprised by the sudden shift in energy.

Perhaps doing as she was told would prevent him doing her any real harm, then soon she could have his name and the power to banish him herself.

"Wow look at that. I didn't even have to push. Beautiful. I'll tell you something Mattie as you and I will be spending some time together, you're the first person who gave in so quickly to my request to do what I say. I wonder if it is because you're trying to gain something? Hmm?"

"I want to put a name to the person who killed my friend and likely others before and since." Martha hissed losing control over her temper.

This time a bolt of fiery pain went through her core and harsh laughter rolled through her head.

"Oh silly. You should have just said, I killed no-one, their weaknesses did." He said lightly, after ceasing the laughter.

"Well, will you tell me now then?" she asked, ignoring his jibe.

"No. A deal has been struck." Came the harsh reply and Martha felt her spirits sink.

"I suppose it has. What do you want me to do first?"

"Go for a walk." Martha frowned, what a strange request. "I'll be with you the whole way, just be sure to listen out for me when I tell you what is next."

The fog lifted and Martha opened her eyes, disheartened that she had been unable to banish him. Not that she was surprised, just disappointed. It looked like it was going to be the hard way and based on the pains he inflicted on her without hesitation she knew he wasn't messing around. She wondered where Steven was and if he would be able to reach her. She stood up, brushed herself down and then went and put on her worn brown loafers and soft knit shawl for warmth. The evening air could be very cool and she wasn't sure how long she would be out for.

***

Trudging along the streets Martha wondered when she would hear his voice again. When she would hear Steven's voice again. She remembered she needed to go to the police station and tell them about Yeti – but as yet she had not worked out how to word it in a way that didn't make her sound crazy or mean she was putting her nephews in dangers way. She hadn't seen anyone yet and the outside felt lonely, making her wish for the comfort of her home. She felt a little fogginess come over her and knew that she was about to be spoken to,

"Go find the beggar who lives in the park." He whispered to her. Although the voice was not external to her, in her mind she could feel his lips close to her ear whilst he spoke. She shuddered.

"Then what? I won't do your evil bidding!" she whispered and was immediately rewarded with the blinding pain in her head and she tried to shake it away. He held the band of pain there for a moment longer before releasing. He didn't speak, just waited for her reaction. "I'm going." She panted.

Making her way to the park she wondered if he could hear her thoughts, she knew that in a séance the spirits conversed with you mentally but she wasn't sure how it worked with a spirit attachment. Perhaps this was to be her only place of respite, in her own thoughts.

She arrived at the park and it was its usual sorry state and as expected the elderly man was hunched over in his usual position on the slope behind the metal slide. The fogginess she felt a moment ago came in even stronger and something unfamiliar bubbled up inside her. Not sure what she was doing she took two strong strides forward and swung her right leg up swiftly, kicking the paper bag out of his hand. The look of shock that flashed over his face was something she'd likely never erase from her memory. She immediately opened her mouth to apologise,

"You filthy scum, you belong in the earth not on it!" was all that came out and she put her hands to her mouth to silence the poisonous words.

The elderly man was scrambling away in fear and Martha felt her whole being sink in shame and disgust. The voice spoke to her,

"Very good Mattie. You did that very well. Who knew you could be so...direct?"

She bit back the retort that was on the tip of her tongue, not willing to endure more of that pain he seemed so eager to deliver. Somehow he had controlled her and she was mortified watching the poor man running away from her, she turned on her heel and made for home hating every moment that passed. She wished she had her Steven here, not sure that he could do anything but it would have been a comfort.

"As promised, a letter of my name is 'E'." he said, in a playful tone, letting the vowel tail off in a songlike fashion.

"Thanks." Martha mumbled back.

Feeling dejected she made it to her front door, opened it and went inside. She didn't bother to take her shoes or coat off, and just went to Steven's room and laid on the bed curling up in a ball like she did when feeling overwhelmed or sad.

"You look like you need some space, I'll leave you this then so you don't forget me." Came the voice.

A moment later her feet started to seize up and she shot upwards quickly trying to pull her toes back to stop the cramps. She had them terribly as a kid and learned that if you pulled your toes towards you it prevents it from taking hold. She stopped the cramp and waited for the tingling ache to leave but it didn't ease up. After a few minutes she tried to wriggle her toes and the muscles twinged in warning. She heard a faint laughing and it got louder and louder as though approaching her. It stopped abruptly.

"Good luck with that – I was going to just leave you to it but the joy of seeing your confusion was too precious. You know, the constant verging on the edge of cramp is one of my favourites. Your energy drains much faster when filled with negative emotions, which naturally I get to lap up like a kitty-cat with its cream. Look at the state of you, bon appetit to me!"

Once more he left, Martha could feel the empty space where his menacing energy had been just moments before. The thing that didn't leave was the horrible sensation in her feet and she knew she was in for a long night. The only thing that kept her from falling straight into the dark well of depression was that he didn't seem to be able to hear her thoughts. That, and the plan she was slowly forming. Thanks to her natural ability to sense presences she figured she could pay a visit to the local church and find a priest to help her banish this evil entity who she was now going to refer to as 'E', as long as she couldn't sense him nearby, it could work.

She didn't know if she could do it right now though, the feeling in her feet was making her nauseous and just the thought of trying to walk on them was making it worse. But the idea of handling a whole night, or however long it was until E returned, was just as awful a prospect. If this was even half of what Susie had endured at such a young age then she understood why after months of not being able to remove him she gave up.

Chapter Twenty

Steven travelled swiftly down the pathway deep in thought, indistinctive buildings passing each side of him, again he wasn't sure how long he had been gone but he was uneasy thanks to the last interaction he had with his mum. What was he supposed to do? What could he have done? It had felt like he had been hanging on a cliff edge and a maniac picked his fingers off one by one. The rushed movement around him suddenly stopped and he found himself in an unmistakable place, it was the same in pretty much every prison you went to.

The stairs each side led up to a balcony that ran round the entire perimeter, with countless cells dotted along it. The floor was painted a royal blue and the heavy-duty doors were an off white blemished with scuff marks. The area was vacated with the exception of a few uniformed men walking back and forth looking bored. Steven wondered what he was here for and watched as the officer closest to him looked up at the big black and white clock that hung on the back wall of the second floor and huffed to himself. He then stepped briskly over to the railings of the stairs and dragged his baton across them like an oversized off-key xylophone.

"Free time! You know the drills, stand by your cell door hands in front of you. If you do not comply you do not get your free time today."

He inclined his head at another officer standing nearby who nodded curtly back at him, then went and busied himself unlocking the cell doors downstairs whilst the first officer went upstairs to start opening those cells. One by one they clicked open and the inmates stepped out of their dimly lit cells. If they were lucky and on good behaviour they'd be allowed out onto the court, but these officers preferred to keep their inmates inside, easier to keep an eye on them all that way.

Steven watched with some level of bemusement, so many times he had managed to evade the clutches of the justice system and thought he was just a lucky one. He wasn't sure how lucky he felt now thinking about the fact he'd been murdered on his own corner at just twenty-four years old, he felt his rage simmering again as he once more reflected on his misfortune. He tamped down the wrath threatening to burst from him and felt frustration at not releasing it. The feeling quickly turned to grim satisfaction as remembered that the emotions could be stored and used to his advantage, if he controlled them. He had found that even though he was relatively peaceful in his 'resting' state that inner fire was very quick to rile up and get burning, much like it had been in life. He wondered how powerful he could be if he could churn it all up into an inferno, he was new to all this after all and it only stood to reason that with practice he would get better and stronger, the damage he had dealt so far was surely nothing compared to what he could achieve. He might even be able to fend off that other spirit who had taunted both him and his mum, saying he would try and convince her to do something stupid. He wished he was near her now to at least try to help and wondered if the other spirit was still with her.

He was so caught up in his thoughts he hadn't noticed that the inmates had all moved from outside their doorways, they were now all milling about talking amongst themselves. Steven scanned the room for the reason he was here, he was now sure it was going to be something related to Seth or Ross, or both. Soon enough he saw them and he noticed their body language was less than inviting, which wasn't surprising as no-one wanted to look soft in prison. Despite the fact he hadn't seen them in years they both looked pretty much the same as before, just a touch paler and broader in the shoulders. They'd turned into men since he'd laid eyes on them last and they may have said the same of him, if his physical body wasn't currently worm food six feet under. He had a moment of wistfulness remembering when they were all young, but he vehemently shook that off. No time for such weak thinking, he needed to be strong now more than ever, everything depended on his actual energy and he couldn't think small.

He paid attention to his cousins and realised with dismay that something was going down and it looked like they were in the middle of it. He got closer and checked out who the guy at the front was, he was currently jabbing his stubby finger at the air in front of Ross's chest but not actually touching it. He was a burly looking guy with a tattooed face and the typical barbed wire around his upper arm, just visible underneath the sleeves of his t-shirt. Steven didn't recognise him, he tuned into the words instead.

"…little scumbag thinking you can run your mouth being a snitch!"

"Look mate, I don't know what you've heard but we've not said anything to anyone about anyone. What are you talking about?"

This came from Ross, who despite facing off with what looked to be a weathered prisoner who could overpower him fairly easily kept his tone level and direct.

"Cocky prick. Information has been passed down the line and they know you blabbed to that old chick who came in, the dead guys mum of all people. You must be dumb to think that would go unnoticed."

"You don't understand, she was never going to say anything!" Seth put in.

"Why? Because she is your family? You're more stupid than I thought. You really think we didn't know that Brute was your cousin? We've got links and those links know *everything*."

"Ok, so we messed up. Sorry. Won't happen again." Ross said in surrender putting his hands up to show he wasn't going to argue any longer.

Seth was watching cautiously and a shout bellowed from his mouth a moment too late as he saw the guy who'd been challenging them put his hand behind his back and take something from someone behind him, then in one swift confident movement he brought it upwards and thudded it into Ross' neck. There was no glint of a blade and Seth pulled his brother backwards in shock trying to work out what he had just been hit by. Steven oversaw the whole thing, unlike Seth he had seen what was handed over, a shard of wood. Not something that you'd picture when you think about a deadly weapon but hellishly effective if you used it right, like now. The attacker stepped away swiftly and blended into the light crowd of other inmates, but not before hissing at Seth,

"Take that as a warning."

Steven didn't need to look back to know that it was too late, but his morbid curiosity won and he couldn't resist. His cousins were on the floor; Ross was laid on his back with his head resting on Seth's knee whilst Seth held him there looking dumbfounded. He was looking at his brothers' neck and could clearly see the shard of wood embedded there, for the initial ten seconds there was no blood. Once those ten seconds had lapsed everything changed and became more real, the wood itself slowly changed colour, the deep red hue of blood slowly being absorbed by its porous surface turning it from light brown to burgundy.

A tiny droplet of blood gathered at the entry site and dribbled down and round Ross' neck, once that tiny droplet had set a path more followed at a faster rate and soon was trickling steadily from the plugged wound. Ross was in shock staring up at the ceiling, refusing even in these moments of horror to show weakness. Someone was shouting nearby and there was the sound of running feet. Steven didn't need to have any medical knowledge to know that there was no hope for his cousin now, strangely he found himself grateful that it was Ross of the two as he was frankly useless. Seth had shown loyalty, strength and promise – problem was he squandered it by defending his brother all the time.

He turned his attention to the culprit responsible for Ross' untimely demise and found him lurking in the corner studiously looking away from the commotion. He had another inmate next to him acting like a meerkat, craning his neck over the crowds to see what was going on and relaying it in a not particularly discreet manner out the corner of his mouth. Steven knew the exact moment that Ross died because his murderer nodded grimly, a smug look coming across his pitted features, in his head, it was a job well done. Steven wasn't going to allow him to revel in his supposed glory, he let his fury rise and bubble in his core and centred himself right in front of his intended victim. With an explosive roar that only he could hear he unleashed and the guy doubled up from the sudden intense wave of pressure that hit him in the stomach, then in slow-motion he lifted off the ground and flew backwards into the railing cracking his head on the way, his friend leapt out of the way in surprise and went on guard.

  The whole room now erupted into chaos and the officers on duty struggled to control the situation. Steven knew he had depleted his reserves but felt good knowing he did what he could to fight for his blood. More than it felt anyone else had done for him so far and if it was the last thing he ever did in this plane he would see to it that Yeti got what was coming to him too.

Chapter Twenty-One

She couldn't handle it, the constant nauseating fizzing was proving too much and Martha pulled herself off the bed and put her feet tenderly on the floor. This was her opportunity to get help in severing the attachment, he obviously thought she was weak and unlikely to do anything other than lay there mewling and she was determined to prove him wrong and banish him. She tried to step and cried out, then tentatively put her other foot forwards and bit her lip in concentration.

"You can overcome anything Mattie, just put your mind to it. Pain is just a sensation and not permanent. One foot in front of the other." She murmured to herself, forcing strength back into her dwindling resolve.

It worked, she stepped again, the pain was present but she overrode it with gritted teeth. Another step, and then another. Soon she was at her door and she tried to not allow the closed door to hinder her speed too much and quickly pulled it open and stepped outside. She had to keep pace because despite the crippling sensation in her crunching feet she was moving, the further she got before her mental power gave out the better. She hobbled along rapidly humming to herself that it was just around the corner and she was nearly there, grateful for the cool pavement under her bare soles. She was right of course as it really was just around the corner but when walking was such a painful task it felt like miles. By the time she was within one hundred metres she was about ready to give up and began to run, her feet bending inwards from the contracting muscles.

She smashed into the heavy door of the church and fell through as it swung inwards, sprawled on the floor she let out a whimper before hoisting herself back up using the concrete seating in the entrance for support. She sat on it for a moment and allowed herself to breathe, her feet were in agony and she felt it would be less painful at this point if they actually did cramp and release her from this limbo sensation of will they, won't they. She heard footsteps approaching and made a solid effort to gather and present herself as a strong-willed woman and not one who was close to snapping after a very short period of hosting an evil spirit. Martha looked up to greet the approaching figure and was pleased to see a friendly face.

"Are you ok?" the elderly lady said kindly.

Martha wasn't sure why she thought of her as elderly as she looked not too much older than she herself was. She was in a knitted sweater which had a sweet daisy pattern on the chest and bootcut jeans over a pair of tatty white trainers. Martha nodded at her before opening her mouth,

"Yes. Well, no actually, I lied, I'm sorry. I need help urgently." She said with a grimace.

"Is someone chasing you?" the lady asked, a deep frown creasing her lined brow.

"Sort of, I need help of a spiritual nature if someone can please help me?" the lady looked taken aback and wasn't sure what to say for a minute, clearly assessing whether the newcomer in distress was to be taken seriously. She put her hand on Martha's shoulder after her considerations, looked her in the eyes and spoke,

"You just sit right there OK? I'll be right back with help."

Martha allowed her head to drop back onto the wall with a thud and closed her eyes trying to block everything out, she was completely exhausted. Before long she heard two sets of footsteps coming and she opened her eyes reluctantly. It was the lady who had greeted her and she had brought what looked to be the priest. He was wearing his robes but he looked a little dishevelled.

"I'm sorry, I have disturbed you. I wouldn't have done so if it wasn't absolutely necessary." Martha said breathlessly and the priest stepped towards her quickly with a shake of his hands dismissing her words.

He had a look of deep concern on his face,

"Oh my dear. You have picked up the wrong sort on your travels haven't you?" was all he said.

Martha smiled grimly in response. He waved away the lady and she obliged with a small smile and a wave.

"Don't worry. She spends most of her time here since her husband passed on. Now tell me your name."

"Martha. Please, my feet. He has put them in a state of spasm."

"A state of spasm?" the priest responded, unable to conceal the surprise in his voice. "How?"

"I don't know. He was speaking with me and when I spoke out of turn he inflicted quite intense pains in my head or stomach. He left me for the evening telling me that this was one of his favourite forms of torture."

"My oh my, that is really something. This may not be a simple task and something tells me you know that already. How did this even happen?"

"Please sir, if we can stop this pain I can tell you all you need to know." He nodded at her,

"You're right, please accept my apologies. I need to prepare for the ritual but I will get you a bucket of ice-cold water to try and alleviate the pain in the meantime." Martha gratefully accepted, anything to ease the pain was more than welcome. A few long moments later the priest returned with a dusty looking black bucket lapping with water. He placed it front of her and gestured for her to use it.

"How long ago did you say you were cursed with these feet?" the priest asked, Martha plunged them into the water inhaling sharply as the iciness shocked her but the relief was immediate.

"No more than a few hours since he was last in my presence."

"My goodness that's truly awful, how did you get here? Your feet are black and blue!" the priest asked, astounded.

Martha nodded sadly, her feet were heavily bruised. She wasn't sure why they'd bruised though, maybe it was the running and walking on them whilst they were constantly contracting and releasing.

"Driving was out of the question, I walked. This is not the first time I've encountered him I'm afraid as he attached himself to a dear friend of mine many years ago. Decades, actually."

"You said he inflicted other pains upon you as well, he is evidently strong and must be regularly sapping energy from someone, or multiple people perhaps. To cause these pains on you he will be expending plenty too." The priest was half talking to Martha, and half to himself. He turned his gaze back to Martha after looking around the room. "How did you get him to detach from your friend?"

"Death." Martha replied, sourly. The priest flinched at this, he had thought as much but hoped for an alternative answer.

"I see. Well, our first goal here will be for that not the be way this time, we know death is of course an effective way to sever the attachment but it goes without saying it is not a desirable option. However, if you are under his power and enduring whatever he inflicts upon you then he will be steadily draining your energy, meaning you're not in the best condition to fight him off. Have you got his name?"

"No. He told me he would give me a letter every time I did something he asked of me, he made me attack an elderly man in the park." Martha muttered, her voice cracking with guilt. "He gave me the letter 'E' for it. The thing is I didn't really have control of myself, he gave me instructions and somehow my body just complied. Said words I'd never say. It was awful, like I was a puppet. I have already tried to banish him myself and I think that is what lead him to all of this." she said, gesturing at her feet, "I envisioned my aura and him leaving it, but he overpowered me almost immediately and it all went wrong."

"I am not surprised you couldn't do it by yourself, I know you said you've had experience with this entity before and I'm sure that isn't the extent of your knowledge on matters of a spiritual nature, but you are dealing with a particularly malevolent being here. I will help you be rid of him once and for all, how are your feet feeling?" he asked.

"Sore, but manageable with the ice."

"Will you be alright if I go and prepare myself?" Martha just nodded in response, "May I ask one other question before we continue?"

"Go ahead." Martha replied, cautiously.

"You say this entity attached itself to your friend years ago, right?" he asked.

"Right…" Martha wondered where he was going with this.

"Why did it wait so long to attach to you? If you kept him at bay for this long what happened to make you drop your guard? Spirits can only usually attach in moments of extreme emotions or open spiritual channels." Martha hesitated before replying, eyes downcast.

"It was the latter. My son was killed recently and he was my only child. I live alone and only have a few members of family left. I decided to try and contact him to make myself feel better, I haven't practiced in many years, not since my friend Susie took her own life to escape this evil spirit. I made a promise to my family to stop my practices because they were afraid the same may happen to me. I proved their fear right and I messed up again, I forgot to take protective measures and left the pathway open. I don't want to hear anything more on that, I am paying my dues for such a stupid mistake. He must have been waiting for me, he even said he was going to see how long it took for me to go the same way Susie did."

Martha made sure to leave some important details out, it was not the his business what she had being doing or why, she just needed his help to remove E.

"I see, I'm sorry about the loss of your son." The priest said with pursed lips, not giving his thoughts away.

"Father, please just help me." Martha pleaded.

"I'll do what I can." He said, this time with more kindness in his tone.

She could tell he disapproved of her dealings with the other side but pitied her the loss of her son. She nodded her thanks and watched as he walked away whilst trying to ignore the sensation coursing through her sore feet, hoping that she would be able to sever the connection to E tonight with the help of the priest. She realised belatedly she hadn't even asked his name, although in light of the circumstances she was sure he wouldn't think much of it.

****

With a little effort they retired into the room off to the left of the altar. To Martha's surprise the priest had come back with the lady who had initially greeted her, and they each helped her get here and placed her feet in a fresh batch of icy cold water. Despite not having sat for too long with the first lot of water it had warmed up rapidly, perhaps thanks to the heat of her seizing feet.

"What are your names?" Martha asked them.

"That is father Robins and I am Irene." The reply came from the lady.

"Thanks Irene. Nice to meet you, despite the circumstances." Irene smiled lightly back at her.

"You too. I bet you're wondering why I'm here, I am a spiritual worker and I will assist father Robins in removing your unwanted guest."

"Martha, are you ready?" the question came from the priest. She nodded in return, not sure what to say other than it was pretty obvious she was ready, how could she not be? "Good, I thought as much I just needed confirmation. What is your last name?"

"Tawn."

"Very well, let us all join hands and close our eyes."

They all obliged, Irene took a moment to straighten out her knitted sleeves before taking their hands and closing the circle. Martha closed her eyes first, allowing herself to be completely in the hands of these two people she had only met tonight.

"Great Holy one, I call upon you to assist in removing a malevolent earthbound spirit from Martha Tawn. The entity currently known only as E has created an unwelcome bond with Martha Tawn and we require assistance to sever the connection."

Martha felt the room start to sway, a multitude of shifting colours waved in front of her eyelids and she struggled to keep them closed, as though her thoughts had been read Martha felt Irene squeeze her hand a little tighter. Despite having her feet in the icy water Martha felt the pain intensify suddenly, then a familiar voice spoke to them,

"You think you can remove me? Mattie dear please tell them you know me and invited me, more or less." There was an evil leer to the tone and Martha started to shake her head. Father Robins continued.

"Spirit known to us as E, you are no longer welcome here. Sever the tether you have created with Martha Tawn and remove yourself. You are *not* welcome!" he said powerfully, his voice echoing around the small chamber.

Martha's feet were causing her to cry out, the ice water completely useless now, she was trying to hold it in but it was impossible.

"Silly Martha who does this guy think he is? Do you think if there was a God he would let me do this? Well actually by all accounts he is quite a sucker for punishment, so perhaps he would indeed allow me to do this!"

The pain in her feet abruptly stopped and just as she let out a sigh of relief a blinding pain ripped through her temples and eyes causing the sigh to turn into a shriek. She pulled her hands up to her head to try and hold it but both Irene and father Robins held her in place to keep the strength of the connection. Martha couldn't stop herself and she opened her eyes. The pain disappeared but everything was completely white.

"I can't see, everything is white!" She said, panic panging through her like electric shocks.

"Thought you might appreciate it my little Mattie. You are blind but you'll never have the respite of darkness again!"

"E, speak to me! I command you with the power of the Lord above, speak with me and tell me your full name!" father Robins demanded, a hissing noise came now, E showing his annoyance.

"What do you want 'father'?" he said, the word father said with pure venom.

"I demand you tell me your name." the priest said firmly.

Martha sat completely still, immobilised by the blindness and fear, her breathing shallow.

"Ah, why didn't you just say?" E laughed.

"I demand you, tell me your name!" he repeated.

"You called me E, did you not? Then that shall be my name." came the sneered reply.

"Tell me your given name!" father Robins roared, the power in his command made the invisible connection shake, and a moment later the voice of E came through again.

"Keith! You disgusting human, meddling in my business. You'll pay for this!"

"Keith. With the power of the Lord above you and me I command that you, spirit known as Keith, detach from the being known as Martha

Tawn." There was silence for a moment, and father Robins started to speak again. "I father Robins, command you…"

He was suddenly interrupted by manic laughter,

"You may have my name but you do not have the power to remove me and you should know that your lord is wasted on me, it is only you he controls! You command nothing when it comes to me."

Martha could feel father Robins bristling at being goaded and despite all she was feeling right now she was surprised that Keith was able to garner such a reaction from the priest so quickly.

"Keith I ask of you to disconnect from me. Your presence is not welcome nor wanted and there is little to be gained from me and you know it!" She said, with a lot more power than she knew she had in her at that moment.

"Hmm, bored of me already are you Mattie? We've only just begun. I thought you were going to be much stronger than this but I guess your dead son made you weak. How dull and predictable you have turned out to be."

"Don't listen to him Martha, he will be using a lot of his energy to maintain your blindness and if he can cause you more pain or negative emotions he will be able to draw it from you instantly. They're just words, ignore him."

The completely calm voice of Irene came from her right, Martha nodded to herself, she needed to hear those words.

"I call upon the help of the powers above us to assist in removing this dark entity from our presence!" came the voice of father Robins again.

Martha blinked, her eyes were itching and she realised she had been straining so hard to see that she hadn't blinked in a while. She noticed there was some red creeping in around the edges of her vision.

"I too call upon the assistance of the powers above us to remove you, Keith, from our presence!" called out Irene, her voice sounding more powerful than Martha would have expected from the gentle looking lady.

"I, Martha Tawn, demand you leave our presence and break your attachment to me!" Martha said.

The room fell silent, the three of them had now made their official request for Keith to remove himself. Martha felt something fizzling in her head and blinked multiple times, each blink bringing more shapes and colour into her vision. All the while she could feel the weight of the presence lifting, and both her companions breathed out low breaths.

"He has gone." father Robins said. "Did it work?"

They all looked at each other and Martha smiled grimly.

"Well, my feet don't hurt and my vision is back. I can't feel him near me." She said.

"I don't know." Irene said, simply. "It seems he has gone but I don't know if the attachment is broken. Unfortunately, we will have to wait to see, you should do some cleansing at home with small chants and visualisations. Your energy is incredibly low right now so you'll be susceptible to reattachment even if we have successfully severed this one, so you'll need to be cautious for the time being."

Despite not being what she wanted to hear, Martha knew she was right.

Chapter Twenty-Two

Steven found himself being whisked along on a flashing journey, he had to focus to keep up with the images being shown to him and realised this was all relating to the death of Ross. He was now looking at his aunt Alicia who even though he couldn't hear anything, he could see from her heaving back that she was sobbing. Darkness took over his vision then when it lifted he could see his cousins mourning their lost brother.

Lily was rocking back and forth clutching her favourite teddy and Tom sat with a tear-streaked face staring at nothing. Darkness.

His nanna Jess was shaking her head back and forth in sorrow, Alicia on her knees in front of her having just delivered the news. Darkness.

Seth sat on a rickety looking cot in prison, his arms were covered in red marks, Steven didn't have to wonder for long what they were from as Seth crossed his forearms, then gripped and pulled them in to his chest and squeezed until his fingers and the arm shone bright white from the pressure. Then he exhaled slowly and repeated the process, Steven realised he was trying to deal with his feelings silently, there were no tears in his eyes just a terrible sadness that dulled the whites. Darkness.

Yeti was pacing around his dingy flat, clearly in yet another rage whilst a petite girl stood off to one side nervously fidgeting her hands. He was roaring something at her and she clearly didn't give the correct answer because Yeti flew forwards and grabbed her by the head and threw her sideways. She went limp in advance to lessen the damage and allowed herself to fall into the wall and slump there, looking up at Yeti who sneered at her then resumed pacing and shouting. Steven wondered what event in the recent times was the one causing this meltdown. Darkness.

Some shadowy figures hunched over, aggressively gesturing at each other whilst talking about something. The room they were in was dark, it was again one of those places that despite the fact he couldn't smell, he was absolutely sure he could smell it. Before he could work out who he was looking at darkness moved him once more.

Now he looked upon his mum sprawled across the sofa in the living area of her home with one foot up on the arm rest and the other on the floor, he noticed she had support wraps on both of her feet. Despite being asleep she looked exhausted, her face deeply lined and sallow, the sight causing guilt to course through him as he wondered what she had gone through in his absence. He needed to learn to control where he went and when, he should have been able to protect his mum from a ghost. Anger boiled inside of him and he stored it away, envisioning a little cabinet with shelves made to hold bottles of his unexpressed anger, ready to be used when needed like ammunition. Darkness.

His aunt Alicia was clutching her phone in her hand and crying wildly whilst hitting the call button, lifting it to her ear then pulling it away again a moment later and doing it again. He watched her do this six times before he was pulled away. Darkness.

Back with Yeti again, this time he was storming down the street. Steven recognised the place, it was the spot that you used when you were fairly new to the game and still had to earn your place in the ranks. Steven was pulled along with him, interested to see he could actually see the air around Yeti fizzing like electricity, charged by the immense anger he was barely containing. He approached a hooded figure stood off to the side of the streetlamp and Steven recognised him, it was Grid. He was on his own, not that being in company would make any difference if Yeti wanted to confront him about anything as Steven had discovered first-hand. He tamped down the rage again at remembering the injustice of it, hand to hand combat he would have put up a fair fight and had a chance to win. He focused back on what was happening in front of him. Yeti was looming over Grid and Steven had to hand it to him, Grid didn't even flinch which Yeti began to shout in his face and jab him in the chest. Steven began to feel frustrated at not being able to hear, he wished he could hear what was being said. Suddenly the whole view jolted and he felt the sensation of dropping and heard a popping sound. He looked back to the two men in front of him and realised he could now hear them loud and clear, like someone heard his wish and it had been granted.

"I know you've been hanging with Shells and he was tight with Brute, so you're going to tell me what you know. Someone thought they could get away with screwing with my stuff and now there is a price to pay. Was it you? Trying to be a big man and make a name for yourself?" Yeti was shouting, spittle spraying everywhere.

"I don't even really know you man, come on. Yeah I've been hanging with Shells but he ain't said nothing about nothing, you know? We just smoke and hang." Grid replied in a flat tone, Steven could hear from his voice he was high as a kite and could explain his overly calm reaction to Yeti confronting him.

"Bullshit. I took Brute down and he only had one guy on his side and that was Shells, you can't tell me that Shells hasn't said anything to you about me." Yeti retorted, jabbing Grid in the shoulder with his still bloody hands after every other word.

It was clear as day that Yeti was itching for a fight but Grid was standing his ground and not taking the bait despite being stabbed in the shoulder over and over by a furious madman.

"Why would he talk about you to me? I guess I'm just too low down on the streets to be told any of this stuff man. I didn't even know you took Brute out, I didn't hang with him. I just assumed it was a deal gone bad, or he'd been taken out by an officer getting trigger happy and they played it off to make it look like one of us did it. Remember Jose?"

"Obviously I remember him." Yeti spat, annoyed he wasn't getting the answers he wanted. "I'm watching you and Shells. Either of you step out of line I'll crush you both, hear me?" he leered.

"Got it, no worries Yeti." Grid said, nonchalantly.

This riled Yeti back up and Grid didn't see the blood crusted fist as it swung upwards, it struck him squarely on the left side of his jaw. His head snapped back but he didn't go down and Yeti smiled grimly at him.

"Fuck you." He hissed before storming off.

Steven had completely changed his opinion of Grid after the last two occasions he had witnessed him, he had loyalty and backbone. He didn't even fall to the ground when Yeti sucker punched him which was saying something. Maybe he would turn out to be more than just a lowly runner in the end, it was looking like he had the makings for it. His view started to fade and Steven allowed himself to be pulled back into the darkness, hoping his next stop would be with his mum again so they could talk.

He needed to get a physical form again, he had a renewed desire to go and combat Yeti and fight him like a man, fist to fist. To do that he needed a body and amongst all the confusion of everything else he was sure that his mum had mentioned that there was a potential vessel for him to use. As he thought about it he wondered what had become of Ross, on some level he had expected to see him in a ghostly form after he died. He needed to ask his mum about that and why he didn't encounter any other spirits as he moved around.

Chapter Twenty-Three

A persistent loud rapping noise disturbed her less than restful slumber. Martha stirred and struggled to pull herself back to reality. Her dreams had been vivid and confusing, full of fast changing images and nothing that made any sense. She saw Steven, he was there almost constantly off to the side in some way but never physically, even in her dreams he was physically gone and her heart ached. In the dreams it was a host of random everyday things that seemed to be going wrong, like placing something back on the shelf in the supermarket only for it to teeter and drop off but her hands were too slow to respond. At some point she put on a pair of shoes and walked out the door to realise they were on the wrong feet, then stumbled down some concrete stairs that hadn't been there a moment before as she turned to go back and fix them. She watched a car pull out at a red light and a lorry that couldn't slow down in time smashed into it, the sound of metal tearing and being dragged on the floor was deafening.

There had been a whole host of other events that she could hardly recall now, as was the way with dreams, she couldn't make sense of any of the disasters she dreamt about and hoped they were not symbolic. She could still hear the rapping noise that had stirred her from her sleep, after a moment of confusion the sleepiness lifted and she realised it was the door and with a gasp leapt up off the sofa and ran to it, only as she reached it did she remember her bruised feet and quickly grabbed the side table for support as the burning ache crept over them. Grimacing she pulled open the door as it started to knock again, it sounded urgent and the pain in her feet went to the back of her mind. Her heart sank when she saw it was Alicia with a tear-streaked face and furious expression. How long had she slept? She knew Alicia had wanted to go to the prison today with her to see Seth and Ross, maybe she had knocked earlier and

Martha had slept through it but that wouldn't explain the level of emotions her sister was clearly feeling.

"Alicia? What happened? Are you alright? Where are Tom and Lily?"

"My baby is dead!" Alicia screamed, the pain in her voice rendering Martha motionless for a moment before she came back to the present, reeling from the shock of her sisters words. Not her too! Their family didn't deserve this much heartache.

"What! Come inside quickly." Martha said, not giving her any choice and putting her arms around her sister and pulling her inside. "Where are Tom and Lily, Alicia? Who was it?"

"Not them Mattie, it was Ross. He was killed in free time at the prison, he died in Seth's arms." She sobbed.

Martha's heart broke listening to her, knowing the pain all too well, now both of them had lost children to the hands of others. She wondered what they had all done in a past life to deserve such pain or if it was simply terrible luck. She brought her sister in for a tight embrace whilst feeling her already broken heart strain under the pressure of this new sadness.

"I'm so sorry, I don't have words to make the pain better. What do you need from me?" she asked.

"Just be here for me please." She cried whilst burying her face into Martha's shoulder.

"Always." She replied, knowing she would do anything to take this pain away for her.

She wondered if it would be the same as what happened with Steven, if Ross would be stuck here earthbound waiting for release. Something told her he wouldn't be as he wasn't at all spiritual and she couldn't begin to envision any unfinished business he may have here despite being murdered.

***

A short while later Martha looked down at her sister who had laid across her lap seeking comfort for her broken heart. Martha had sat quietly, listening to the wracking sobs and mewling. Eventually she ran out of energy to make sound and just laid there staring at nothing with tears rolling down her cheeks silently, then soon the crying ceased too. She had now fallen into a fitful sleep and Martha gently sidled away from her, put her head on a pillow, and moved cautiously over to the kitchen area to make a tea and get some painkillers for her feet.

She wanted to contact Steven to tell him more about her plans. She wondered if he knew about Ross, and how Seth was doing. Judging by the previous interactions she had had with Steven he was being shown many things and this was a good thing in most ways as he could experience and learn, and come back to her with important information, but the flip side of that was that he would see things that would scar most people. She popped some tablets out of the packet and downed them with a glass of water. After everything that had already happened, she felt ashamed to admit to herself that although it was incredibly upsetting, she mostly felt numb about the passing of her nephew now the initial shock of the news was passing. She didn't know why, maybe she had reached maximum capacity for the amount of grief she could feel. The news of Ross being murdered did however spur her on and she decided to take action with the information she had already about Steven's death, she was going go to the police and speak to the officers who had initially told her they were handling the case. The same two officers who unsurprisingly hadn't contacted her since that day in the hospital.

She picked up her phone and did a quick search for the local police station and hit dial whilst hobbling down the hallway to her bedroom. It rang for multiple minutes before being picked up by a tired sounding agent,

"Hello? I am calling to speak with either officer Bridges or officer Gord please." Martha asked, keeping her voice low but steady.

"May I ask what this is regarding?" the lady on the line asked.

"Of course. Regarding the murder of my son, Steven Tawn."

"I see. Are you with him now?" she asked, a slight hint of excitement in her voice.

Martha bristled at this. She didn't expect the desk clerk to know every case that went through the station but she did expect them to know that if she was in fact stood next to a murder victim she wouldn't be calling the general line.

"No. I would have called 999 in such an instance. This is an open case and I was told to call if I ever had any more information that could help close it."

"Do you?" came the reply.

"No, I'm calling to say I don't have any new information and I am trying to waste your time!" Martha said, her voice raised in frustration. She checked herself and spoke again, "Sorry. I do have further information that could be used to help close the case."

The initial sarcasm and consequent apology seemed to be missed and the clerk carried on,

"OK, give me a moment I'll call through to officer Bridges for you. Do you happen to have the case number?" she asked.

"No, sorry." Martha mumbled, realising she didn't know it and feeling like she should. Had she been told and forgotten it?

"No problem, one moment please." And with that she was put on hold and a tinny rendition of some decade old pop song started playing in her ear, causing her to wince and move the phone away. She could hear it even from arms distance. After some more minutes the lady came back on the line, "Mrs Tawn?"

"Hello."

"I couldn't reach officer Bridges but I managed to get through to officer Gord. He asked if he could call you back shortly as he is in a meeting." She explained.

"Fine." Martha replied, she left her number and hung the phone up and waited for the call back.

She sat massaging her feet, already feeling some relief from the ibuprofen she had just taken, when she heard a light knocking at her front door. She frowned and looked at the clock on the wall. It was early evening, who would be coming round at this time? The only person who ever turned up unexpected was her sister, even her mum called beforehand on the rare occasion she visited. Thinking about her mum sent a wave of sadness through her, she had barely heard from her since Steven passed. She was sure she blamed her and her parenting skills in some way, now Ross had succumbed to the same fate as Steven, Alicia may have to deal with this too – or perhaps not as their mum was often softer on Alicia than her. The door knocked again a little louder this time and pulled Martha out of her train of thought, she jumped up and winced at the jolts that went through her feet then went to the door as fast as she dared. As she pulled it open she couldn't hide the surprise on her face.

"Tim?" she said, taken aback to see him here. He was stood there looking down at her, straight faced and serious as ever but with a look of concern on his features.

"Martha. I hope you don't mind me coming around unannounced. You don't have to invite me in but I was just sat at home and you kept crossing my mind for some reason. After all that talk about spirits and so on the other day, I think I am probably overthinking it, but I became worried for your wellbeing and I needed to know you were ok. Despite my feelings about the general human population you have become someone I actually care about so it is in my best interest to check in on you."

Martha looked up at him, thoughts whirling around her head. She was impressed he had been so open to her pushing a connection with him, but had not anticipated him being receptive to his intuition telling him something was wrong. She had to think objectively, with her goal in mind, she couldn't have herself feeling any bad emotions when his true purpose to her came to light. He was meant to be a loner, someone disliked and for good reason. Not someone who could form a genuine connection with her and maybe a true friendship, something she found hard to achieve. She shook away the feelings and gave a small smile.

"Well yes. As a matter of fact there is something wrong, we've just had another unexpected death in the family," she shifted to one side and gestured at Alicia asleep on the sofa, "my nephew Ross was killed. We don't know why or who by at the moment."

"Oh dear. I am sorry, I guess. Let us hope it isn't three for three then." He replied.

Martha fought the urge to react to such a thoughtless comment, it did help her remove some of that guilt that had begun to creep in a moment ago though.

"Well, as long as you're ok."

"Actually Tim, I'm not, I have hurt my feet in an accident as well and to be frank nothing seems to quite be going right. How are you? Have you had any ideas on how to go forwards in your life? Give me some good news." She said, watching to see if he took the bait.

"An accident?" Martha pursed her lips, wrong bait.

"Yes, nothing serious thankfully. I couldn't tell you why as I don't know, but I decided to hop along the curb and didn't quite do it as gracefully as I thought I would and toppled off. Both ankles twisted and a lesson learned!" she said, hoping it sounded even a little bit believable because in this moment she couldn't think of a reasonable explanation for how she had severely bruised both feet at the same time. She realised she could have said she dropped something heavy on them and inwardly sighed.

"I should think that lesson is learned. What a childish thing to have done, serves you right. Can I help with anything?" he asked, clearly hoping she didn't request anything but his strange pull to her made him offer anyway.

"Yes very childish. Would you like to come in and tell me about your plans for your future or have you not thought on it yet? I could use a distraction from all that has been happening."

"Well actually I do have some news on my side. I was going to wait until things were more cemented but I don't see the harm in telling you about them as it won't change the outcome. Unless you work at the bank of course." He replied. She laughed quietly in response, stood back and welcomed him in.

"Come, we must not be noisy though, I'd hate to disturb Alicia as she needs all the rest she can get."

"Right. Do you want to come back to mine for coffee?" he asked, even as he offered he regretted offering it despite knowing if she said yes he would let her.

"No, I don't want to leave her alone here. If she wakes up and I'm not here I wouldn't forgive myself. Come through to my room, I have a couple of seats in there. Do you want a coffee?"

"Sure. If I'm imposing just let me know." Martha knew this was his way of asking leave but wasn't able to be his usual abrupt and dismissive self around her. Well, not completely anyway.

"No, not at all. Like I said, I could use the distraction. Go down the hall, first door on your right. The light switch is on the left as you open the door."

He nodded at her and walked away avoiding looking at Martha's emotional guest, whilst she walked gently across to the kettle and made him a coffee. Steaming mug in hand, she made her way to the bedroom and found him perched on the edge of one of the chequered chairs. She registered the look on his face and recognised it as the same one that he had given the first night she asked him to come round. She decided to shut it off quickly, she didn't need to draw that kind of attention from him.

"My nephew was stabbed. My son was stabbed. What is this world coming to?" she said, her voice breaking slightly. He reached forwards and took the mug from her.

"What do you expect in an area like this? The world is full of lowlife scum and you're surprised? You seem more switched on than the kind of person who asks a question like that." He said sternly. Martha nodded.

"You're right, I am. I guess I am just worn down, it feels like one bad thing after the other."

"Sure. But think about those who lost so much more, in childhood no less. If they can get through some emotional pain unfettered, then you as a fully grown woman should be able to too." Not entirely unfettered, she thought bitterly, then shook it away.

"You're right. I should be more together than this. Tell me Tim, you said you had some updates you could tell me." She said, and sat back whilst he spoke about his plans.

Chapter Twenty-Four

As she trod the pathway towards the shop Martha thought about what lay ahead. Her evening had been a difficult one but that seemed to be becoming the new normal recently. Alicia had woken multiple times throughout the night and begun the painful howling of a mother who had lost one of her young too soon. Martha felt her pain, but selfishly for her own loss. The consolation she had regarding her own loss was that she had spoken with her son after his death and soon would be able to hold a physical form that contained his being again. She couldn't offer that to her sister, she had tried a couple of times in the night to call upon Ross, making sure to protect herself each time just in case she had a repeat of another evil entity intruding like Keith had. She had wanted to reach out to Steven but knew the right thing to do was check that her nephew wasn't lost in a confusing state like Steven had been initially. Nothing came, she didn't even sense a presence trying to come through. She knew that if she conducted a séance with Alicia he would be able to come through thanks to the strong tether they had of mother and son, but as his aunt with her own mourning heart she wasn't able to do it by herself. Either way she felt comforted knowing that Ross will have already entered into the spirit realm and his suffering was over, something she would relay to Alicia when the time was right.

In the morning, once Alicia had gotten herself together enough to function on a basic level past the pained weeping she had silently embraced Martha and left, presumably going off to see her mum, Tom and Lily. Martha needed to go and buy some more incense and candles as she wanted all the assistance she could get for the next step in their journey. Tim had inadvertently told her he was ready last night, not by outright saying the words 'please take my soul out of my body and use the empty vessel to get your son back', but by informing her that he had been accepted for a large business grant from his bank and had instantly gone and handed in his notice at his current practice. He was going to invest in a private practice and be rid of all the things he classed as a burden, all he had to do was put in a successful offer on a new office and he was set.

Martha had again re-evaluated her opinion of Tim, for a brief moment she had wavered but in reality he was not a good example of what a human should be. He was bitter and hated the world, full of sexist and ignorant opinions. No one would miss the original version of him, and he didn't really seem like he was enjoying living, the fruits of life were wasted on him. He would be renewed, his physical form utilised by someone who deserved a body and an existence on this earth. It wasn't like Tim would suffer, she would put him in an out of body state and Steven would come in and take his body, Tim would then discover he couldn't return and spend a short time roaming the earth until he was returned to the spirit realm, hopefully of his own accord but Martha would help if it came to it. Painless, and easy, if it went well. She just needed to contact Steven and run through it all with him so he would be prepared, she sensed his hesitation last time she mentioned the subject and would soon be able to put his mind at ease. She also needed to have that Jake boy, Yeti, sorted.

Officer Gord hadn't called back last night and she still hadn't heard anything as of this morning, it had slipped her mind after Tim's unexpected visit. One positive this morning was despite the lack of sleep her feet were recovering remarkably fast and she could walk with next to no pain now as long as she stepped softly. Pulling her phone from her pocket she dialled the police station, waiting impatiently for them to pick up.

"Hello you're through to Katie how can I help you today?" Martha felt relieved, at least this girl sounded kind and efficient.

"Hi Katie, I'm calling to speak with officer Gord or officer Bridges, they're dealing with the case involving the murder of my son Steven Tawn. I did call yesterday and was informed he would return my call but I haven't heard anything yet."

"I'm sorry to hear that. Can I ask your name please?" she asked.

"Martha Tawn. You can call me Martha." She replied.

"Thank you Martha. Hold the line for just a moment I'll see if I can get hold of either of the officers for you."

"Thanks." Martha muttered, just as the line fizzed and that awful tinny music played in her ears again.

This time it lasted less than a minute, which was good because she was just leaning against the wall of the shop. She didn't want to walk around the shop talking on her phone, she hated when people did that. She also didn't want to talk in a closed space with however many ears listening in about her recently deceased son and his killer.

"Hello Mrs Tawn?" came the voice of a young sounding officer.

"Hello officer Bridges. Please, call me Martha." She said.

"Hello Martha. I understand you're calling with information regarding your sons murder. I hope this information has come from a reliable source?" he said.

Martha laughed inwardly, of course it was a reliable source, it was the victim himself. Of course she couldn't say that which is why she had gone and spoken to Seth and Ross. Guilt panged inside her and she suddenly wondered if what happened had anything to do with her visiting, then dismissed the idea. No one could have possibly heard, and she hadn't spoken to anyone about what they had said.

"Yes, I have been informed by a reliable source. I wouldn't be calling if not, I don't want to waste your valuable time." She replied smartly. "Are you able to meet to discuss this or are we to talk over the phone?"

"We can do this however you prefer Martha, we are here to help and of course would like to close this case as soon as possible."

"I would prefer to discuss it face to face as I am currently out shopping. Could you come by mine this afternoon?" she suggested. Officer Bridges paused for a moment before responding.

"That would be fine, I'll come by with officer Gord."

Martha sighed with relief, she didn't know why but she hated doing things over the phone, marginally more than she hated being out and about socialising. Not necessarily anything to do with anyone else, she was just introverted. She thanked the officer and gave her address again, despite being sure she had given it before. She knew that they wouldn't have been looking into the case at all being that it was a street killing with known drug runners, but they wouldn't be able to admit that and they wouldn't be able to ignore her reporting further information on a murderer without coming under fire. She pocketed her phone and headed inside the shop and straight to the same section as before, picking up a couple more of their white candles.

They'd recently restocked their scent section too and she was pleased to see they had some sandalwood. That was a perfect scent for meditation, not far off what she was looking to use it for. She took the items to the counter and paid the woman, giving her a brief smile before heading back out and going home. The officers were going to be there within the hour and she wanted to be ready for them.

Chapter Twenty-Five

He found himself in his mums living room and everything was bright and open. All the curtains were fully drawn and it must have been around midday. He could hear something bubbling and looked to see the kettle boiling away in the corner. His mum was stood beside it looking a little anxious, but he was relieved to see her standing with seemingly no problem after seeing her with the bandaged feet before. He was watching her for a moment and he wasn't even surprised to see her lift her chin up and smile, then speak,

"You there Steven?" she said. "I was going to try and reach you later, I have so much to update you on. Soon we will have you back walking and talking." She said.

He watched as she second guessed herself about whether he was there or not. He moved over to the kettle and focused on the switch and flicked it off, then on again. His mum smiled.

"You're getting good with the control. I won't get the board out yet or open a connection with you as I have the police coming to discuss your case."

Steven wondered what she wanted to discuss with them, they wouldn't do anything even if they could. This was all bigger than them, the highest ranking police officers were paid off regularly by the highest ranking suppliers and runners in the streets. Before he could even attempt further interaction with her the door knocked neatly three times, a typical no nonsense police knock. His mum brushed her front down, making sure her flannel shirt and jeans were relatively presentable before moving over to the door. He noted that she walked carefully and realised her feet were still injured. It was hard to work out how much time was passing between him coming in and out of different places.

As the door opened he saw the two police officers standing there looking sceptical, already he was annoyed at their presence and not just because of his obvious and long standing distaste for all things law, they didn't hide the fact that they didn't want to be here.

"Mrs Tawn." Officer Gord said with an incline of the head, officer Bridges just nodded in acknowledgement.

His mum invited them in and they all sat on the sofas in the living area facing each other and he was glad to see she didn't even offer them a cup of tea. He moved closer to them, not because it affected his ability to hear them – he had found that if he focused he could hear things no matter the distance as long as he had a visual – but because he wanted his mum to feel his presence supporting her close by.

"I wanted to inform you that I know the name of my sons' killer." She went straight in with it, no hesitation.

Steven was shocked by this and felt a little pulse come out of him. He thought they were going to get Yeti by themselves, make him pay. He had already started formulating plans in his mind for what he would do once he had a body to do it with. His mum frowned lightly and tilted her head in his direction, showing her awareness of his less than joyful reaction to her informing the police of this information.

"You do? Please tell us all the information you have." Spoke officer Bridges leaning forwards on his knees to show his interest. Officer Gord on the other hand remained upright and maintained a poker face.

"I only have his first name which is Jake but he goes by the street name Yeti too. You'll also find he is responsible for the murder of his landlord too – you may have already taken him in for this actually. But I wanted to inform you that I have it on good authority that he is the man who raised a blade to my son."

Officer Bridges kept his eye contact, and Steven was impressed that he was actually now seemingly taking an interest in the information being given by his mum. Again, officer Gord was sat back and simply observing, allowing officer Bridges to lead.

"I see. It is unfortunate you don't have the full name of the alleged criminal as that would be quite helpful to us. Is there any other information about him that you've been told?"

"He lives in the corner flats on Jewel Street. I don't know what they're called." She replied, thanking her good memory for retaining that information.

"We know the place." Officer Bridges said stroking his chin thoughtfully. Steven watched on with curiosity as he watched officer Gord subtly bump his colleague with his knee. He wasn't sure his mum noticed it.

"Yes, we have a patrol that works that area occasionally. We can send someone to check it out." Officer Gord spoke up. "May I ask the source of your information? We need to know it is reliable."

"Well yes. I don't want to name anyone though." Martha replied.

"I understand that. Let me reassure you that this information is strictly confidential and is solely for us to ascertain that the information is reliable and true." Officer Gord explained, offering a small smile her way in a bid to try and reassure her.

Steven didn't like this one bit. Officer Bridges was fidgeting his hands, seemingly uncomfortable.

"I see. In that case I can tell you." She started, pausing to take a breath and shoot a warning look in the general direction she thought Steven was in, "His friend was with him that evening, Shelly I think his name is. He came and told me who had done it. I believe on some level he wanted to alleviate the guilt he was feeling for leaving my boy bleeding out in a gutter, and sought forgiveness from me. I am trusting in you officers to look after an older woman and not get him in to any kind of trouble. He hasn't done anything wrong."

Steven bubbled with anger. He had never really felt anger towards his mum, nothing more than a typical teenage tantrum anyway. How could she throw his friend under the bus like that? Sure she got his name a little wrong but of course the police who regularly circled the area knew the nicknames they all used for each other and would be able to easily deduce that Shelly was Shells. What was she playing at? He wondered. Was it to protect Seth? He got lost in his thoughts and suddenly felt himself being pulled along again. He found he had transported to the other side of the room by the front door. Somehow some minutes had passed and the police officers were bidding his mum farewell. His business with them clearly wasn't over as he was feeling a strong pull towards them so he allowed himself to follow them and listen in. Once they'd cleared the pathway they turned left and walked a couple metres down to where they had parked the car. They were wordless up until the point they were both seated, Steven had entered behind them and waited to see why he was being drawn to them.

"Why'd you stop me?" asked officer Bridges.

"That wasn't relevant information to the case. You were blabbering." Came the curt reply of officer Gord.

"I didn't give anything away, it would have been a comfort to her to know that the person she believes to be her sons' killer is already on our radar." He replied.

"We aren't here to comfort. The sooner you learn that the better. We don't just go and arrest people on mere hearsay. If this Jake fellow had really killed his landlord do you not think something would have come up?" officer Gord reasoned.

"I suppose it is unlikely something like that would be missed. Do you think her source was lying?"

"Probably, he was just another runner filling our town with more drugs. He was likely high and doesn't actually know anything. Who knows. Maybe her source was the killer. Maybe he was covering for the real killer or maybe he was telling the truth. Maybe he doesn't know anything and he somehow thought it would make her feel better. It is a whole lot of maybes, and we don't work with maybes. Remember that if you want to get anywhere in the force." Spoke officer Gord, looking meaningfully at his younger colleague.

"So are we going to check it out anyway? It is still a lead." Pushed officer Bridges.

"We can report it and they'll send another newbie. I'm not wasting my time today. Heck, you can even check it out yourself, I don't expect it'll amount to anything, you'll just be using up valuable time that would be better used elsewhere."

Steven wasn't even surprised at the interaction he was witnessing; it was completely in keeping with what he knew of the local force here. They loved to throw their weight around but were absolutely useless. It did happen to work in his favour though, if they were not going to follow up the information given by his mum that meant that Yeti would remain on the streets, and what she had said about Shells would go no further. He didn't trust that in the event Yeti had been pulled in for questioning the officers wouldn't have thrown Shells' name in for effect in a bid to get him to crack. He felt the tug pulling him away again and he was grateful, hating the fact he'd spent any of his precious time near them at all. He still felt if he could have the choice, he would have sought instant retribution for his death then headed straight off into the afterlife. This being stuck here, watching the still living beings of his previous life doing all these things and him not actually being able to do anything was wearing thin.

Chapter Twenty-Six

They crept in through the front door, the security latch had been broken long ago and was never fixed. The building was eerily quiet, perhaps something they were only noticing because they were trying to be silent. They actually had no idea where Yeti was at the moment and no matter how well they could hold up in a one on one with him they knew that his unpredictable rage and willingness to fight dirty made him a substantially harder opponent. They'd heard through various people gossiping that things had been going down for Yeti and everything was closing in on him, so he was even more prone to lashing out. They themselves had been the source of one of the events that was sending him crazy, but that wasn't the most interesting one they'd heard about. Apparently he had confided in his long suffering girlfriend that he was being attacked by invisible forces, including objects being launched in his face. She had spoken to her girlfriends about it, who naturally blabbed to their boyfriends and the infamous game of chinese whispers was well underway by the time it reached the ears of Shells and Grid. They didn't know how much faith to put into what they'd heard, Yeti was high more often than not and it wouldn't be much of a surprise to hear he was seeing and hearing things, but the suggestion that something invisible was attacking him was a bit much and they were waiting to hear from the source herself if these rumours were to be believed. They pulled their ski masks over their faces so that if they did accidentally encounter him they stood half a chance of legging it and assuming they got away, he wouldn't know who it was. They got to the stairs and started to climb, keeping their ears alert for any noises in the silence. Although neither of them lived in particularly nice accommodation this was a different level of squalor, the whole building seemed to stink of something awful, a combination of uncleanliness, urine and decay.

The place could have been nice if it was maintained by the owner but it looked like he must have given up long ago. They split at the top of the staircase with Shells keeping an eye on the stairs and Grid creeping over to Yeti's door, it was unmistakable thanks to the numerous splintered holes and dark stains. Grid moved close to the door and listened for any sounds. Turned out he didn't need to go as close to the door as he had, he could hear Yeti thumping around in there muttering loudly enough that he could be heard through a closed door. He nodded his head at Shells and took a couple of steps over to him when he heard the unmistakeable sound of a door clicking behind him, his heart thumped a heavy beat in his chest when he realised it could be one of two doors behind him and he prayed it was Yeti's neighbour. He dared not look behind him but the sudden widening of his friends eyes told him all he needed to know and he dashed the last metre of the hallway and bombed down the stairs hot on the heels of Shells. They ran down the flights without a glance back and slammed out of the entry door, grateful for the broken latch once more. They didn't stop until they'd rounded the next corner and leapt behind one of the hedgerows lining the side of the building, hunched down they looked at one another, panting.

"Do you think he followed us?" Grid hissed under his breath.

"Don't know, to be honest I don't know if he even saw us when we both legged it. I just knew we didn't want to be in that hallway long enough for him to recognise us. He was texting on his phone and hadn't looked up. Might've done when we ran though." Shells answered.

Neither wanted to come out from their hiding spot until they were certain Yeti hadn't pursued them, to him it must've been strange seeing two people suddenly start running – or not, based on what he had allegedly been experiencing recently. They waited for around five minutes before deciding it was unlikely he was going to be coming this way after all, as they stood to leave they heard a car starting up close by. They looked around, they were pretty much next to the ramp of the carpark. The car started revving and they knew instinctively it was going to be Yeti in his BMW, they were both surprised it still drove after all the puncture wounds they'd inflicted on the bonnet. Sure enough it tore up the ramp and braked harshly at the top, rap music was blaring out of the speakers and grey smoke was billowing out of the drivers' window. The front of the car was a state, and it was almost certain Yeti could barely see out of the smashed windscreen. Grid and Shells had ducked back down when they heard the car and they watched on with satisfaction. They may not be able to finish wrecking his car but they could hit his flat now, they waited a moment after he had pulled away before moving.

***

Back upstairs they tried the handle of Yeti's door to find it was locked, Shells pulled a card from his pocket and slid it neatly down the gap between the frame and the door and heard the mechanism click back. No fancy security systems here. They walked in and were instantly hit by an intense smell of something like rotting meat with a pungent fruity undertone. Holding their hands over their already mask covered faces to try and stop more of the smell coming through they looked around. This place was a literal dump, punch holes lined the walls, burn marks covered all surfaces including the ceiling, there was rubbish littered everywhere and at least two of the windows had no glass in. The main source of the cloying smell seemed to be coming from the sofa which was heaped with dirty old blankets, coats and even shoes – it was like a huge stinking laundry pile.

"Shit!" came the surprised voice of Grid. Shells jumped and looked around to see what was happening. He reeled back in disgust, Grid was stood holding the edge of one of the blankets from the sofa but it wasn't the sofa that had shocked him, it was the grey mottled face staring blindly up at him with a hole in its head and dried blood crusted all around it.

"What the f-" Shells began, then realised who it was. "no way. Shit that's Max, the guy who runs with Yeti. Wonder what happened."

"Man I don't know." Grid replied, dropping the blanket with a cringe, "Looks like he shot him in the head, a while ago I'm guessing. He came for me the other day when I was selling and starting asking questions about who was messing with him. Could've been me on this sofa maybe."

"Nah, that doesn't make sense, I've never seen Yeti with a gun. Either you're wrong or someone else hit Max. Weird he has him here though, maybe he forgot he was there under all this shit." Shells replied. "Let's see if we can find his stash, I hear he is pretty much on the line now. One more mistake and he is cold in the ground."

"Surprised they let him live so long. C'mon let's do it." Grid said, moving hastily away from the rotting corpse on the sofa trying not to inhale too deeply. As this was a studio flat they didn't have many places to look and they were confident that the cocky Yeti wouldn't have put too much thought into his hiding spot for his stash because he'd assume that no one would dare mess with him. How wrong he was now. They moved over to the dingy kitchen and thought for a moment,

"Let's make this fun, I wager first dibs on the new chick Kelsey that he stashed it up behind the sink." Grid said, his mischievous grin was hidden by the ski mask but his sparkling eyes gave it away,

"You're on, I bet he stashed it on top of the cupboards." Shells replied with a snort. Shells went to put his hand up to feel around and thought better of it after realised there could be anything stashed up there. He swept the rubbish and cutlery off the kitchen side and scrambled up. "Hey don't make a mess he'll know we've been here!" Grid said, maintaining a serious composure before laughing it off and crouching down to raid through the cupboard under the overflowing sink.

Shells poked his head into the space on top of the shelves and was greeted by a variety of things, thick nests of spider webs, empty baggies and a handful of blades – one of which was covered in dried blood. The laughter that had only just come from Shells was abruptly forgotten as he thought about the fact it was likely Brute's blood on that blade. His switch into darkness was only lightly relieved by the dusty black bag he could see on the right-hand side. He carefully trod his way over and reached for the bag, grabbing it and hopping back down onto the floor next to Grid who was squinting up at him.

"Damn, I thought I was onto a winner there. Fine, but when she rejects you its fair game!" he joked. Shells jovial nature was strongly affected at this point and Grid sensed it, "Come on man, lets bounce."

Shells merely nodded in reply, both of them grateful to get from this place and its rotting inhabitants.

Chapter Twenty-Seven

Martha was sat in the middle of her living area once more. She was cross legged and breathing deeply, allowing herself to fall into a state of meditation before attempting to call Steven's presence. She needed to talk him through what was going to happen before she set it all up otherwise the whole thing could be lost through disruption, something she wanted to avoid.

"I call upon the powers above me to grant me protection from any ill wishing entities. Do not allow any dark entities to enter my presence and grant me protection from that which intends harm. I now call upon Steven Tawn to join my circle." She spoke clearly and powerfully, making sure to enunciate to avoid any issues.

She was apprehensive after the whole Keith ordeal and didn't want to risk anything like that happening again. She also couldn't face going back to father Robins and Irene and explaining that she had ignored them, proving their doubts in her abilities to be well founded. They had both told her that she shouldn't try to handle anything supernatural, as it was far too risky, using her experience with Keith as an example of that. Father Robins tried to console her, telling her she would feel Steven's presence if he visited whilst Irene had settled for just giving her a long hard look, to get her point across.

Martha didn't care, she was going to get her son back no matter what and no priest or his helper was going to stop her. She focused her thoughts back onto Steven, and only Steven. After a couple of minutes of silence she tried again,

"I, Martha Tawn, call upon the spirit known as Steven Tawn to join me in my circle whilst I am under the protection of the powers above me."

This time about thirty seconds passed and she felt the air in the room shifting, she kept her eyes closed and waited. The shift indicated that the energy being summoned was now aware of the request to be present and could choose to resist or attend the séance. She anticipated his displeasure at her pointing the police in the direction of his friend, but hoped he would understand she was protecting her other nephew. Martha was sure Ross's death was unconnected to her but didn't want to risk it.

She felt the air around her contract and become denser and knew he was present before he even spoke.

"That was interesting." Was all he said.

"Steven!" she exclaimed, her excitement at hearing his voice hard to hide.

"Shells? What were you thinking mum?" he asked pointedly.

"I'm sorry. I knew that would make you unhappy but I have terrible news, and once I tell you it you'll know why I did what I did." She said.

"What is the news?" he asked, not sure they needed more bad news at the moment.

"It's your cousin, Ross." She started, and he interrupted.

"He's dead. I know, you don't need to tell me that. I saw the whole thing."

"With Alicia?" she asked.

"What? No. I did see some things that looked like her telling people amongst other things but I was also there in the prison. Seth is in a pretty rough place and should probably be put into isolation. What has that got to do with you naming one of the few people I actually respect?"

"I was worried that if I named your cousins as the people who told me, they would call Seth in for questioning and then it'd be pretty obvious what happened if this Jake boy suddenly ended up in prison. I was trying to protect him." She explained.

"Mum, they know that Seth and Ross told you about Yeti. That was why a hit was taken out on Ross, Seth got a warning too and I don't know if he'll get hit next, but I don't think so."

Martha was silent for a moment and Steven wished he could see her whilst he spoke with her, he wasn't trying to hurt her but she needed to know. He was pretty sure she was safe for now, judging by everything he was seeing Yeti wasn't long for this world and Steven just wanted to get there in time to be the one to end his life before anyone else got the pleasure. He could feel the hurt and worry in his mums' energy as she spoke,

"I'm so sorry. I didn't mean for this to happen. I told myself that he was killed for any reason other than someone knowing that they had spoken with me, I didn't want the guilt. How do I tell Alicia?"

"I don't know mum, maybe you don't have to. The police won't know that was why he had a hit on him. Seth won't speak because he will be next if he does. Now tell me what happened with that other spirit."

"Oh I haven't explained that really have I?" Martha said sadly.

"No, like a lot of things. But we will start with this."

"It was the evil entity that I accidentally introduced to Susie when we were teenagers. Back then, he attached himself to her and taunted her for weeks and weeks, tortured her, didn't let her rest – drained every ounce of her being until she was just a shell of herself and took her own life to sever the tether that bound her to him. Turns out he had been waiting for all these years for me to open up the channels and not protect myself, which is what happened when I contacted you again. In my haste to speak with you I forgot to request protection and he took the opportunity to attach himself to me."

"Where is he now?" Steven asked.

"Gone, I tried to remove him by myself but he was far too strong, so I went to the church down the road and one of the priests there and a spiritual worker helped."

"Was he the reason for your hurt feet?"

"Yes. He put the muscles into a state of spasm for hours and I think the bruising was because I walked to the church with them like that. They're much better now."

"If I ever see him I'll…" Steven started getting angry, when his mum interrupted.

"You'll what? There isn't really much you can do. The form you are in now is the best one to realise that all this materialistic living does nothing for one's soul. Carrying grudges and ill wishes does nothing to help you in this life or the next. Let it go."

"Aren't you helping me seek revenge for my death?" Steven pointed out. His mum laughed lightly.

"True. But that's different. I am choosing to pursue revenge despite knowing all this." Steven didn't bother answering, he knew when his mum was set on something and there wasn't any point wasting words, so he went back to the subject of the police.

"You needn't have worried about reporting anything by the way, the police aren't going to do anything, I heard them after they left." He said, Martha tutted harshly in response.

"Scum." She hissed, then changed her tone, "We don't have much time left I can feel you fading. I am going to set up a meditation session with Tim Panel, he is the one whose body you're going to take, I will run you through it as we go you just have to be present and ready. I need you to go and gather as much energy as you can as it is going to be a huge undertaking."

"Ok." Was all he managed before he found himself in a cloudy haze and was pulled away from the connection.

He looked upon his mum once more as she was opening her eyes, she seemed to look directly at him and for a moment he forgot he wasn't a physical form anymore. It was like she could really see him. She smiled sadly and spoke once more,

"Go, rest and recuperate." She instructed and with that everything faded away.

Chapter Twenty-Eight

He stormed around his flat booting the debris on the floor away from him in a fit of rage. Someone had been here. Someone had broken into his place, his refuge. That someone was going to pay. He was beyond reasoning, and he considered himself to be a reasonable man. Sure, he had a temper but those who pretended to not were lying to themselves and everyone around them and he was no liar.

The place stank, even he knew that, probably in part thanks to Max. He hadn't been bleeding anymore when Yeti had picked him up off the table after he'd been shot by Lance, so he had figured it would be fine but it looked like he was wrong. He didn't know where else to dump his body. Usually he left people in the streets, dead or alive, and let someone else deal with it. Problem he had with Max was Lance told him he had to dispose of the body and clear up, which meant he needed to be discreet, not that he would have wanted to leave Max behind anyway.

He pummelled his fist angrily into the wall. Fucking Brute. This was all his fault, everything that was happening was his fault. Since that prick died because of a measly stab in the leg everything had gone bad for him. How was he to know that there was some big artery in the thigh that could cause someone to bleed out in minutes? Useful to know now, and probably handy down the line but a pain that he just so happened to hit Brute in it. He was only trying to warn him, assert his place on the streets because Brute was one of the ones they recommended keeping on side or there would be trouble. Yeti wasn't going to be told what to do or whose ass to kiss, so he wanted to make a point of not being pushed around by him. If the guy had just accepted less cash for a bag Yeti was sure he would have returned the favour if ever needed, maybe. He wouldn't have asked if he wasn't just waiting for his next stash to come in. Thinking of stashes, he roared in anger again, someone had broken into his home and stolen his gear. He couldn't even get the landlord to install cameras now because that idiot was also dead and rotting in a pool of his own blood upstairs. Thinking about cameras reminded him of his car, his pride and joy.

Someone was messing with him and they were going to pay with their lives, he just had to work out who or just kill everyone who gave him a bad feeling. He had a feeling about Grid and although he was believable, he had been hanging out with Shells a lot if the talk on the street was to be believed and he knew full well that Shells was a sneaky bastard. He wondered if it was those two who he saw bolting through the building when he left yesterday but dismissed the idea, they wouldn't be so dumb as to willingly incur his wrath especially after he warned Grid the other day.

He glanced over at where Max lay and disgust flooded through him when he spotted that part of his face was exposed, it seemed to be melting into itself and he grimaced, he'd not seen a body that had been dead this long before. Something ticked in his brain for a moment then he had a eureka moment, the exposed face meant that whoever had been here must have seen Max. He wasn't worried they'd report him to the police because if they were going to the police would have been here by now. The police! Yeti grinned darkly as the pieces fell into place, he knew there were many corrupt officers on the force and he dealt with them regularly, he was willing to wager that it was a dirty police officer that came snooping around and saw an opportunity. Question was, what did he do now?

He needed to replace the stash and fast, his girl was off working the house parties tonight which meant she needed to have some on hand to shift – and he wasn't going to be able to *not* pay Lance and his superiors. In all fairness if he was honest with himself people had been eliminated for far less than the shit that had been happening around him and he wasn't sure if he was about to join Max. The anxiety this thought process induced was too much and he dropped to his knees and dug around under the sofa, ignoring the pungent smell leaking out of Max that threatened to suffocate him and located his little black box of magic. He pulled out a dirty metal spoon, loaded up and took himself off to another planet, grateful for the respite.

Chapter Twenty-Nine

A couple of days had passed since Ross was killed and Martha was concerned about Alicia. She knew she had her three other kids to keep her going but Martha knew how painful and all-consuming it was to know you had outlived your child. She had tried to call her a couple of times since Alicia stayed the night but the line kept ringing out and she figured she must need her space and time to heal enough to speak. She had been considering telling her about what Steven had told her but she had no reasonable way to explain that at the moment. She figured it was best to simply not talk about it just yet and if her instinct told her it was time, she would then bite the bullet and do so. She was worried about her though and although her and her mum had barely spoken since Steven's death she decided to call her and ask for an update.

She grabbed her phone off the little coffee table and as she did so the Ouija board box caught her eye, she shook away those thoughts as that was going be her next focus just as soon as she knew Alicia was alright, as much as she could be anyway. She pulled up the number and hit dial with baited breath, her own heart still aching at the fact her mum hadn't been there for her when she needed her. It rang twice before she picked up,

"Yes?" was all she said.

"Mum?" Martha said, holding back the tears that instantly threatened to engulf her as soon as she heard her voice.

"What is it Martha?" she asked.

"What do you think mum? Why won't you talk to me?" she exclaimed, the tsunami of emotions she always tried to contain found a crack in the dam she had built, and smashed through without warning. "Why are you so angry at me, what have I done? I lost my only child and you've turned your back on me. I can see now that the treatment was reserved solely for me and I don't know why. Why am I not deserving of your support and love too, mum?"

The line went silent aside from the slightly laboured breathing on the other side, she heard her mum inhale deeply before she replied,

"Martha. I didn't know you felt like that." Was all she said.

"How could I not? We've done so much as a family, always been together and the moment my son is killed everything changes."

"I've always been here for you, I'm always open to you. You never call or come round anymore." She said.

"I've been in mourning! I've been trying to pick my life up since everything happened, he was my whole everything mum! I did my best to raise him against all odds and he was taken from me, I thought you could try to understand that or at least have a spot of empathy!" cried Martha.

"I do, and I didn't want to overwhelm you. You've always kept yourself to yourself when it comes to personal feelings and life matters so I assumed this would be no different, that you would want extra space to heal and then you'd come back to us when you were good and ready. We've been mourning too and we are now having to mourn another loss in our family, it seems our pain will never end. We're all dealing with our feelings as best we can, I didn't know you felt so strongly about it."

"I wasn't trying to make this call about me or my feelings, that wasn't at all the intent of this call believe it or not. I know we're all dealing with the loss of not only one but now two family members, your grandchildren, your daughters' babies. I think when I heard your voice then I just couldn't ignore how I felt anymore."

"Oh Mattie, we all need each other now more than ever and I'm sad to know you feel this way as it wasn't my intentions. Your sister is in an awful way too. Have you spoken to her since you saw her?"

"No, I've tried to call countless times but she never picks up and her voicemail is off so I can't even leave a message. It's actually why I called, have you seen her?"

"Have I seen her? She hasn't left since she came back from yours except to go and collect Ross' belongings from the prison. She saw Seth as well I believe but hasn't told me how that went or how Seth is doing. She came back and locked herself in my spare room, I've been taking Lily and Tom to and from school and caring for them. They need their mum, she seems to have forgotten that it isn't just her who lost someone, they lost their older brother too."

Martha was surprised to hear all of this, Alicia was the most emotional one of the two of them but locking herself away and not even looking after her other kids was a step too far.

"Mum, I want you to go to her room and hand her the phone. If she doesn't take it put it on loudspeaker and lay it next to her. She needs to speak to someone or she may get stuck in a dangerous spiral." She said.

"That's my girl." Was all her mum said and Martha couldn't help but feel a pang in her heart.

She listened as her mum walked down the hall towards the bedroom and knocked on the door gently, there was no response and she knocked harder, this time following up by opening the door.

"Alicia? I have the phone for you."

"I don't want it." Came the muffled reply.

"It's your sister."

"I don't care."

"Talk to her." She commanded.

"No." Alicia said gently.

"I'm just going to put this here. She is there if you want her."

Martha heard the phone rustling like it was being placed on a blanket and muted footsteps retreating. She waited until she heard the door click closed before speaking.

"Alicia?" she said, but there was no reply. "I know how you're feeling, you just want the earth to swallow you up and you can stop feeling all these awful things but that won't help anything. You've got Lily and Tom who really need their mum right now, they probably feel like you aren't there for them right now because it is past their comprehension that you can't cope. I am here if you need to talk, shout, cry or whatever it may be, but we all need you to come out of the room and try. Your kids need you."

She heard a shuffling, and it sounded like the phone was picked up, then her sisters voice came through the phone loud and clear,

"If I need to talk, shout or cry? What about if I need to ask what the hell you were thinking when you asked my sons information about Steven's killer? Now my son is dead too because he trusted you!" this hit Martha like a wrecking ball.

"I never told anyone what was said! I never even reported it to the police, I promise! I have no idea how anyone could have known that they told me, I knew how stupid it would be to report it especially straight after seeing them. I just needed a name to help find closure even if I couldn't do anything."

"Must be nice, having closure." Alicia spat.

"I don't have it, if I am honest with you. It didn't work." Martha replied bluntly.

"Good. So it was all in vain then." Alicia said, and Martha felt awful as she heard renewed crying down the line. She began to tear up again.

"No not in vain! Your sons were brave enough to tell me information even though they knew it could be risky! You should be so proud that they did the right thing, I feel now I didn't by not reporting what they told me." She cried.

"No, you did what I would have done if I'm honest. I don't really blame you, I just hurt so much Mattie. So damn much I can barely breathe. When does this grief end?" Alicia asked woefully.

"It doesn't, you have to grow around it. The grief doesn't shrink or lessen, you just learn to carry it with you and accept its presence, some days it interferes more than others. I'm still too early on in my journey to tell you more."

Then after a moments thought she decided to tell her one small bit of information,

"Alicia, I should tell you. I tried to contact Ross." This was met with echoing silence, so she continued. "He wasn't anywhere in this plane, which can only mean one thing. I don't know if it will be of comfort to you, although it should be, he has already moved on into the spirit realm and is free of the tethers that bind us here."

"You tried to contact him?" Alicia asked, her voice sounding hollow.

"I did." Martha replied quietly. "I'm sorry, I should have told you before that I was going to try to. I know I promised so many years ago I wouldn't do that stuff anymore but I needed to know."

"Have you tried to contact Steven?" Alicia asked, although she was confident she knew the answer already.

"I don't think I am ready to talk about that right now." Martha replied.

"How could you not be? You are talking to me about trying to contact my dead son but cannot talk to me about contacting your own?" came Alicia's fraught voice, her emotions getting out of control again.

"I'm sorry. I am just processing too. I will tell you everything when more makes sense I promise."

"Does that mean you spoke to him?" Alicia asked, despite her overwhelming emotions she was intrigued and slightly in awe.

"Yes. He is trapped here and hasn't been able to move on yet." Martha replied, not wanting to go into it. Alicia thankfully accepted this.

"When you're ready then. We can get through this together, right?" she asked.

"We can. I love you."

"Back at you Mattie. I guess I should go and face Lily and Tom." Alicia said, voice cracking.

With that they hung up and Martha returned her attention to the next task of the day.

Chapter Thirty

Further chaos was unfolding in Yeti's world, he was coming down off his latest high and rapidly. Reality was clawing at his consciousness with its dirt encrusted nails and he didn't want it, not yet, not ever. He looked in his little black box again even though he knew it was going to be as empty as it had been the last three times he had checked, taunting him. He remained hopeful though that he just somehow missed something in his haze and there would be enough remnants of his go to release to give him the sweet satisfaction he so craved.

The low mood was beginning to make his head feel like a barren wasteland and he knew he needed to pull himself out of it but every which way he looked he hit a wall. He needed to find out if it was the police who took the drugs, or someone else. He didn't want to entertain the possibility of it being the latter, if people started thinking they could get one over on him he was going to have to up his fear game even more and he wasn't sure yet what he could do to achieve that without signing his own death warrant. He knew full well that if he didn't have the cash for at least half the gear he was meant to be shifting by the end of the week Lance would end him anyway. He wasn't going to consider getting a job somewhere because that would be giving in and letting whoever messed with him win, plus he wasn't really cut out for your typical nine-to-five. No, he was going to get to the bottom of it and find out who broke in to his home, stole his gear and smashed his BMW up.

He pulled himself up off the floor and ignored the fogginess that was sweeping circles through his sodden brain and threw the blanket back over Max's still exposed face whilst fighting the urge to pound him for repulsing him so much. Maybe he could kill Lance, he would deserve it after all. In fact, all of them did and if he could work out how to take them all down he would run this town and then no one would shoot his buddy in the head or treat him like this. He could think about getting clean and not ingest all his profits, his girl would be happier and if he was true to himself he might be too. He had started seeing things and hallucinating strongly even when he wasn't actively high, to the point he had convinced himself that an ornamental dog had been launched out of thin air at him and nearly broken his nose.

  He stomped his way over to his front door and made his way down the stairs and into the garage, got to his sorry looking car and scowled. The deep lines the expression carved into his face abated slowly, transforming into a grim smile, what people failed to realise was that this only ended up empowering him and made him stronger. He would come back and take everyone down in his path no matter who they were, he wasn't a small fish in a big pond, he was a shark in a tank of goldfish masquerading as predators and it was clear he needed to remind them of their true rankings. He climbed into his passenger seat, retracted his legs up to his chest and in one neat kick booted the already smashed windscreen outwards, then he climbed out and went to the driver's side to repeat the process on the remaining shards jutting out. That was better, it hurt him to cause further damage to his car but the last time he drove it was sketchy, the holes in the windscreen kept sucking the smoke out through them the last time he drove and he couldn't see properly. He turned the key in the ignition and roared out of the garage, hoping for anyone to push him today so he could show them he wasn't to be messed with.

  A few minutes later he came to a screeching stop outside an old one storey brick building and climbed out of the car, ignoring the smoke trickling lazily out of the puncture wounds in his bonnet. He walked over to the black metal door on the side of the building and rapped neatly three times, checking the parking bay next to the big oak tree to make sure the person he was visiting was here. The gleaming Bugatti Veyron sat there taunting him with the reminder his own ride once looked so beautiful, but seeing it did also confirm that he would find what he was looking for here. A minute passed and the door opened inwards and as expected there was no-one standing there to greet him, no-one in their right mind in this business would provide such an easy target. Yeti spoke,

"Lance, it's me Yeti. I've come to talk to you about a proposition." He said.

"Very well." Came the crisp voice of Lance. "Come in."

Yeti walked into the badly lit room and looked around, he knew that Lance would likely be alone but he wanted to check first.

"What is this…proposition?" Lance asked.

He was sat at the very same chair that Max had been in when he was shot by him. It went against everything Yeti knew to control his rising temper but he did, for the moment.

"Things are getting out of hand on the streets. People forgetting their place and stepping on other peoples' turf." Yeti said, barely controlling his voice and keeping it steady.

"Right, what does this have to do with me?" Lance replied smoothly. "You're meant to keep your own operation in check and if what I am hearing from various sources is in any way true, you have failed to do so. You know what happens when our representatives show us they're not up to their job."

"I am. I've been shifting gear all over the place, I've just hit a few hitches in other areas, I was actually coming here to ask you to up my quantity. I have a lot of people waiting for gear and I've run out."

"Run out? Then I assume you've got the cash to exchange." Came the steady reply of Lance, cocking his bushy black eyebrow at his visitor.

"Well, funny story that. Like I said people have been stepping onto the wrong turf. Mine. Someone broke in and stole the cash I'd made from the stash." Yeti lied, better for Lance to think he shifted the entire lot of gear than to know it had been stolen.

"I should hope you're trying to be funny." Lance said shortly and Yeti knew he was on thin ice.

"I know who took the cash and you know I'm good for it. I'll get it back and make them pay. But I had no problem selling out the gear I had so I can move the next batch just as quickly. I won't smoke any, and won't have no profit just to make it up to you."

"Will you now?" Lance asked, a dark expression came over his face then he pulled one side of his thin-lipped mouth upwards in a vague attempt to smile. It came across as more of a leer. "I'll tell you something. I won't tell anyone any of that idiotic plan and you go and get that money back for me. You will sell the next batch we give to you and you're right, you will not consume even a milligram of it nor have any profit. You will not however receive the next batch until you return the money to me in full for this one, you have two days."

Yeti stared at him, wondering how it would play out if he launched himself at him and broke his neck, that could solve this problem of being told what to do as well. Might mean that he would have the big bosses after him though and he wasn't ready for that.

"Right boss. I'll sort it." Yeti said, still itching to launch at the man treating him like a worthless puppet.

"Don't even think about it." Lance said, the leer remaining firmly in place.

Yeti noticed Lance's hand was in his pocket and he now heard the unmistakable clicking noise of a gun being cocked.

"Do as you're told. The only reason your still standing is because we don't need three dead street boys, but don't think we won't accept that outcome if you step out of line."

Yeti nodded, refusing to look away or back down and show weakness.

"Get out." Lance muttered, gesturing with his free hand to show he was tired of this meeting. Yeti left, feeling furious at the way he had been spoken to.

Chapter Thirty-One

Martha was sat at home meditating, waiting for her door to knock. She had called round to Tim earlier and asked if he was free to talk, he had seemed apprehensive at first and she realised in her eagerness she was likely coming across as manic and eased off a little. It helped and he immediately became more responsive and agreed to come to her when he was ready. She had smiled at this because she knew he was unlikely to have been busy but was trying to retain some control when it came to this relationship he had with her. She had gently put her hand on his upper arm, palm completely flat to him and nodded, then sashayed away from him. It worked like a charm and she knew he wouldn't take too long, just long enough to express a little rebellion and show her he wasn't at her beck and call.

She needed to make sure the air in her home was light and welcoming to help guide Tim's decision today. It wasn't the end of the world if he said no for now but it would set her back and she didn't want to wait any longer. Martha craved good news, something positive happening. She knew in her heart that being able to hug her son would satiate that craving and like a broke addict hell bent on finding their next fix she would do anything to achieve it. She felt herself drift into a blissfully calm trance like state and consciously held it over herself like a comfort blanket and reached for the candles she'd set up on the board, she lit them one by one, taking care to impart love and tranquillity to each flame as it flickered and took hold. Next, she reached over to the sandalwood incense that was in a wooden holder and lit it, inhaling deeply as the earthy rich plume rose in a mesmerising swirl, she placed it back in its place and sure enough the door knocked. She rose from her position and walked to the door making sure to open it slowly and with a smile on her lips.

"Coffee?" Tim said straight away. Martha laughed lightly back at him.

"Sure. Come, sit down." She gestured the sofa near her set up. He looked at it then back at her quizzically.

"Am I interrupting something?" he asked.

"No of course not, that wouldn't make sense for me to invite you if you were." Martha replied, "I was just doing some meditating. Have you ever tried it?"

"No. Can't say it ever appealed to me." Tim said flatly, but still glanced once more at the area with a bit of curiosity.

Martha turned her face to hide her joy at his interest, even if he wouldn't admit it yet she could see the lure was working. She moved over to the kitchen and flicked the kettle on whilst he settled down. Martha silently berated herself, she should have had more faith in her plan, she wasn't certain that Tim would have enough interest the first time she introduced him to this and so hadn't called upon Steven to come yet. If Tim did try a little meditation session she would have to discreetly reach out to him, or better yet get Tim completely under and then start a séance. Yes, that would work perfectly too. She fought the urge to clap her hands together in glee at the plan forming, Tim would wonder what was wrong with her and everyone knew that cheering too early was begging for bad luck.

She made the coffee quickly and took it over to Tim making sure she had the energy of calm and peace emanating from her being as she handed him the cup. It was working, as he took the coffee he brushed his fingers against hers and his eyes widened ever so slightly. She smiled at him and let go, taking a seat next to him ensuring she was sat just close enough that her knees were almost touching his but not quite.

"So Martha did you have anything in particular you wanted to talk about? Or can I tell you about my latest news?" he said, clearly enjoying the fact he had someone he actually wanted to tell his news to.

"I do, but I am more than happy to wait. I'd love to hear what has been happening with you." She replied.

"Good. As you know I handed in my notice so I could leave that miserable dentist office, well I was told just yesterday they were willing to let me go without working the full notice period. When I tell you that I am relieved to see the back of that place I mean it, those grimy little brats and their social media mums can become a thing of the past whilst I handpick my future patients. I've already been looking at places to rent and I think I've found one just down the road. Not far from the one I just left actually, but if the clients are worthy of my dental care they'll choose correctly, assuming I get the place that is. At some point I'll be able to view it and put in my pitch to secure it. I will be in need of a receptionist of sorts, someone to work administration. I can't work with someone like the wench I had at my last place, I would likely burn the place down. This is where you come into the picture, would you be interested in coming to work for me?"

He looked at her expectantly, not registering that he had just said a lot about his character again and then asked her to work for him. She took a subtle deep breath and spoke,

"Wonderful news you don't have to work your notice period. It means you can chase your dreams even earlier. Fingers crossed about the new place, how gratifying it would be to show your old place your true worth." She replied. He inclined his head at her.

"And the idea of working for me? Was that too forward of me? From what I've gathered so far you are quite the woman and I can say I've never met anyone like you. I'd like to hear you say you'll at least consider it." He said.

"I will consider it. I am flattered you want to work with me, I'm not particularly people friendly." She replied.

"You've mentioned this before and I still cannot see how. Not that it changes my opinion nor request, as you know I myself am not overly keen on people."

"I'd say the lack of long-term friends and relationships is a good indicator of me being the incompatible one." Martha shrugged it off, having accepted long ago that this was how it was and, in all fairness, suited her introverted ways just fine.

Up until recently she had her son and their close bond had sufficed for her by meeting the low quota of social interaction needed to get by. Now he was gone she was not just the mourning the death of a child but a friend too. She figured this was why she had a weak moment the other day in feeling some way about using Tim, luckily he opened his mouth and reminded her that what she was doing was the right thing.

"Maybe you're right. But in my books that has made you the kind of person that appeals to me. I think we were meant to cross each other's paths, for reasons unknown to us perhaps." Tim said. Martha smiled at him,

"I think you're exactly right Tim. We were meant to cross each other's paths, and I'm very sure that reason will come to light at some point or another." He nodded at her in appreciation of her agreement. "Can you feel that warmth?"

"Warmth?" Tim asked curiously.

Martha leaned forwards and put her palm on his chest, the sudden contact made him flinch a little but he didn't remove her hand. He looked down for a moment to gather himself then looked back up at her.

"I am feeling something warm yes. What is that?" he asked.

"That is a connection between us. The tether that formed between us when we first met is being strengthened by our experiences together." She replied, removing her hand.

"How interesting. Is this normal? Do other people get this?"

"Not many, it is an experience reserved for the few who have the gift of higher perception. I knew when I first met you that you had this gift." She explained.

"What do I do with this gift?"

"You can do a lot. You can see and feel things outside of the average person. It also means you can meditate on a new level."

"I've never meditated before so I wouldn't know what that means." He said.

"Well, put it this way. You would be able to have something commonly referred to as an out of body experience."

"I've seen something about that in a movie I watched once, I thought it was nonsense."

"Not at all, nonsense to someone who doesn't have the natural ability and power to actually achieve it. It takes great mental strength and concentration, do you think you could do it?" she asked.

"Great mental strength? Surely that is easy." He scoffed. "Have you done it before?"

"A few times. It is quite phenomenal. I'd always recommend having someone nearby to reground you if you drift too far though."

"Do you believe I could achieve this?" Tim asked, looking her dead in the eye challenging her to say no.

"I think I do. Do you?" Martha flipped it back on him, trying to hide the triumphant sensation prematurely trying to flood her system. Not only was it going better than she could have hoped, she was sure she just felt a presence in the room which meant it was all aligning. The signs were telling her this was the right time.

"Shall we try? I'm curious to see if it really is nonsense. It doesn't put me at any sort of risk, does it?" he asked, now a hint of dubiousness coming into his voice.

"Not at all. It feels incredibly liberating and you're in safe hands here. Just feel the air around you, use your intuition, can you tell you are safe?" she pushed.

He sat and thought about it for a moment and she could see he was making an effort to feel the room around him. She pushed out her feeling of peace and comfort and knew that combined with all the other factors he would be feeling at ease.

"I think I can, what do I need to do?" he asked.

Martha was impressed with Tim's interest and almost giddy with delight.

"Well, I wouldn't recommend finishing that coffee for a start, that will increase your heartrate and make it harder for you to fall into a state of meditation." She said, nodding her head at his half-drunk cup. He reached across and put it on the side table without pause. "You need to be as calm and collected as you can be, and envision yourself in a different state of being, you may find it easier if you are laying down."

"Ok, where shall we do it? I'd like to try this and see if all this is true or I need to run a mile because you're out of your head crazy." Tim said, and Martha could tell this was his weak attempt at humour and he clearly wanted to experience something new and more stimulating than the reality he currently lived in, and despised so much.

"Well if you'd like to try it now, you can either lay back on the sofa you're on or I can put a mat on the floor for you." Martha offered.

As expected, Tim snubbed the idea of laying on the floor and proceeded to lay himself back on the sofa. Martha knelt on the floor next to him.

"OK now close your eyes and count backwards from one hundred. I'm going to sit here and be present so you don't need to worry about anything."

"Like I would." Tim retorted, "I know I'm in good hands." He added.

"Right. I need you to picture yourself as a whole, from the top of your head all the way down to your toes. Once you have that image in your mind make sure you focus on it in its entirety and not any one singular part. After a while you'll become aware of the weight of yourself, then you'll feel everything lighten and in turn, won't be able to sense the things in the room around you anymore. As soon as that happens you need to make the image in your head of you rise up away from the heavy weight that is your physical being, this will be the out of body moment and if you lose your focus you will cut the experience short and have to start again. This is the hard bit. After you've made yourself rise up and out of your body your perspective will change and you'll find yourself in the room looking down at yourself, try not to be alarmed by this. You'll be able to move around the room, even outside of the room if you are brave enough to venture that far. I will be here to guide you back to your body in the event you move away and cannot find your way back."

Martha looked at Tim, laying there with his eyes closed taking in what she was saying. She felt her excitement grow, the moment she had been waiting for was within reach. She cast her eyes over his chest and watched as he went through the process she had described to him, he should still counting at this point, a great exercise for centering and calming oneself. She took this moment to feel the room once more and check that her senses had been correct, she could feel him near but couldn't speak out yet as Tim would be disrupted. She waved her hand above the lit candle and made the flame dance in disturbed airwaves, Martha did this three times then placed her hands back on her knees. She watched as the flame flickered once, twice and then a third time and smiled in acknowledgement.

Focusing back on Tim she could see his breathing had deepened and was steadily getting slower. She calmed her own and began to meditate in order to better channel both Tim and Steven. Eyes closed she could see swirling shapes all around her in a multitude of shades of orange and red. She fixated on one of the strands and it came into focus, her heartbeat sounded all around her and the visual danced gracefully in the rhythm, it showed her Tim standing staring into space. He was nearly there and ready to move away from his physical form, he had taken well to the process and Martha was sure it was down to sheer stubbornness and a refusal to fail that he did so because achieving a successful out of body experience on the first go was almost unheard of. That or the spirits that protected her were helping her out, something she would be happy to believe too.

She unfocused from Tim's frame and moved to another swaying shape close by and with happiness saw Steven there in a very blurry format. He wouldn't be seen in his original physical manner unless he actively chose to present himself as such, and she felt a flash of pride that he had already discovered a great way to preserve energy is to not hold on to the body you once had. She called silently out to him to come closer and he obliged, now he was within reach of her but still untouchable. Not for long. Removing her gaze from Steven she looked over to Tim again and could see him now waving his arms around himself, clearly fully immersed in the experience. Martha couldn't see the surroundings in this state, only the energies and she watched as Tim looked down directly at her and waved. She smiled in response and waved him away, showing that she could see he had achieved the thing she told him was difficult and knowing full well he wouldn't be able to resist pushing it to the next step.

That was why she had planted that seed, saying that he would be able to travel further when he was able would have only made him want to do it all and prove himself. Sure enough he did a mock salute back at her and slowly moved away, blissfully unaware of the presence of Steven waiting to take his place. Tim didn't hesitate to move outside of the room and very quickly faded from view, she felt now was a safe time to speak,

"Steven, you will be doing the reverse of what I just told Tim to do. Rest your energy in his vessel and count to one hundred. Imagine you are one with the body and feel your being fill it bit by bit, see yourself fitting into it and wearing it. You will likely find it sluggish to respond to start with but we will work on that later. You must believe it is your body, your vessel to control. Now go." She demanded.

With that she opened her eyes and watched Tim's inert body closely for signs of movement. Several minutes passed and Martha began to feel concern edging in, perhaps Steven wasn't ready yet and she was pushing him too soon. He had seemed so strong and advanced that she had assumed he would be capable of this. He had been gone for a couple of days so he should have his full energy capabilities, the problem she now faced was not wanting to try and communicate with him right now in case it pulled Tim back or potentially halted whatever progress Steven was making in taking over Tim's body. She stared at him for what felt like an eon and her heart started when his eyes shot open. She gasped in surprise, she didn't want to admit it but on some level Martha worried it wouldn't be possible, and she chided herself for this negative thinking.

"Steven?" she whispered, reaching her hand up to his. He turned his head to look at her, and a smile started at the corners of his mouth. "Steven!"

she cried and threw herself on his chest to embrace him. She felt his arms come around her and hold her tight for a moment.

"That does indeed feel peculiar after all these years." He said. Martha stared at him, mouth slowly dropping open. "You're right, I do feel a touch sluggish but I'm sure I'll get used to that in no time."

Martha felt the world around her crumbling, her legs felt weak and if she hadn't already been knelt on the floor next to this man she would have fallen.

Chapter Thirty-Two

Something snapped in the atmosphere around him and broke his previously blissful state. Tim had been floating along the streets picking random houses to peek into unseen, listening to passers-by conversations and enjoying swishing his hands through people but now he sensed something was wrong, a feeling he would have probably ignored had Martha had not enlightened him about the importance of listening to his intuition. He wasn't sure what he must do to return to his body except hope that she would do that grounding thing she had promised she would do at the first sign of trouble, or simply head back of his own accord. He decided to start moving back the way he had come and wait to be pinged back somehow, he wasn't sure how this all worked. He had to admit this was quite the feeling though, the liberation of not being touchable by the general population, unheard and unseen in the best way. Tim was unsure what people usually used this state for but he was sure as hell going to be exploring a lot of different ideas. He would be able to spy on people for a start, he wasn't sure who he would choose to gift his time and energy to yet so he would have to mull it over.

He had shown Martha that he was more powerful than she had thought he would be, he found it a source of great amusement that she had expressed doubts that someone could achieve this on their first try and he had done so almost effortlessly. His intuition continued to sound its alarm and he had a strange sensation coursing through him that he couldn't put a finger on. He moved along at a fair pace not bothering to move out of the way of anyone also using the path, choosing to simply float through them like they were nothing, the idea that he himself was the thing with no substance failed to cross his mind. Tim hadn't realised just how far away he had gone and was annoyed at the inconvenience of having to travel all the way back and not be fast-tracked like he thought he would be, a bone he would be picking with Martha when he was in her presence again.

Choosing to change the scenery he moved to the middle of the road and felt immense power at not having to move out of the way of the incoming vehicles. He tried to jump over one to see if he could make it and discovered he could jump really high, a couple of metres in fact, then he found he could hold that height and not come down. He shook his head at himself for being so obtuse, of course he could, gravity didn't apply to him right now.

This out of body stuff was going to be his new favourite thing, he could feel it already, it trumped his usual go to hobbies like crosswords and watching game shows. The first one angered him when he couldn't work out the words and the latter irritated him because of the people. Soon he found himself outside Martha's home and something stopped him in his tracks, although what that something was did not become apparent straight away. His instinct was telling him to ready himself and he wondered if Martha had keeled over in his absence and died, it would explain why he had the weird feeling and why she didn't bring him back herself. She had been going through quite a bit lately, and despite the fact he was pretty sure she was dramatizing some of it she was fifty something and heartbroken. Stranger things had happened, although he did hope in his core that this wasn't the case.

Tim passed through the door and looked at the scene before him, Martha was sat in the same place but now bore a dumbfounded expression with silent tears weaving tracks down her face. Whilst it gave him a moments pause a quick scan of the surroundings put his confusion about her state out of his mind, shock pulsed through his being when he saw that the sofa he had been laying on was vacant. Tim felt everything around him fizzing with static as his panic built up, Martha whipped her head around as though she sensed him. He ignored her and moved through the house room to room trying to find his body in case she had for some mad reason decided to move it, but it wasn't there. He came back into the living area and tried to shout at Martha but it was in vain, she couldn't hear him. He could still hear though, and Martha spoke to him in a choked voice,

"Tim? If that's you something terrible has happened, I cannot even open a séance to explain it to you right now because you'll be too weak to communicate and maintain the connection, as am I. So, I'll just let you know this before you go, an evil entity has possessed your body. We will fix this and I am so sorry, I shouldn't have let you go so far from your body on your first time. This is my fault and I know what we need to do, I will find where your body has been taken and banish the evil spirit from it and you can take it over again. I don't claim have an expansive knowledge of these things but I do know some things. Once the evil spirit has left your body you have around four minutes to return to it and repossess it yourself otherwise your body will die and with it, you."

Tim tried to absorb this information and struggled to see straight, everything was waving around in front of him as his panic at the situation and hatred for unexpected things clashed. He had no body? Did this make him a ghost? He couldn't be a ghost, he wasn't dead! If what Martha was saying was true, as far-fetched as it all sounded, he could be in some serious trouble. The room was fading in front of him and he tried to force it back into focus but it didn't work, but one thing he did notice before it all faded to black was there was a shadowy silhouette of a man suddenly standing near Martha. He wondered what he was doing there and if she knew he was so close to her.

Chapter Thirty-Three

It finally happened, that endless waiting around for the old bag Martha to make her next move was so worth the pay off. He wished he had thought of something like this before but the desire to taunt those he had attached himself to had always been far too alluring to ignore. During the session where that priest and his assistant tried to remove him he sensed a deeper darker energy about Martha and his intrigue only grew as he listened to her lying to them, in a house of god no less. Not that it mattered to him, even in death he had found no reason to become religious. He had been trapped earthside for what felt like forever and his only lot in death was to draw the energy from living beings, meaning that even if he had been a good intentioned human in life he had no choice but to become what he was now in order to sustain and feed his existence.

He didn't mind this one bit as it was a fantastic source of amusement when it was going well, the only real issue he found was when he made the mistake of attaching to someone who turned out to be not quite so useful or entertaining as there were only three ways to sever the attachment; firstly, if you were strong enough and the attached spirit wasn't, you could do what Martha tried by expelling them with your own energy, secondly through external assistance from a spiritual worker or lastly by death. Keith had in the end learned to be pickier in who he chose to attach to, actually observe them for a while before making the move. He had been watching Martha for years and had only attached to a handful of lucky souls since Susie, something had told him it would be worth it once he got to connect with dear Mattie and it turned out to be true. Look at him now, with an actual physical form again strutting down the same streets he once walked many years ago.

This body was younger than his had been when he had died, he had been forty-seven and in his prime. The ladies had loved him and he loved them, even the men if the mood struck but back then it was better kept under wraps on that front. He had been a real player, jumping from bar to bed, bed to craps table, craps table to bar. He wasn't ready to call life quits yet when he was in a drunken car crash, seatbelts were not really a thing back then and no-one blinked an eye if you got behind your ride a half-cut.

It wasn't even a big crash, the road surface had been slick and he'd spun out, not thinking in his alcohol sodden mind to take his foot off the accelerator or control the steering, instead aggressively turning the steering wheel any which way hoping it would stop the spin. The car had suddenly stopped its wild skidding and launched forwards into a tree, Keith got launched into the windshield. The glass was thick and sharp and it broke into jagged chunks which made quick work of impaling him and causing him to bleed out in a gory mess on the bonnet.

He remembered everything going light around him and an invisible pressure all around him trying to pull him away, he had resisted the lure, he assumed in that moment that if he didn't go he could potentially survive. This hadn't been the case, so he had been here since. Soon he had tired of learning how to control things with his energy and harassing the living, then he realised he wasn't sure how to get his invite to the spirit realm back, so he ended up just stuck in the loop of constantly seeking replenishment for his energy and being bored.

He learned quickly that if he didn't absorb energy to recharge he became weakened and it felt as though he would simply cease to be, fade into nothingness and the energy mass that was him would become unbound and have to reform elsewhere, afresh. Somehow that seemed more intimidating than his initial death because this version was eternal nothingness, a destruction of all that he had ever been. But now Martha had kindly given him a second chance at life, and he would be able to forget about that void for a while.

Keith was strutting along, aware that it was more of a heavy traipse but the feeling of the thudding footsteps was like a comforting old friend and he was resisting the urge to start dancing along the street with glee. He had decided that the first place he wanted to take his new body was somewhere he hadn't been since his old body was barely out of the rigor mortis stage and being obscured with clumps of mud. He had attended his own funeral and it was a miserable affair. Not because of mourners, it was rather the lack of any. His sister had been present and a couple of other people not even worth the mention but he had really hoped his bigger than life attitude and multiple connections would have yielded a larger gathering to celebrate his life. He had gone from being surrounded by many laughing at his jokes and bending to his will to nobody being affected enough by his passing to even say goodbye as his corpse was buried six feet under.

The hurt he felt at this revelation fuelled his bitterness for a while but that wore thin as the years passed. He had done what was needed to maintain his powerful range of abilities as an experienced earthbound spirit – or an obsessor as some would call it, based on his tendency to attach to living beings – but really had been biding his time for something, *anything,* to come along and pique his interest again. Who could imagine such a thing as a bored ghost?

He had fun with Martha in all fairness, she actually got some of his finest work right from the outset as punishment for keeping him shut out for so long, it had been hard for him to not inflict more of his favourite forms of torture on her but he had needed to keep himself invisible until the time was right. Now look at him, nearly two decades younger and fighting fit. He had arrived at the cobbled driveway that led up to the church and the adjoined graveyard.

Keith had forgotten how heavy a body was to lug around and could feel all the muscles in his legs and feet working, luckily this Tim fellow was in good shape but it would still take some getting used to. He trudged up the pathway into the graveyard and made his way to the back near the gigantic oak tree that provided shade for many long forgotten final resting places, overgrown and sunken in spots. He felt lightly amused and paused as he passed a very fresh-looking headstone that sat a couple of rows in, his instinct telling him who it was before reading it.

> Steven Tawn
> Beloved son, nephew, grandson and friend to all
> He will be forever loved and missed

Shaking his head to himself he carried on with what he came here to do. A minute later he found the headstone he was looking for and bent down to try and read the markings, no easy feat considering the headstone was covered in an abundance of stains, cracks and moss. He wiped some of the growth away to read it, despite knowing what it said underneath:

> Here lies Keith Buchan
> Rest in eternal peace
> Born 4th August 1865
> Died 13th April 1913

He smiled grimly down upon the unloved stone and the lack of caring sentiments emblazoned upon it, especially disgruntled after seeing Steven's considering the kind of character he was. He centred his energy and tried to release it, only to be dismayed that nothing happened. In the very least the furry growth on it should have been blasted away and at best the stone should crashed backwards. It took a millisecond for him to register he was in a human body again and he laughed out loud, that would take some time to get accustomed to. Determined to carry out his initial intention, he swung his right foot forwards making sure to tip his toes back and delivered a hefty kick to the sorry excuse of a gravestone and watched it give out and smash backwards in a dusty pile. That would do.

"Goodbye Keith Buchan, was nice knowing you." He uttered at the mess before him, before turning on his heel and walking away.

Chapter Thirty-Four

Martha sat on the floor, still reeling from what had transpired here not so long ago. She couldn't even cry, nothing seemed real to her anymore. She knew she needed to speak with Steven but had been rallying the courage to do so and was actively shutting him out until she felt ready. He had been moving around the room shifting things to show her he wanted her attention and answers. After some deliberation and realising that stalling wouldn't change anything she accepted it was time, Martha glanced at the candles still flickering away and noticed the incense was out so clambered up and got a new one out of the packet, choosing frankincense this time. She lit it and resumed a seated position then placed her hands on her knees palms skyward and took three deep breaths,

"I call upon the powers above me to protect me from ill wishing entities and prevent those who wish me harm from reaching me. I now call upon Steven Tawn to join me in my circle."

Within a few moments the inky blackness filled her mind and she knew she was connected with him.

"What happened mum? I thought he was gone, you said he was!" Steven said accusingly. "Now what are we going to do?"

"I don't know, I truly thought he was gone. It seems incredibly unlikely that an entity so powerful and evil could have been attached to me without my knowing but I was obviously wrong, again. Now we need to fix this instead of mulling over my mistakes."

"Where is that Tim guy now then?" he asked, he heard the sharpness in her tone and didn't bother to argue the rest.

"He will have gone to gather energy and will be back within a day or two like you were. For all intents and purposes he has now passed away, but he will likely not pass to the spirit realm too easily given the nature of the situation."

"Could he take the body back?"

"No. Not unless Keith voluntarily evicts himself or we perform an exorcism." Martha replied, "Which also means you'll have a difficult time ahead of you. It's quite obvious that Keith is a more powerful being than you so you wouldn't be able to overpower him, we just have to handle the situation as it unfolds."

"Right. This is all more than a little messed up mum, do we even know where he went?"

"No, I was so surprised to realise it wasn't you I froze and didn't know what to do. I'm sure he won't be able to resist coming here again, in the very least he will want to boast of his progress. We need to wait for that time to come and I'll be ready to try to trap and banish him from Tim's body. We can then try again to put you in the body but you'll have to be quick, I may need to call in some help for this." She explained.

"So, I have to spend more time in this bodiless form? We don't have long, I think the world is coming down on Yeti soon and I want to be the one to deliver his final blow, so the sooner we fix this the better."

"I know son, he will pay for what he did to you it's just unfortunate the whole process here is a little more complex than I'd anticipated. I haven't heard back from those officers like you said by the way, so they won't be a problem."

Despite what Steven had told her about what he had overheard and her true intentions for dealing with her sons' murderer, she was still annoyed at the awful example of their local law enforcement.

Before Steven had travelled down the more frowned upon path in life she would have sworn blind that the police were there to help the general population, but she now found them to be lazy and incompetent at the best of times, even when they were trying. Martha also wouldn't usually agree with the path of revenge but this was different, everything that had transpired since Steven's murder was linked back to that lowlife and he was going to get his comeuppance.

"Yeah, like I said, they won't. It isn't them that's the problem, it's everyone else in the streets. For now I'll go out and see if I can find Keith before Tim comes back from wherever he is."

"True, yes. OK, you do that and I'll contact the church, I don't know about father Robins but I would like to have Irene on side to help, she seemed very switched on."

"Then we need to make sure that I can get Keith to a planned location to do this, right?"

"I guess so, I hadn't really thought that far ahead yet as I'm still trying to process what just happened."

"Process it mum. We don't have time." Steven said harshly.

She could take all the time she wanted in the future to process things and in fact most of these things she wanted to process wouldn't even be relevant once they'd finished what they planned to do.

"You're right. You go and see if you can find him whilst I head down to the church. I'll be waiting for a sign from you, perhaps until we know the best place to do the exorcism we should hold off of making any moves."

"Fine. I'll find him and come back to you." Steven said, and Martha felt him pull away taking the inky darkness with him.

She opened her eyes and waited a moment for them to adjust to the light in the room then stood up ready to face the next task. She grabbed a cereal bar from the cupboard to eat on the walk, realising her energy was low and knew she would be no use to anyone in a state of lethargy. She walked at a brisk pace to the church and felt immense gratitude for the lack of pain in her feet, a huge difference to the last time she came here. She strode through the already open door and after what father Robins had said she wasn't at all surprised to see the dainty frame of Irene sat in one of the pews at the front. She turned to look at her almost immediately, despite barely making any noise Irene had clearly sensed Martha's presence.

"Martha, how are you?" she opened, simply, as though this wasn't at all an unexpected visit and Martha picked up on this and smiled sheepishly.

"I'm alright I suppose, personally anyway. We have however encountered a terrible problem and I once again have to seek your help before it is too late."

"What's happened?" Irene replied, looking at her visitor with curiosity but no surprise.

"The entity that had attached to me didn't move on as we had thought he had. He followed one of my close friends, Tim. I'm not sure what to do now," she broke off and had to hold back her tears, clearing her throat before continuing under Irene's patient gaze, "myself and Tim were trying to contact Steven, I know I shouldn't do it anymore but I'm only human and I miss my son, but whilst we were doing it Tim somehow ended up having an out of body experience and he has been possessed by Keith, evicted from his own body."

Irene looked at her pityingly and shook her head almost imperceptibly before replying,

"I see. You don't have much luck with this sort of thing and I stand by my recommendation to you. There is a reason I don't contact my husband, we should allow them to rest and be freed into the next realm – it is not up to us to hinder their progress in this universe. You have made another grave error Martha and we will do what we can to fix it but this will be a lot harder. Do you know what has become of the soul of your friend? You realise he will be stuck in limbo at the moment?" she asked.

"Not quite, I managed to communicate with him briefly before he went away and he will try to find his body and lead us to it. I just know I cannot fix this by myself, so I've had to come to you again and hope you'll forgive my foolishness once more."

"He must be in a state of great distress to find himself without a body, impressive he had the energy to speak with you before he went away." Irene said whilst itching her chin in thought. "I will confer with father Robins and we will formulate a plan to get Tim back in his body, and eradicate Keith once and for all. He has clearly taken a liking to you and those around you."

"You don't say." Martha replied drily. "If I can count on you to help me get my friend back, I'll go home and await his return and hope he can bring me some information soon. How is best to get hold of you when I know where we need to go? I don't know if I will have time to come here to tell you so do you mind if it is a phone call?"

"Just call one of us at any time and we will come straight away to wherever you tell us. Be careful Martha, you have a dark aura around you. Protect yourself." Irene warned. "I also agree with you, you made the right choice seeking our help again, for the sake of your friend we will do whatever we can."

With that Martha bid her goodbye and left with a sense of sadness, not once in her life had her aura been a dark one and she was pretty sure she knew why it was now. The things she had been doing and planned to still do played on her mind, she now wondered how far was too far? Sure, she wanted her son back and they had been seeking revenge on Yeti, but so many people were being dragged into this now and it was becoming a full-blown saga. Martha found herself getting more and more worked up about her energy becoming darker and knew she needed to do something either now or later to balance it out.

Chapter Thirty-Five

For the first time a true feeling of uncertainty was rippling through Steven's being. He hated to admit it to himself but he was questioning his mums' abilities to complete this task efficiently. It wasn't that she had messed up once in a small way, it was that she had messed up in huge ways many times now and he wondered if her heart was really in it. He had been dubious about the idea initially as it seemed so outlandish but he had put faith in his mothers' words and realised it would be the best way to achieve what he wanted, revenge.

Once he got a body again, he was going to seek out Yeti and make him pay for everything he had done to him and everyone around him, but then what? Would he have to try and infiltrate the local drugs rings again as a nearly thirty-year old and be treated like a dumb little street rat? He had no plans to do such things and could perhaps see it as an opportunity to start anew and make a different life for himself, he had always had a vague interest in cars so he could try to work out something to do with those. But this all depended on the plan his mum had made and it was seeming less likely with every passing moment that it was going to work. Now the body that had been intended for him was possessed by some wild evil entity and was even further from their reach.

Steven kind of felt bad for Tim but the feeling faded quickly as he pondered how he would make better use of having a physical presence than Tim ever could. At least Steven made a point of living and enjoying his life, his mum told him that Tim did nothing but complain and hate everything and everyone. He wondered how easy it would be to just go ahead and possess someone else, he was sure his mum referred to some state of mind called the fugue state which was what she described as the weird zone you find yourself in when you're almost asleep but semi-conscious, and the world gets a bit weird around you. She had told him that in that fugue state she would see and hear things, even sometimes having what felt like an out of body experience. She had never liked it and he figured now it was because she wasn't controlling the contact and the connection. If not during this period maybe Steven could search for people who choose to have out of body experiences and do what Keith did to them, just sneak in and take the body. If his mums' plans failed he'd have to do something along those lines.

***

He had been moving around the streets for some time and not seen anything out of the ordinary yet, but he kept finding himself distracted at his thoughts. Making the conscious effort to concentrate on this current task at hand Steven decided he needed to take a smarter approach to finding Keith. It was unlikely he had gotten very far, thanks to the sluggish movements he'll have had after taking over the body but that weighted movement would ease up the more Keith got used to it, so the sooner he found him the better.

He found himself drawn to the church and approached it, the sense of unease he always felt around Christian structures washed through him. He wasn't religious in any way and the reaction the building garnered from him annoyed him, especially as now he had died and *not* seen the pearly gates. Perhaps it was just the power that the structures contained. The ability of the attendees to believe in something without proof, and live a life by rules in a book that had been amended multiple times just didn't sit well with him. That said, a part of him wished he could have had that feeling of passion about something, that re-assurance and love that the devout said they felt.

A disturbance nearby pulled him from his reverie. There was a scuffling noise and some muttering coming from the other side of the building and Steven moved closer to see what was happening. The hunched figure of

Keith was swearing under his breath whilst trying to close the latch on the walkers' entrance gate to the cemetery, his fingers not quite as nimble and efficient as he wanted them to be. Steven resisted the urge to do something to alert Keith of his presence, instead he watched on ready to follow as soon as he moved. After a few more seconds Keith gave up and thumped his hand down into the wood angrily and started trudging up the pathway, past where Steven was idling patiently. Aside from a small incline of his head Keith made no motion to suggest he was aware of Steven being there, confirming Steven's suspicion that Keith would be far too preoccupied with trying to control the body and work things out to pay much mind to his surroundings.

Already he could see that Keith's control over the body was improving rapidly and he was already moving at a reasonably paced thudding walk. Luckily for both Keith's energy and Steven's patience the walk wasn't long and they'd only crossed two streets from the church when Keith turned right onto Newstation Road, slowly making his way down the row of narrow terraced houses and coming to a stop outside number thirty-three. He moved closer to the door, raised his hand and knocked on the door heavily a few times and Steven wondered who on this earth this man could be visiting. The door swung inwards slowly and behind it stood an older man in his mid-sixties or so and he frowned when he saw the tall form of Keith standing in his doorway with bunched fists. Keith followed his gaze to his hands and laughed,

"I'm so sorry. I have nerve damage in both my hands, they don't straighten very well." He said by way of explanation. The old man looked at him with a raised brow.

"Right. How can I help you, young man?" he asked, it was clear from his raspy voice he was either a long-term smoker or had a cold of sorts.

"Well, it's a funny story really…" Keith started, and paused for the man to give his name.

"Gareth." He replied tersely, clearly not up to dealing with whatever tricks this late afternoon visitor was playing.

"Gareth! Wonderful name, truly. I have to inform you that I am home. You are in my house, and this is your notice to leave." Keith said enthusiastically gesturing his hands at the run-down homes pathway as though Gareth was just going to hop down it with a wave over his shoulder singing 'ta-ta!'.

"Excuse me?" Gareth replied in surprise.

"I'm sure you heard me, do you need me to repeat myself?" Keith said with his smile still firmly in place.

Steven could see a manic glow glinting in his eyes and wondered if Gareth could too, a part of him wanted to try and interfere in some way but aside from knowing that there wasn't exactly much he could do, he liked to live by the notion that whatever happens, happens. He wasn't going to be the one that stepped into fates way, and based on the ridiculous amount of shit luck that had hit him and his family he felt it was about time someone else had some, even if it happened to be this unknown old guy just minding his own business. Who was he to interfere with fate?

"You don't have to repeat yourself. Leave my property now or I will call the police to remove you." Gareth replied. Keith let out a low laugh in response. "I have lived here for sixty-seven years and my father and grandfather before him lived here too. That is nearly one hundred years this home has been in my family, so I am afraid you have the wrong house." Steven was impressed as despite the tall and imposing stance Keith was holding Gareth was not giving in.

"You should be afraid." Was all Keith muttered back.

"You have thirty seconds to be out of my sight." Gareth growled, and to Steven's surprise Keith nodded at Gareth with something edging on respect, then plastered a big smile on his face,

"You know, you must be right and I've got it confused then. Terribly sorry and please forgive my intrusion so close to your bedtime. It must be going on for five now am I right?" he said. Gareth was taken by surprise by the strange turn of conversation.

"Not quite, and just because I'm older doesn't mean I go to sleep at teatime. Eight is closer to correct, not that it is any of your business." He retorted.

"No, it isn't. Good day." Keith said and turned on his heel and made his way back down the street, Gareth closed the door with a confused look upon his face.

Steven waited a moment then followed Keith, he had stopped and settled himself into the narrow space between the rows of houses, within minutes he had looked at his surroundings then rested his head against the wall, eyes closed. Enough time passed for Steven to assume he had fallen asleep and grew restless so he started practicing lifting and moving the tiny rocks that lived in the cracks of the pavement. He had no idea of how much time had passed when he heard Keith stirring and quickly ceased what he was doing, feeling the effects of using even the smallest amounts of his energy reserves. Keith rubbed his eyes and spoke out loud as though he just wanted to hear his own voice,

"I forgot how it felt to sleep. How unusual that experience was to have once more."

Then he repeated the last word but with a different inflection.

"More."

He laughed, and tried again. He said the same word six or so times with different tones and accents, perhaps simply enjoying the feeling of using a voice box again and having it echo back at him in the restricted space.

Keith bored of this quickly and rose to his feet. His movements looked as though he was merely a little stiff now. Keith shook himself to shake the last tendrils of sleep and made his way back down the now darkened street. Based on the darkness Steven was going to guess it was sometime after eight or nine in the evening and he had a feeling he knew what was about to happen. Keith trudged back up the same path he had retreated down a few hours ago and approached the door cautiously, he could see the windows were all dark and it was likely Gareth wasn't lying about his bedtime. Keith tried the handle of the door, not being too surprised when it didn't open, and started looking around the area immediate to it, he rummaged around the plant pots and under a grumpy looking ceramic gnome, then stood back up scratching his chin muttering to himself,

"Bound to be somewhere."

He then looked up at the slightly overhanging doorframe and smiled, then skimmed his hands across it barely containing the triumphant cheer that threatened to burst out of him as he found what he was looking for. He held a tarnished key in his hand and slid it into the lock, pulling the handle towards him so there was no click as the mechanism came out of its slot when he turned the key.

He had gained entry now and Steven wondered what his plan was, he surely didn't think he would be able to just come in and dispose of the old guy, where would he put him? These places didn't have much to boast about with their gardens, so he couldn't bury him. Steven had to begrudgingly acknowledge his foe's abilities as he silently walked down the hallway laid with a frayed grey carpet. He came to the bottom of a staircase and put each of his feet at opposite sides of the step and went up them one by one not making the slightest noise, even his breathing was muted. Once he reached the top he peered down the landing assessing the three different doorways. Steven had no idea what room was what but if what Keith had said was true about this being his home from before he would have full knowledge of the layout of this place.

Steven felt the urge to give Gareth a fighting chance and smash something, but that would also alert Keith of his presence and he didn't want to do that, he might bolt. If he had half a mind about him he would know that once Martha regained herself after the shock she was unlikely to let him go. Keith did an elaborate hop from the corner of the landing to the middle of the doorway on the left to avoid any creaking floorboards, surprisingly light-footed and once more displaying his quick adjustment to being in a body again. He then peered inside the darkened room and could make out the bed in the far corner with the figure of Gareth just about visible. Keith didn't hesitate to enter the room. Ever careful of his footing he reached the wardrobe that sat at the end of the bed and quietly opened the door, finding what he needed instantly. He pulled one of the weathered trainers from the bottom and unlaced it, then wrapped one end of the lace around his left hand and held the other in his right, then with a grim expression he took three swift steps to the head of the bed and brought it down over Gareth's throat and applied full body pressure.

Steven found this to be an unfair battle between men and lost respect for Keith's strength, it seemed one sided in the worst way, the same way Yeti fought. Steven had often had the advantage of strength and speed thanks to his natural build and so when someone did actually dare to physically confront him it had always gone in his favour, but despite being easily triggered he never fought dirty. Tim's body was a solid build too and Steven knew that if Keith was to play fair he wouldn't have had an issue taking Gareth out – but it had been clear from day one that Keith did not play fair. Gareth barely moved, his legs flailed a little and his arms pumped but very quickly his peaceful face of rest became a bloated and bloodshot purple mess and his body stopped jerking. Keith released his weight, barely out of breath from the exertion and he smiled grimly down at the dead form of Gareth.

"Sorry buddy but I did ask you nicely. Thanks for keeping the place up for me." He said, then rolled Gareth sideways to tuck the blanket under him, then made him do a full roll over to the other side of the bed completely encasing him in the duvet. "You're a heavy bugger aren't you? Tired me out already, no worries though I can see you've kept a spot warm for me. Not sure I know you well enough to share a bed with you just yet though!" he patted Gareth on the arm in a chummy way as though he wasn't chatting to someone he just killed in cold blood.

Steven was confident that Keith was planning to stick around here so gratefully took himself away and made his way back to his mum hoping she had done what she said she would do to prepare.

Chapter Thirty-Six

Yeti had been driving around the streets aimlessly in his smashed-up car for ages and wanted to give up, but he knew he couldn't. Despite how he felt about the bosses he wasn't about to piss them off further by not getting their gear back – or money as they thought. Truth be told Yeti wasn't even sure where he should start looking, his initial conviction that it was police had worn off at the same time as the last lingering effects of his high and nothing seemed to make sense to him again. Still in the mind-set of second guessing himself he realised that getting clean probably wouldn't be that great, he could be so successful that he could ingest all he wanted, then he wouldn't have to deal with *this* feeling anymore, he hated being sober.

He parked up at the back of the parking area of the bowling alley and decided he just couldn't do anything without clearing his head a little, and opened the ashtray in the centre consol. He knew there'd be nothing he could light up right away and had to settle for a butt roll-up, you always knew you'd hit rock bottom when you resorted to that. He grimaced whilst filtering through the pile of stubbed out joints trying to find any with a notable amount of content left in them. Once he had a dusty little pile on his leg he closed the ashtray and began splitting them into a new paper and rolled it up, the smell of the weed and tobacco was tainted by the stench of stale smoke but that wouldn't be a problem once lit. He flicked his lighter and brought it to life and lifted it up to the pungent joint now hanging from his smirking mouth. Yeti took a deep draw and held it for ten seconds, then let it out slowly making a grey plume of smoke rise up from his mouth and spread out on the car ceiling. The relief he felt was immediate and Yeti knew he could now carry on with the task ahead more level headed.

He gazed through hooded eyes at his surroundings and he could see a group of young lads over near the bowling's entrance, hanging out on the hoods of their kitted-out Golf's and Peugeot's, donning bomber jackets. They couldn't have been older than seventeen or eighteen, acting bigger than life being rowdy and drawing the wrong kind of attention.

They had now spotted Yeti assessing them and were glancing over at his sorry looking BMW looking confused but wary and rightly so. This reaction gave him pleasure and he fought the urge to laugh, this was the reputation he needed and craved so no-one was dumb enough to mess with him. He stared at each one in turn through the broken windscreen and then slowly climbed out of his car, closing the door gently behind him. He could feel the gentle fogginess induced from his smoke calming his previously sketchy and frantic brain, he moved with purpose towards them, planning to enlist them to get the information he needed, paying in fear and threats. They all stood to attention and he counted them as he approached, five of them. Even if these scrawny street urchins got bold he would be able to quickly put them back in place.

"Yo. Who runs the best out of you all?" Yeti said as he got level with them. They all looked to one another unsure of what to say. "What's the matter? What you scared of?" he said, and bared his stained teeth in a purposefully mean smile.

"Nothing man, we just running these streets as a team ya know?" came the voice of a younger looking teen on the left.

He stood fairly tall and had a mouth full of metal, his eyes were obscured by the shadow cast by his cap.

"Nothing? Seems a bold statement. Is it you then, as you spoke for them?" Yeti waved his hands at the 'them' standing with hands in pockets watching the exchange.

"I guess so. What's it to you?" he replied, clearly deciding to take one for the team he just professed to be a part of.

"Well since you asked, I need you to find something out for me. Get some information, quietly. I'm sure you know what will happen if you screw around." Yeti said the unspoken threat causing a visible swallow from the kid he was talking to.

"Yeah. I hear you. What do you need to know? We don't have that many links yet so we might not be able to get the info you're after."

"What's your name?" Yeti asked.

"Bell."

"Right. How so?"

"I'm a good watchman, I make a bell noise when someone comes near when there's a deal going down."

Yeti cocked his eyebrow at the youth in front of him, curious but also lacking any real desire to get him to demonstrate. He was clearly one of the last generations of runners with any real hope, at least people of his group got names through what really mattered, physical prowess and reputation. Yeti was obvious, he was a beast. Brute was exactly as it said on the tin, in hand to hand combat he was hard to beat. Max was owing to him literally taking everything to the absolute limit even when losing, whether it be the amount he charged a bag or pushed his luck with his bosses – something that became the end of him. Shells earned his from stealing his dads' shotgun when he was just emerging as a runner and shooting down the first people who tried to deal on his turf, the guy got lucky as Shells shot wide and he fled with his friend clutching a bloodied arm. But a nickname because you could alert your friends to unwanted prying eyes making a dinging noise? Pathetic.

He was about to reply when all five of the boys in front of him suddenly looked surprised then fearful, and all except one of them ran off. Yeti didn't bother to look around to see what startled them,

"Failed there didn't you Bell." Was all he said, then gestured at him to go away with a scowl.

He turned to see what had caused the reaction and he couldn't hold back the smirk. Police, and not just any, it was his old friend. He pulled up in front of him and lowered his window casting a questioning eye over the cars behind Yeti.

"What do you want?" Yeti sneered.

"You've had a lot of heat lately and our deal isn't exactly cutting it anymore. I'm not that far off retiring with all the perks so this arrangement we have needs to be worth it. I'm sure you understand." Yeti looked at him, struggling to keep his instantly rising temper in check.

"You're taking the piss right? So it was you!" Yeti shouted accusingly.

Officer Gord's head retracted in surprise, he knew Yeti was a loose cannon but wasn't expecting him to blow up on him instantly.

"What? I protected you. Someone told me you have been popping people off one by one lately and frankly I am tired of it. I don't give a damn what you lot want to do, but stop doing things that draw attention." He replied hotly.

"You broke into my place, stole my gear." Yeti retorted, then slammed his fists on the roof of the police car and enjoyed watching its driver visibly shrink.

Getting his credibility was going to be a piece of cake now he was back on form, seeing this initially bold police officer quaver at his rage fed his confidence.

"No I didn't! Why would I do that? Listen to me, that wouldn't make sense and you know it."

"Well, you can't go back to getting gear from evidence room and you're now coming at me asking for me to cut you a better deal for watching my corner? Makes sense to me." Yeti replied, squaring up and getting ready to pull officer Gord out of the car if he even dared to move defensively.

"Alright, yeah when you put it like that. But I swear to you it wasn't me." He pleaded.

"So, you didn't break in, smash my car, see Max on my sofa?" Yeti drawled, wondering why he was dragging it out when everything lined up and pointed at him now.

"Max? I haven't seen him in a while."

"And that is exactly what you would say." Yeti was working out the best way to deal with this, as a police officer it was harder for him to exact revenge.

"Look Yeti, listen to me. I'd heard there was a little extra something going on where that Grit guy deals. I've not checked it out, but he's been drawing in a lot more of an audience. Could it have been him?" he suggested.

"Grit? You idiot, It's Grid and there's no way, he knows his place." Yeti waved it off then played back the last interaction he'd had with him, the look in Grid's eyes showing him he wasn't afraid of him. He gritted his teeth.

"Fucker." He hissed and booted the car door, glaring at Gord when he jumped and shouted out.

He walked away ignoring the officer sat behind him, got straight into his car and skidded out of the car park at full speed.

***

He arrived on Grid's corner with his rage barely in check. Grid was stood handing over something to a couple of kids and looked up as Yeti steamed towards him, the reaction he failed to conceal was enough to show Yeti that he had found his guy. Thinking back to the hallway when he saw those two masked men running away he realised that Grid could have easily been one of them and likely with Shells, he kicked himself for not trusting his thinking before and dismissing it so quickly. Foolish of him for sure but doubly foolish of them to think they'd get away with it.

Grid ushered his buyers away and stood to attention, his strong form and square build a fair challenge for the incoming fury of a wronged madman. Yeti didn't hesitate to go straight in with a gut punch and Grid doubled over, then threw himself forwards into Yeti's legs and forced him to the ground.

"You prick!" Grid shouted into Yeti's midriff.

"Fuck you!" Yeti yelled back and brought his elbow cracking down onto Grid's skull.

This dazed him for a second and Yeti rolled out from under him and bounced up, the effects of his high fading and causing him to flag for a moment before regaining himself. Luckily, he gathered himself before Grid did and he brought his heel down on Grid's chest and stomped full strength, grinning at the crunching noise. Grid sputtered and tried to grab his leg but he brought it down hard a second time and laughed whilst doing it, revelling in the easy victory. Everyone in the area had cleared the moment they saw the fight break out because no-one wanted to be a witness, and Yeti felt a touch of deflation that no-one could see first-hand his abilities, it'd be a great deterrent for anyone thinking about crossing him. Blood was coming out of Grid's mouth and Yeti crouched down, not worried he would be any threat to him now,

"Let that be a lesson to you and Shells." He hissed, watching for a few more moments as Grid shuddered and drew his last breath.

He put his hand on Grid's chest and felt around, then smiled to himself pleased at the effort, the ribs where completely snapped and had likely punctured a whole trove of organs. Then he sifted through his pockets and fished out a handful of happy looking bags and cash then took a leisurely walk back to his car to have a celebratory smoke, knowing it wouldn't be too long before the news of Grid's death would reach Shells. He would be looking over his shoulder from that moment right up to when Yeti exacted his revenge. He was well on the way to being the top dog in the area, he could feel it in his bones.

Chapter Thirty-Seven

Martha was sat on her sofa, trying to stay awake but the events of the last few weeks were taking their toll on her. She wasn't certain what was real anymore, everything was merging in a surreal blur as the dreams teased her with the promise of sweet release every time she blinked heavily, the flashing colours and temptation to submit herself to unconsciousness almost too much.

Just as she decided that it didn't hurt to rest a little and allowed her eyes to close she heard a thudding noise nearby. She dragged her heavy lids open and looked around the room, not sure if it was a sign from Steven or if she was hallucinating. The thudding happened again and she looked at the candle on the floor to see it rising up in the air and falling back down. The sleepiness that had been overwhelming a moment ago lifted immediately and she sprang into action, jumping down onto the floor and closing her eyes, not bothering with the candle and incense as they were both well practiced now – she didn't even protect herself this time as she was confident the only entity that wished ill upon her was currently otherwise occupied. She tuned the world out and waited for the inky blackness to consume all traces of light shining through her eyelids, it didn't take long.

"I found him. He isn't far away from us, thirty-three Newstation Road. I think it was his old house from when he was alive, at least that is what he said to the guy who opened the door. The man who lives there is dead now, he killed him. Keith was saying he was tired before I left so I'd wager he is going to sleep some point soon." Steven went straight in with the facts.

"Oh gosh. This is all just too much, there is so much death. I don't know how much more I can take, my own soul is becoming tainted with the darkness." Martha said.

"We're nearly at the end mum. We just need to get over there and finish this. He is getting stronger by the minute. Let's go, I'll meet you there."

Martha blinked away the darkness as Steven left, knowing he was right. They were so close to their goal that they couldn't back down now. She had to do right by her son, and give him a second chance at the life he had stolen from him. She picked up her phone and found Irene's number, it rang a couple of times before her tired sounding voice sounded down the line,

"Is that you Martha?" she asked.

"Yes it is, I've got the address where he has taken my friends body. He is tired, apparently, so potentially will be sleeping soon. What do we do?"

"We should head over there, he will need a lot of sleep as it'll be hugely draining in the first days for him to use a body. Let me know the address and we will meet you there." Irene replied.

Martha could hear a man's voice in the background and she was surprised to realise she recognised it, turns out father Robins would hear the news earlier than Martha had anticipated.

"Thirty-three Newstation Road." Martha said, "I don't know who lives there but I do know that he is inside the house."

"Oh no, that's Gareth Grange's house!" Irene gasped. "I hope he is alright and Keith hasn't brought any harm to him." Martha kept her mouth closed, she didn't have the heart to relay what Steven had told her.

"Let's go there now, the sooner this is over the better. I'm sorry I went back on my word and I promise not to have any dealings with the other side after this."

"I hope you mean it this time as you've not only put your friend in grave danger you have now endangered the lives of others." Irene said quietly, and Martha could hear father Robins in the background telling her to be gentle.

"You think I don't know this?" Martha responded heatedly.

She heard the phone being taken from Irene and father Robins' voice came on the line,

"We know you didn't have bad intentions. Come, let's make haste to get this sorted. Your friend must be terrified finding himself without his body, and more so having seen someone else using it."

Terminating the call, Martha slipped on her shoes and headed to the door, grabbing her shawl off the hook as she went. The evening air was cool on her face and she breathed it in deeply, filling her lungs to capacity and she exhaling slowly. She did this three times and began to feel a little woozy but better, the conversation with Irene had distressed her and she had started to feel panicky.

She walked briskly to Newstation Road and stood at the top of it for a moment, gathering herself for what lay ahead. She was struggling with her resolve and knew that it wasn't going to get easier, she was having to lie once more to the priest and Irene to get them to carry out the exorcism. Just a few weeks ago her life was so simple, made up of family dinners and cleaning her home. Nothing too strenuous with the exception of worrying about Steven sometimes, and now everything was anything but the serene easy style she had forged for herself.

She hadn't even heard from Alicia, despite having told her she needed time before she spoke about everything, she hadn't expected her to listen and now wished she hadn't. She made a mental note to call her in the morning after all this was over, her sister needed her right now too. She heard voices to her right and looked to see who was wandering around this late, forever conscious of the sorts of people who trod these streets at night. Relief coursed through her when she saw it was Irene and father Robins, they were talking in hushed tones and stopped when they saw her. She didn't say anything as they drew level, just gave a sombre nod and they walked together down the pathway in silence, Irene spoke first as they came to a stop outside number thirty-three.

"Gareth is an old family friend and my sister used to come and clean this house when we were younger, there was always a key on the top of the doorframe, father Robins check for me please I'm not quite tall enough." She whispered.

Father Robins nodded at her and reached up, his mouth downturned when he came back empty handed.

"I guess that answers how he got inside the house. I couldn't imagine Gareth inviting just anyone in. Luckily I used to tag along sometimes and I know that unless it has been fixed, which is unlikely, the back door doesn't lock. He told us once that it had been broken for as long as he could remember and he's not very into fixing things up, let's go check."

With that Irene made off and they followed close behind her. Martha wondered where Steven was and if he was close by like he said he would be. They walked down the narrow alley a few houses down and turned sharply right down an overgrown pathway littered with faded packets and exposed tree roots, Irene stopped outside one of the gates and turned the rusted handle but nothing happened.

"There's probably a latch on the other side, could you jump it?" she asked father Robins, who looked dubiously at the top of the fence which was level with his head.

He was no athlete. Martha felt a wash of fuzziness come over her and just as soon as she felt it, she heard the latch on the other side click and drag out of its locked position. Father Robins jumped at the noise whilst Irene's eyes glazed over for a moment before she refocused and looked directly at Martha, wordlessly she tried the handle again and the door swung inwards, showing the tiny area outside the back of the house which had nothing but a few concrete slabs and bins. As she had guessed, the back door was unlocked which was astonishing given it would have been many years since she had last been here but very in keeping with what she remembered of Gareth.

Irene took the lead as she knew her way around. They moved silently through the house and up the stairs taking care with the old floorboards, coming to a stop at the top to listen for movement. The only sound was a slightly laboured breathing coming from the room on the left and they moved towards it being careful to step as lightly as possible, father Robins tried to go around a shoe that was discarded in the middle of the floor and trod straight on a creaky board. The noise penetrated the silence and they all froze with baited breaths to see if the figure on the bed they were creeping towards would wake and they all breathed a collective sigh of relief when he did not.

Father Robins got to him first and pulled some rope out of his jacket, counting out four lengths and handing two of them to Irene. They made quick work of binding him to the posts of the bed and Martha was astounded that he didn't wake up from the movement let alone the pressure on his wrists and ankles, then remembered what Irene had said about how tired he would be. Sensing her thought process Irene spoke to her,

"In a possession like this the spirit will be exhausted from the exertion of using a real body again and won't have full sensation of the extremities yet. Glad we found him so early really."

Father Robins and Irene met each other's eyes and nodded gently.

"I've sensed the presence and we know he is near – in fact we know he is surprisingly powerful for a young spirit as he physically moved something in this plane for us with great control – no easy feat as we know." She said, and once more looked at Martha with a hint of sadness in her eyes as she spoke.

Martha noticed and wondered how much she knew, she had already shown herself to be intuitive and if she read what was just said correctly Irene was telling her she knew the entity present wasn't who she had said it was.

"Are we ready? What is his name again?" father Robins asked.

"Tim." Martha replied quietly whilst avoiding looking at Irene, whose gaze she could feel upon her.

"Then let us continue." He said, they both nodded at him soberly. They linked hands and bowed their heads with closed eyes, and father Robins spoke,

"I call upon our lord and saviour to protect us in this moment of voluntary exposure to those who have wronged the living in this plane. I call upon our God to grant us his guidance and safety as we remove the evil entity known to us as Keith from this body he has stolen."

The air became unsteady around them as external forces became aware of the planes merging, Martha fought the urge to look up when she heard the voice of Irene next to her speaking clearly,

"I call upon the holy lord above us to deliver his love and protection as we return the rightful soul to this body. I request of the powers above me that any beings that do not belong in this body are not granted entry and only the true soul bound to it can return to its rightful place."

She spoke with such power that Martha could feel the electric pulses coursing through her hands. In that moment Martha knew without doubt that Irene knew and her heart sank heavily. She heard a roaring shout nearby and felt the air clasping at her as it was being wrenched away, she knew that it was her sons' soul being rejected from their presence, and within moments the stabbing pain in her heart told her this journey wasn't over and she couldn't give up on her boy yet. Then a new shouting noise started up but this was very close by, in the room with them.

"Open your eyes!" Father Robins called out and they let go of each other and looked to the bed where Keith was writhing around trying to break the bindings. "Keith you are to leave the body of Tim, you are not welcome here. The lord above has granted us power and you are to remove yourself."

Keith's crazed eyes darted around the room and landed on Martha, he began to laugh manically.

"You dumb wench! I'll tell you what, this life of the living is exhausting and not nearly as fun as I thought it'd be, I don't know why you all hang on to it for so long. I don't want this damned body anyway! I thought this would be a great way to spend time and avoid the void but frankly, I can't see the point if you sorry examples of fellow humans are what I can expect to have to interact with."

"Leave the body of Tim and allow his soul to return to its rightful place. I command you to exit and leave the vicinity never to return."

"Yes, yes. Quieten down now old boy we will get there in time. Don't suppose you have discovered the little gift I left for you?" Keith said, exposing his teeth in a menacing grin.

He spoke clearly but it was obvious from his writhing body he was in some discomfort.

"Judging by the looks on your faces you haven't. Irene, it's not too difficult to recognise you, and boy haven't you aged. Your sister was so young when I saw her last, I watched you both enter my home and scrub the toilets I had emptied my bowels into many times. Speaking of, I'm sure you must be aware that there is a cesspit in the basement. Sure it had been covered up but luckily ole Gareth had popped a few tools down there so it wasn't too much work to open up."

Irene had covered her mouth with her hand and struggled to conceal the horror in her eyes,

"It's you!" she gasped, tears filling her eyes. Father Robins looked from Keith to Irene in confusion.

"Yes dear, it is me. Don't look so surprised, few are resilient enough to stick around as long as I have and your sister was one of the many who kindly gave me energy to sustain my existence here."

"You killed her! I have hated you for so many years, you took my sister from me!"

"Technically she killed herself, let us get that fact straight. I didn't tell her to jump in front of a train did I? Or perhaps I did. You'll never know!" he laughed.

Father Robins put his arm out in front of Irene as her hurt and rage bubbled over.

"I call upon the almighty and powerful lord above us to command this entity to leave our presence and never return!" he bellowed.

Keith suddenly screamed out seemingly in agony and his whole body contorted, the veins on his neck bulging to the point it looked as though they may burst. His mouth was wide open and eyes became unseeing, a sudden gust swept around the room and smashed into Martha nearly sending her flying, then everything fell deadly still. Irene fell to the floor sobbing, and father Robins knelt to comfort her, whilst Martha teetered on the spot in shock and battling exhaustion.

"Martha?" the voice made her jump, it sounded weak and confused.

She looked at the bed and Tim was laying there looking at her with a mixture of confusion, fear and revulsion.

"Tim! It worked, you're back!" she said, trying to put in all the energy she would have done had it been her son there.

She sensed Irene looking at her, perhaps to see if what she had deduced was in fact true. Father Robins put his hand tenderly on Irene's shoulder before reaching to untie the bonds securing Tim to the bed, Irene stepped forwards after wiping her face and helped him.

"What the hell happened Martha?" Tim hissed whilst rubbing his wrists.

"You were possessed by an evil entity that had attached itself to me a while back and I thought was gone, but had been waiting for a moment to strike once more. I'm so sorry Tim it won't happen again." Martha said, putting her hands on his shoulders.

"You're damn right it won't. You nearly killed me and I was dumb to trust you, you're a witch." He said flatly and shrugged her hands off his shoulders.

His words stung but Martha couldn't blame him, right now she couldn't think straight.

"We need to find Gareth." Irene said bluntly, her voice strained from holding back more tears. "There is a cesspit and it sounds like that's where Keith put him. We need to call the police to come and investigate."

"I'll get on it. Tim, I can't even offer you anything to make you more comfortable now as this is a crime scene and I can't let you leave," Father Robins said, Tim glared at him as he said this, despite his fragile state his hatred at being told what to do shone through, especially after the experience he just had. "it's best you just stay put otherwise we may touch things we shouldn't. Although I suppose your fingerprints will be on things."

"What the hell are you talking about?" Tim asked, ignoring the way father Robins flinched when he said hell.

"Well, during your possession it seems the entity used your body to end another person's life, namely the gentleman who lives here. We don't know for sure yet but he said that we needed to check the cesspit, we won't do that but are going to call the police to do it for us." Father Robins was stuttering a little, the whole thing proving to be too much of a strain and Martha tried to talk to Tim.

"You won't be held accountable for the murder – due to the nature of the situation you will be interviewed to check you were in fact under demonic possession and ultimately released because you'll have the word of father Robin's to defend you, and prove an exorcism had to take place to liberate you. Whilst uncommon these cases have occurred in our history and are dealt with quietly due to their sensitive nature."

"Held accountable? Let them try! I should be able to just leave." Tim scoffed, completely unfazed by the idea that his hands had killed someone, far angrier at the idea that he could be blamed for it. The reassurance Irene had offered fell on deaf ears.

"Look, we all know that if any of us leave now we will be arrested for leaving the scene." Martha reasoned and no-one responded.

Father Robins excused himself and went into the hallway to call the police, coming back into the room with a grim expression a few minutes later.

"Are you ok Irene?" he asked, concern clear in his expression.

"I will be. I know it has been years and if I'm honest I was already feeling some way about returning to this house. I had never been sure where she had picked up the entity and now I know, maybe it will provide some kind of closure."

"Where did he go?" Tim asked, not able to fully hide the trepidation in his voice.

"I think it is a safe guess that his interest in you is gone so don't worry, he suggested that the physical life was not for him anymore. In a way you may have helped an earthbound spirit finally pass into the spirit realm, or in the very least prevent future possession attempts." Irene explained.

"Go me." Tim replied tartly. Irene turned the corners of her mouth down at him but didn't respond.

"What did the police say?" Martha asked father Robins.

"They'll be here soon." Father Robins said with a shrug. Before long there was a knock at the door.

Chapter Thirty-Eight

Two dead in the streets. Two people who once upon a time had shared lewd jokes, ran their corners and passed a joint between friends. Two who should have still been here now telling him it wasn't worth it, only pick battles that better his life not worsen it. Shells was sat tucked up in the corner of his sofa, idly running his fingers over the stripy print of the throw that covered it whilst thinking about the call he just had from Lance. Lance never called anyone, never left a digital trace, always had one of his lackeys reach out on disposables. That should have been some kind of comfort to Shells but at this point he was wondering if he was somehow the common factor here as two of his friends had been killed by the same guy.

His teeth gritted in rage as he thought about Yeti, wishing he had poured that fuel can all over his car at the outset and lit it with him inside, then in the very least Grid would still be alive. Lance hadn't sounded happy but why would he? One of his own runners had killed two of his other runners, in broad daylight no less. Everyone knew Yeti had drawn the blade on Brute but more or less got over it as a one-off fatal disagreement between sellers – despite them being on shared turf – but now an enraged Yeti had sought out yet another and brutally killed him with multiple witnesses, there was nothing that could be said to cover for him this time.

Shells was pretty sure the only reason Yeti got away with the whole Brute mess was because Lance didn't want to have to have two of his strongest runners taken out in a short time. Sure, Yeti had only recently taken on a bigger role and been dealing in more public spots but he was renowned in the streets, stories of his temper and history had filtered through the people for some time before many met him, and his reputation preceding him meant that him being killed would bring even more attention. Something best avoided, especially as the competition was always waiting for a window to take more turf. However, the way things had been going meant that Yeti was more a burden than an asset and Shells felt that Lance was warning him that Yeti was on the warpath, but he was on his radar and something was going to go down before long.

If Yeti found him before whatever Lance had up his sleeve happened, he knew it'd be rough. If he was honest with himself he knew he couldn't win in that situation because Yeti fought dirty, and Shells wasn't stupid enough to risk his life for the sake of street rep now two of his boys were dead. He had to keep out of the way for the meantime and knew that his mums would be the place to go, out of town. He stood up having made his decision and grabbed his old backpack from the bottom of his wardrobe, it was the one he had from his school years, barely used thanks to the lack of attendance. He stuffed some pants and t-shirts in there haphazardly then considered packing some gear but knew if his mum found it he'd be turned back around and out the door, so left it alone. In the unlikely event that Yeti was wise enough to find out his address and come here, he would probably find the last of the stash that he got after splitting it with Grid but he wasn't worried. The chances of that happening were slim, Yeti would simply wait for the opportunity to strike out in the open and Shells wasn't about to facilitate that. He headed out the door and pulled it closed behind him, made his way to his car and started the short drive to his old home.

Chapter Thirty-Nine

Tim left the police station feeling worse for wear and angry at the world. They had done all sorts to get him to confess that he was in fact 'himself' during the whole saga on Newstation Road, and he was somehow convincing three people to lie on his behalf about being possessed. As Irene had said, they had a way of dealing with these rare-occurring cases and it worked in his favour that no-one knew what had happened and neither him nor Gareth had too many acquaintances. Had it been a case with more reach he'd have likely been sent down or sectioned. Thanks to the backing of father Robins and Irene he was being allowed to leave without further charges unless something came up to prove he was in fact 'present' for the murder, bunch of bullshit as far as he was concerned and he was just glad to see the back of the station.

He was also peeved that the period between leaving Martha on her living room floor and seeing her son looming over her and arriving back in his own body was blank, not a single memory as though it hadn't happened despite a fair period of time passing in between. He didn't know when Martha, Irene and father Robins had been released but he guessed it would have been a while before him. He was adamant he wouldn't cross paths with Martha again, when he came back into his body and laid eyes on her he had initially felt relieved that this woman he had come to trust in had in fact come through and managed to bring him back, but within moments he registered the disappointment in her eyes as she looked at him and all that connection he had felt with her previously was instantly severed.

He felt like whatever spell she had been holding over him was gone, seeing now that she had been holding him spellbound and manipulating him, he now knew he had been dealing with the sorcery of a witch and it explained a lot. He had seen a show during one of his many sleepless nights whilst skipping through the less frequented channels, it was about modern day witches and their abilities and how they walked among the normal people of the world casting out their intentions willy-nilly, without a care. He couldn't believe he had offered her a job at his new practice and was definitely taking that back if she ever dared to contact him again, although he was sure he had made his feelings towards her clear.

As far as this whole adventure was concerned he was done and moving on with his life fully intending to resume it to its previous status of doing what he wanted, alone. It suited him better and he had enough to focus on now what with the plans to get the new place under his belt and consequently up and running, last thing he needed was a 'friend' who endangered his life and was disappointed at his successful return. No, he was going to go back to what he did best and in a happier state for it. The main perk he was going to take away was that he now knew he would be able to do the out of body experience himself without assistance, Martha had said that it was possible but just recommended you didn't in case you needed to be grounded. She had failed at that and in spite of her failing he had come back from a long way and found her, so he knew he would be able to do it again with no problem. Maybe not right away though.

Chapter Forty

Martha had been talking for a while, non-stop and fast. When she finally ceased speaking, Alicia had to take a moment to process all she had just been told. She was sat across from her sister reeling from all the information, with her clammy hands clasped in her lap. Before Ross, she wouldn't have been able to fathom what had come over Martha to have taken such awful measures to get her son back. She knew the maternal pain now, she knew the gut wrenching feeling of knowing her boy would never once walk back through her door or speak her name. On some level she understood, the pain that flared up in her core with every inhalation since Ross was murdered was too much to bear some days. That was just a part of missing someone and one day that pain would hopefully become a pang instead, not painful, just present, and she could remember him without wanting to rend devastation on everything and everyone around her.

Alicia was well aware of the risks her boys had taken in the path they chose in life and she'd be damned if her youngest did the same, the only saving grace of her boys' situation was that Seth was being his own person once more. The trauma of having held Ross as he died was on the edge of being too much to process but he had delved deep within himself and found a new calling. He wanted to be an IT technician and was now studying it through an in-prison rehabilitation program, clearly realising that the life he had been leading up to that point was not one for him, or anyone at that. He would be her success story whilst Ross was her sorrowful tale, her own ying and yang.

Alicia knew she couldn't fully understand Martha's actions because she herself didn't have the natural gift of seeing and communicating with those who had passed on. Supposing she was able to she may have done something similar although possessing another living persons' body was out of bounds, no matter how much pain you were in. Because of Martha she had known that Ross had passed on almost immediately to the spirit realm and she realised she maybe had it a little easier, knowing that your deceased son was trapped here must be awful. She could see Martha was desperate for something from her so she inhaled deeply and spoke slowly,

"I cannot condone what you've done Mattie. But I think I understand what drove you and I don't blame you. I do wish you had come to me sooner."

"I couldn't. To start with I was doing something I'd sworn I'd never do after what happened with Susie, although after speaking with her and watching her be released I realise it wasn't all my fault, just a terrible mistake. Thing was, I just couldn't bare knowing that Steven was nearby, lost and confused. I spoke with him a couple of times, then that didn't feel enough and I needed to be able to give him a voice and a physical body once more, a second chance at life – I don't know where the idea came from but it felt *right*. I didn't just pick anyone Alicia, I picked someone who is quite despicable and alone in this world. He would be better off living in a different plane freely than trapped here miserably."

She paused for a breath quickly and held her hand up to Alicia to show she wasn't done, just gathering herself.

"But the thing was it all got so out of hand, people got hurt and killed. I was already having my doubts about everything, but during the interrogation with the police after they found Gareth I knew that I'd come too far to back down now, all that has happened would be in vain, even Ross' death in a way."

Alicia flinched at the mention of her sons' death and its relation to her sister and nephew.

"So, you're telling me that even after everything that has happened you're considering it still?"

"I know you won't approve and I don't expect you to. I don't even approve but something in my core is telling me this is what I am supposed to be doing. I can't explain it. I feel so terribly sad and guilty about what has happened to the other people but everything has aligned and given me the signs that this was the right path, it just seems to have become quite confused and difficult along the way. If Keith wasn't a factor it would have gone smoothly and happened already, and I believe he was an unpredictable hitch in the plan. Now he is out of the equation there is nothing else that can cause harm to anyone else."

"Except this Tim guy, he will die, right?" Alicia pointed out sharply.

"It doesn't hurt and he will finally be free of this life. Speak to him you'll see, he hates it and everyone in it. I had to use every trick I know to get him to even speak with me for more than a minute."

"I don't want to speak with him Mattie. I don't want any part of this, I'm sorry."

"No, I didn't think you would. I'm sorry too, I just needed to talk to someone about it all, I don't feel like myself anymore."

"I'm not surprised, you're not behaving like yourself. Grief does crazy things to us Mattie, give yourself space and perhaps stop what you're doing. I can't have anything happen to you too and it sounds like you had an awfully close call with that evil spirit attaching himself to you. I'm not going to ask you to stop contacting Steven because if the shoe was on the other foot I'd do the same regardless of risks, if I could contact Ross I would." Alicia said with a sad sigh.

Martha assessed her to see if the idea that bloomed in her mind was a good one, it was something she had planned to offer to her at some point anyway.

"You know you can, right? I can set up the channel for him to reach you and speak with you. He will use me as the carrier of his messages. You won't hear his voice but it will be his words."

Alicia stared at her for a while, the seconds passing felt like physical thuds vibrating through the air between them before she slowly nodded with tears filling her eyes.

"I would like to, very much. Please." She whispered, barely audible. Martha leaned forwards and clasped her hands between her own.

"It'll be ok I promise. Maybe it will help you heal a little to know how he is doing."

Alicia nodded nervously at her sister who in typical fashion true to herself instantly busied herself with the next task at hand. She watched as Martha went and fetched a white candle and packet of incense sticks, this made Alicia scowl a little as she hated incense sticks. They were too strong for her liking but she would deal with them if it helped her speak to her boy once more. In the least she could now say goodbye, an option she hadn't been given.

They'd not even had the funeral yet as they were holding his body whilst the investigation was ongoing. The smell of the incense burning filled her nostrils and she inhaled tentatively to see if it would be bearable, pleasantly surprised to smell frankincense, she burned frankincense and myrrh candles at home all the time.

"Are you ready?" Martha asked, concern flitting across her features.

"As much as I ever will be I suppose. What shall I do?"

"Just be comfortable, and don't be afraid otherwise the connection will be frail and harder to maintain. He is in the spirit realm now which is further to reach, the bond he has with you is what creates the tether he can utilise to come to you when you call him in a séance." Martha explained as Alicia knitted her brows, concentrating. "You're better off closing your eyes as well to avoid visual distractions, but you don't have to if you don't want to."

Alicia shook her head no, and chose to look at her sister instead, waiting for her to begin. She watched as she took some deep breaths, shook herself and then spoke very clearly,

"I Martha Tawn now call upon the powers above me to protect me and my companion as I contact a loved one in the spirit realm. Protect us from that which wishes us harm or holds negative intentions. I invite the spirit of Ross Brindle to come forth and speak with his mother Alicia Brindle, using myself as the vessel of communication."

Alicia's lip curled a little at hearing her married name out loud, it reminded her she still needed to get it legally changed back to Tawn after all these years. She jumped when she felt a hand on her knee and refocused back on Martha who was looking at her quizzically.

"You need to be present Alicia, don't go off in your thoughts or we cannot contact him."

She nodded apologetically back at Martha, who proceeded to say the same thing again and this time Alicia remained focused with a clear open mind. She could feel something around her shifting and her gut was telling her it was Ross. She watched nervously as Martha's head dropped back heavily for a moment and her body shuddered, then when Martha brought her head back upright her eyes were glazed over but she looked at her dead in the eye and smiled.

"Hey mum." The voice was Martha's but the words were from Ross.

Alicia fought back the tears, a moment she thought she'd never have was happening, albeit in a very different fashion to what she would have liked. Something akin to shock was coursing through her and she had to draw a deep breath before continuing.

"Hey son. I miss you." She croaked.

"Don't. It's pretty cool here, and I'm staying out of trouble like you always wanted. How's Seth?"

"He is studying to be a mechanic." She replied, "You should be here too making and chasing dreams."

"I don't think I was ever meant to make it mum, something was always going to happen. You think I didn't know I always held Seth back? He was always protecting me and now he can finally look after himself. I threw away my chances at being worthwhile, nothing ever jumped out at me or made me want to be better."

"You didn't throw your chances away Ross, I don't think you had very many and for that I am sorry."

"Did they get the guy who stabbed me?"

"No, or at least they haven't said anything to me about it."

"Corrupt officers mum. That's how they knew about us telling aunt Mattie about Yeti. It was a hit and a warning." Alicia's focus wavered strongly and she could see the air around her sister shifting. She forced herself back into full focus.

"Do you know who the officers were by any chance?"

"Gord or something like that. Has anything happened to Yeti? He's the whole reason me and Steven are dead, amongst others."

"Not yet." Alicia said, a sudden hardening in the pit of her stomach made her pause. "But it will, I vow to you and your cousin. Me and your aunt will avenge you both."

"No doubt about it, two wily women like you. How's Lily and Tom?"

"Hurting that their big brother has gone forever but I can go back to them after this with more peace in my heart, knowing that you're ok." She replied.

"You can. Keep them in check, you don't need more kids behind bars or dead. I love you mum. Say hi to dad if you see him."

"I love you too Ross, until we meet again."

With that the room suddenly went dimmer and Martha's whole body sank into itself, her head dropping forwards onto her chest. Alicia jumped forwards to pull her out of the slump and met her eyes with her own glistening ones.

"Thank you Mattie. I know what we need to do." She said.

Chapter Forty-One

Officer Gord could feel the walls closing in on him and he wasn't sure what more he could do to hold them back, all these years of toeing the line and getting away with it were precariously close to being wasted. That idiot Yeti was in more of a state than ever before and his unpredictability was becoming a real issue, he couldn't keep taking measures to cover for him just because he supplied him with a little bit of dope here and there, he surely had more self-respect and control over his cravings than to submit to some thuggish murderer. He realised he was nodding to himself and noticed a little old lady stood by the bus stop looking into his open window curiously, one eyebrow cocked at him. He smiled politely at her and wound his window up, nosy cow.

He knew that Yeti had gone straight from him to Grid the other day and killed him in a brutal fashion, stamping on his ribs so hard they cracked and pierced his heart and lungs. His famous temper was out of control now, not that it was ever under control but now it seemed Yeti was on a rampage emboldened by the idea he was untouchable – what he didn't know was that Gord was sick of it now, especially as it would lose him his retirement package if it was found out he was in cahoots with him.

He realised something drastic had to change when he finally went and checked out Yeti's landlords flat to see if what Martha Tawn said had any merit, without any real care as to the wellbeing of the guy himself, and he found the beaten and bloody form of Martin Richard in his own bed. He had cleaned up as best he could and set it up to look like he had a freak accident with the wardrobe and snapped the front feet off to make it look like they'd given out, making sure to scatter heavy items around him so it looked like they'd fallen off the top of the wardrobe and crushed him. Unlikely to be bought by anyone who analysed it for longer than thirty seconds but he was well aware that the teams dealing with this stuff had lost any real passion for finding the truth and accepted things for what they looked like at face value.

He wasn't cut out for this, it wasn't the life he envisioned. He only went into the force because his parents pushed it on him, adamant he wouldn't go down the same path that they had watched so many other youths going down even back then. If they were alive today they would squirm to see what became of the younger generations now – and him, it had all steadily gotten worse and uncontrollably so. Before long he had started to accept bribes to look the other way, then tried to deal with his self-contempt by dabbling in the very things that he was supposed to be arresting people for.

It didn't take long until he realised he couldn't go much time between getting a smoke or a hit, but he at least kept it enough under control that no-one suspected him, until people started to notice the contraband in the evidence locker was being accessed. This coincidentally happened at the same time as Yeti asking for a deal with him, a steady supply to do with what he wished in exchange for not being bothered by the law – how could he say no to that when he knew he had to stop stealing from the locker? It had been an easy enough task to keep his fellow officers away from Yeti when he wasn't being so prolific, oh how it had all changed now.

He scoffed to himself thinking about officer Bridges, so young and still green to the whole scene, thinking he could make a difference. He had felt heavily judged by the young officer when he was pushing him to go check things out, but he had to show him how it was. Thinking about Bridges he wondered where he had got to, he had sent him off to get lunch about twenty minutes ago and he was taking his time about it. He jumped when his radio burst into life and crackled in his ear, he removed it from the holster on his shoulder and waited for someone to speak.

"Officer Gord requesting backup in the deli on Jewel Street."

Gord frowned at this, what the hell was he doing over there? There were at least two places he would have gone past to get there. There's only one reason he could think of, and he hoped it wasn't it.

"What's the situation officer Bridges?"

"I have an armed male holding up the counter, hostage situation sir. I request you report this back to station and come to my location."

"On my way." Gord replied with a sigh.

He hated this job and his gut continued to tell him that it was a field of work that was going to keep getting worse and worse, his only consolation was that he was coming to the end of his career.

With a heavy heart he started the engine and drove over to Jewel Street, making sure to go past Yetis' block of flats in the vague hope he would spot him walking past his smashed-out windows. He didn't. He pulled up out the back of the deli, looked at his radio and decided against calling it in just yet in case he could handle it. He climbed out the car and listened out to see if he could hear anything but aside from the cars whizzing past doing way over the thirty speed limit, he couldn't make anything out. He approached the back door slowly, tapping his belt to make sure he had his baton and taser on him and looked around him to see who was around, happy to see there wasn't anyone loitering on this section of street for once.

To be fair since Yeti had started rampaging most of the hoodlums who had started to frequent this stretch had bailed so as to not be on his radar. He approached the doorway and tried to peer through the beaded curtain but couldn't see or hear anyone, he wondered if he misheard officer Bridges. He stepped through the door into the kitchen area and took in his surroundings. There were a few things knocked onto the ground and he could now make out the sound of heavy breathing through the next door, which led to the storefront. Moving through he was met with the sight of a dishevelled man hunched down on the floor sifting through a pile of money which looked to have been smashed out of the heavily dented till nearby.

"Yeti! What the hell are you doing man?" officer Gord hissed and the figure turned and looked at him with a sardonic grin,

"Working, you?" he said. "Might want to check in on your buddy, just had to make sure he didn't remember my face or we could both get in trouble you know?"

Gord's stomach dropped with the realisation that his annoyance at finding Yeti here robbing the place meant he didn't register the lack of workers or his own colleague who had called him here.

"Where is he?" he asked, voice rising.

Yeti shrugged and stared him in the eye for a moment before laughing, he was clearly high. It took a second for Gord to batten down the rising hatred and fear and look past the crazed man on the floor before him, he quickly spotted a shiny black shoe poking out from behind the sky blue counter and groaned inwardly, Yeti had already gone back to counting his winnings. Gord moved towards the foot and rounded the counters edge and had to stifle the shout of horror at the sight that greeted him. Officer Bridges lay across the lap of what he assumed was one of the staff, although now the light blue apron the worker wore was now stained dark with blood. His cause of death was quite obvious – he had one of the carving blades sticking out of his thigh, another in his chest and one more jutting out the side of his neck. Gord held back a heave as he assessed his colleague, his head was caved in on one side and he stared forwards sightlessly. He rounded on Yeti, blind fury coursing through him.

"What the fuck have you done!?" he shouted, he now noticed blood and matter was all over one corner of the till, he held back a gag.

Yeti looked up at him straight faced,

"Don't raise your voice, you'll draw attention. Surely you know that officer Gord." He said with a sneer. "I figured when he called you in it was easier to just handle it, otherwise he might realise our connection and our sweet little deal would be off. That just wouldn't be on, I was thinking of you the whole time." He laughed uproariously at this before continuing, "Who cares? He was just a filthy cop anyway."

The room swayed around Gord as he struggled to stay calm.

"You killed an officer. A young man, he was barely older than you!"

"Nice to see you care about a death when it is your own kind."

"All for what? How much was in that till?" Gord asked, voice rising again.

"Couple hundred. Had to make back the difference on what those pricks stole from me. Thanks for the tip by the way, just waiting for Shells to come out of hiding and we can even that out too."

"What is wrong with you! I cannot cover this up for you, you must know that!"

"You can, and you will. Imagine after all these years being an upstanding police officer going out in shame, corrupted by the system. Losing all those juicy perks of being a slave to the big guys for all that time. In any case, you utter one word against me and you'll be just like the others who've stood in my way, I'm unstoppable Gord you must see that by now. Never down for long." Yeti said with yet another menacing grin, exposing his stained chipped teeth to officer Gord, who grimaced.

Yeti was right, he was trapped and there was no way out without losing everything, but he had to have some honour as a police officer and respect that young man who still lived deep inside him who had wanted to believe in law and order, even if it was only ever to please his parents.

"Fuck you Yeti. I'm done and it's over, you're going down." He roared and realised his bravery could have been used better when Yeti's face contorted in rage and he swung at him making the world turn black.

Chapter Forty-Two

Steven had been trapped in what had felt like an endless cycle of jumping between various places and scenes, both past and present, leaving him disorientated. He had tried to take stock of what was happening as he flashed from scene to scene but frankly a lot of it didn't make sense. It could have been because he was unable to see past the fury of success being within reach and having it wrenched from him again, so his mind was overridden with negative emotions.

He played back some of the things he saw and realised that there had been a lot of things surrounding that Irene lady and her life. A lot of the scenes depicted her suffering, perhaps he was meant to feel pity for her despite the fact she had stopped him dead in his tracks. She knew what she was doing, he had seen the look in her eyes before she spoke and after too, there was definite guilt in them and he was glad to see it, she deserved to feel bad for that. Now all their hard work was ruined again and he wasn't sure what they could do except find another person as it was unlikely that Tim would risk the same thing happening once more.

Steven tried to look around him now that he had stopped moving for more than a few minutes and could see he was outside his aunt Alicia's house. He moved closer to the window with a light emanating from it to see what was going on inside and he could see his aunt sat on the floor with both Tom and Lily in front of her, he channelled into her to hear what she was saying.

"I think it is important that we always say about how we are feeling and sharing is key to our healing. There is nothing you can say or feel that would make either of you less loved. I want you both to know something, as strange as it may seem I have had contact with your brother." This earned tilted heads and quizzical looks from them both.

"Seth?" Lily ventured.

"No, it was Ross. I've never told you about this but your auntie Mattie has the ability to speak with people who are no longer with us physically, she doesn't like to do it very often but she did this time for me. I needed to know that your big brother was ok and at peace. I am pleased to tell you he is, and he loves you both very much."

They both looked at their mum trying to work out if she was going crazy or telling a truth that simply sounded crazy. They then looked at one another for a moment exchanging a silent agreement and clambered over to their mum and embraced her tightly. Steven then noticed that nanna Jess was sat off to one side in the single armchair watching over the conversation with an unreadable expression. He focused on her for a moment and felt himself being tugged away once more but just before the blackness took over he could have sworn that she looked directly at him and nodded.

***

He was somewhere he didn't recognise, the room he was in was smoky and dull and there was a low murmuring nearby, he tried to work out where he was and it took a moment for the realisation to hit him. This was where Max had been shot and Yeti got his first warning, which should have been his last. The smoke started to disperse and the room became a little clearer, he moved in closer to analyse the faces of the two men sat at the table before him. He recognised Lance immediately, his old boss. His job was keeping the runners in check, something that he clearly hadn't been doing a good job of and based on what he could hear this was the point of discussion. The man with him was unremarkable in appearance, mousy looking but with sharp calculating eyes. They were piercing into Lance as he spoke and Lance was visibly trying to keep his back straight and demeanour calm.

"What you doing to fix this Lance? I've a mind to clear the streets of all your vermin and start fresh, you have lost your touch."

"I've been biding my time boss, waiting to see if he rights himself and comes out on top. With enough respect he will rise through the ranks well, he just needs to contain his temper."

"You've misjudged severely. I have three prime spots uncovered by our guys at the moment because you let one of your rugrats run riot, he isn't even running his own spot at the moment. Profits are down, you know what that means Lance." He said emotionlessly, tapping his fingers on the table casually whilst a bead of sweat formed on Lance's forehead despite the cool temperature of the room.

"I apologise for the error in thinking and you are of course right. I will rectify this situation immediately I just need to locate him." Lance grovelled.

"No, you won't." came the terse reply and Lance stared at him, the growing fear in his usually cold eyes the only thing belying his true feelings in this moment. "I will. This has gone too far and our reputation has taken enough of a hit thanks to your ineptitude. You're in charge of clean up. Impress me or it'll be the last job you do."

"You got it boss. I already cleaned up the deli on Jewel Street to look like a botched robbery. I put the cop out back and dosed him so he should be coming back down soon, he won't say anything anyway as Yeti seems to have him in his pocket, probably why he didn't get killed too."

"The fact he has killed any police near his own turf is a problem, why have you been overlooking this? Maybe I cannot trust you even with this small task. Shit, I don't need to know the details just get the job done, now." He growled. Lance blanched a little and made to stand up but halted when his boss raised his hand.

"One more thing, make sure there are no loose ends anywhere and get all our gear and money back. No. Loose. Ends. Hear me?"

Lance nodded at him silently and stood up, stepping away from the table continuing to hold his boss's gaze. Only when he had backed all the way to the closed door did he turn his back to open it and stepped outside. Steven watched him leaving, he had to buy more time.

He had been holding back so much of his frustration and rage he could feel himself bubbling and knew he could release some of the energy and feel in control again, inflicting some fear on this asshole Lance who couldn't even keep his underlings in check would do for now. Sure, he had accepted Steven and Shells into his 'team' after Tidge met an untimely end but he had allowed a maniac to think he had power in the streets and look where it got him. As far as Steven was concerned they could all burn, and he wouldn't mind being the one holding the match.

He waited for the perfect moment to present itself and watched as Lance climbed into his Bugatti, started the engine and pulled out of the car park on the main road, neatly sliding out behind another car. Steven waited until he had picked up speed and once there was an oncoming vehicle, he expelled a huge amount of energy in two directions at once making sure to isolate two things, Lance's right hand on the steering wheel and the acceleration pedal. The effect was immediate and devastating, Steven allowed himself to drop away from the car to watch the glorious show as Lance crashed into the oncoming bus, thinking to himself grimly that Lance would likely be regretting not wearing his seatbelt as he was propelled through his own windscreen and consequentially speared by the bus's own smashed screen. The blood spatter was reminiscent of a scene from a horror movie and the dazed expressions from the still conscious passengers sprawled across the bus only heightened the grisly scene.

With another task ticked off his to do list Steven felt better, at least that was one less person to stand in his way in his journey to exact revenge upon Yeti. Steven felt his job here was done and allowed the darkness that was tugging at him to take him away.

Chapter Forty-Three

Steven found himself in his mums' house and felt a moment of relief. He had wondered if he was ever to reach her again after the disastrous events over on Newstation Road and the idea of trying to find a new vessel in time, unaided, seemed unachievable. He was glad to see his mum too but he wasn't ashamed to acknowledge that his main source of happiness in this moment was knowing they could formulate a new plan. His doubts in her abilities still lingered but this was one of the rare occasions where he was willing to overlook them and be proved wrong and as they say, third time lucky. His mum and aunt Alicia sat together on the sofa talking in hushed tones with sombre expressions. His mum suddenly stopped and tilted her head in the fashion she did every time he had been nearby, she gave a small smile and Alicia looked around the room curiously,

"What is it Mattie? Is he here?" she asked quietly.

"Yes he is. Steven show us it is you." She said.

Steven assessed the surroundings and settled on Alicia's phone sat on the small table next to the sofa, he channelled his focus and had a moment of reflection about how everything was using less and less of his energy – either he exerted less to complete actions or he was just stronger he wasn't sure – and then lightly pushed the phone across the table and stopped it just shy of tipping off onto the rug. Alicia put her hands to her mouth and looked to Martha,

"Can I speak with him like I spoke with Ross?" she asked.

Steven was taken aback by this, although his mum's true abilities of this nature hadn't been revealed until after he had died he was surprised at how open Alicia suddenly sounded about it all. She had often called anything out of the ordinary 'hocus pocus'.

"That would probably be the best way for us to talk about what we have been discussing. Are you ready now?"

Alicia nodded back at her, clasped her hands on her lap and exhaled slowly giving away her nerves, Martha smiled gently at her then stood up and went about setting up, muttering under her breath about needing more candles. Soon the ambience in the room was set and Alicia deeply inhaled the scent of frankincense, having now associated the scent with her son. They both sat cross legged on the floor facing each other, eyes closed and holding hands. Martha began the ritual by requesting the protection once more from the powers above her and prevention of intrusions from unwanted guests but then stopped.

Steven waited for the connection to be open, and wondered why his mum had paused after the initial requests, then she continued to speak with a more sombre voice.

"I wish to extend my thanks to the powers above that I cannot see for keeping me and my loved ones safe and continuing to keep at bay the spirit that wished us harm."

Steven looked on and saw Alicia nodding and realised that his mum must have filled her in on everything, including the plans involving Tim.

"I call upon my son, the spirit of Steven Tawn to enter our circle and connect with us, using me as the vessel of communication."

He felt everything shift and a strong draw towards his mum, he allowed it and found himself in inky blackness.

"Steven please confirm you can hear and communicate with us." His aunt said with a slight tremor in her voice.

"I'm here. Hi auntie Alicia, good to see you here with mum."

"I am pleased to experience this side of your mums life finally, even if it was brought about in the worst way imaginable. Not only do I speak to you once more, I have spoken to Ross too."

"I'm sorry about Ross, he was brave to the end."

"You saw him?" she asked, shock in her voice.

He realised his mum maybe didn't fill her in on every detail, but then again there was so much to tell it was probably not intentionally omitted.

"I did and I hurt the guy that did it too. I guess you know by now this is all down to that scum Yeti who is still roaming the streets." He hissed.

"I heard, I need your help Steven, I know it is a big ask but I want you to try again. We must avenge your deaths. Your mother and I have been planning and if she can get Tim to on talking terms again we will try with him, but that'll be a hard task. Otherwise, we need to find another suitable vessel. I don't want to disrupt the life of someone undeserving though, that just wouldn't be right." She said.

"I'm down, Yeti is in trouble and we need to move fast. The word has officially been given to take him out and we don't get to claim our revenge if someone else kills him."

"Your mum is going to go and see Tim today. Stick around and we will see what is happening."

"You got it. See you." Steven said and disconnected from the séance.

The urge to go and see if he could find Yeti and make sure no-one else was closing in on him yet was too strong to ignore, he felt bad not to stick around and speak to his mum but he could see they had it all in hand for now. He pulled away and looked over them once more and they were looking a little dazed, emotions high. He forced himself to leave despite the strange pull trying to keep him here, and was suddenly propelled out of the house and down the street, the bricks and concrete whizzing past at what would be a nauseating rate for anyone with a stomach.

He couldn't keep track of where he was going and he wasn't even following pathways, he was melting through all the buildings and countless faces flashed up at him with looks of horror and surprise as though they could see him. He came to an abrupt stop outside a block of flats he knew very well, it was one of his hangouts before being ripped from the land of the living. Shells lived on the bottom floor in flat five, he wondered why he was here and anger started to simmer as the possible reasons why started to filter in.

Without pause he moved around the building to Shells' living room window and moved through the glass with ease these things had become a second nature to him now and were hardly a novelty. He saw what he didn't want to see, Yeti was tearing the room apart, he was obviously looking for something and he was pissed. He stormed into the bedroom and tore the whole room up, swearing loudly to himself before pulling his phone out of his pocket and dialling someone. It rang a couple times before a female voice picked up and Steven quickly connected himself to hear them better,

"Hey baby what's up?" came the drawling sound of what Steven assumed was Yeti's girlfriend, he was surprised that she was still with him or even alive at this point after all he had been witnessing with Yeti.

"I need you to put some feelers out to find that rat Shells." He barked.

"Sure thing honey, I heard his friend was killed the other day though so maybe he is laying low?" she asked. Steven wondered why she referred to his death as only being the other day, it was weeks ago.

"Idiot. I know. Who do you think took him out? Prick stole from me, broke into my place and stole my gear! Turns out it was them who smashed up my baby too, don't you think they deserve to pay?" Steven felt everything darken as he realised it wasn't him she was referring to.

"I heard it was you but you know how it is, a lot of talk not much truth. So, it was a failed revenge story, they tried to get you back for killing Brute and now they both end up dead. You are the king baby." She spewed, Steven could tell she was saying what he wanted to hear and he wasn't sure if it was out of fear or love. Had to be the former because there was no way someone could truly love someone like Yeti.

"You better remember that, later, king Jake is coming for you." He replied.

It was too much for Steven to watch and he was absolutely furious, if what they were saying was true it meant he had killed Grid. He allowed the rage to explode out of him and Yeti's head snapped back in a cartoonish fashion as the force hit him, his phone flew from his hand and smashed into the wall behind him, then his body followed and he crashed down. Shock flashed across Yeti's face not just at being abruptly pulled from his nausea inducing attempt at sweet talking his missus but at the fact the powerful invisible force he had written off as a hard trip the previous times was back.

Steven wished he could laugh out loud for Yeti's ears to hear him and relished the thought that the time was still coming and when it did the laugh would be victorious and deserved. He could feel his energy was heavily drained and his vision faded away slowly as he listened to Yeti roaring in pure rage.

Chapter Forty-Four

Martha tamped down the anxiety that was creeping through her chest and up into her throat, restricting her breathing. She was walking down the street to Tim's home hoping to catch him there, speak with him and patch things up somehow. She needed him back onside, there was no reason for him to suspect anything of her other than minor incompetence and thanks to the banishment of Keith that would no longer be an issue, she just had to make him see it. She was nervous though and knew it was because Tim had made his feelings abundantly clear towards her, and although she had heard he was released from questioning now he hadn't reached out to her, but she wasn't surprised. He had called her a witch and she needed reassure him she was anything but, however it was imperative she calmed herself before getting there though or she would have no chance of connecting with him, a task that felt insurmountable already.

She focused on deep breathing exercises and made conscious decisions on where she placed her foot within the paving slab each time as she paced forwards. It worked and her breathing eased up just as she reached his front door. She drew in one more breath, filled her lungs then lifted her hand to the door ready to announce her presence when she heard someone clear their throat behind her making her jump and exhale harshly.

"Can I help?" Tim said with a cocked eyebrow and downturned mouth.

"Hi Tim, I just needed to come and apologise to you for well, just about everything I'd say." She offered with a self-depreciating shrug and half smile.

"Right. Noted." He replied coldly.

"I have to tell you that I didn't know that all of that could happen, I really believed that the evil spirit that possessed you was gone already and that you wouldn't be at risk. I feel terrible because you were just trying to experience something special and I wasn't able to protect you."

She allowed a slight hint of pleading to come into her tone and turned her body to face him properly. She could see his hard resolve wavering a bit and waited for him to decide his next words. He was clearly mulling over what to say in response and was looking at her with an unreadable expression but Martha was just grateful that he was actually taking the time to think about a response rather than just cutting her down.

"Ok then, I hear you. I understand and don't really blame you personally but I have to question why an evil spirit was hanging around you anyway. You're not quite the person I thought you were."

"I guess I haven't been completely forward about everything but like you it takes me time to trust and confide in someone after a lifetime of feeling it wasn't possible. I didn't think something like an old entity targeting and killing my best friend decades ago, who waited for me to let my guard down to attack, was something I could just casually bring up and not be thought of as crazy. Like I say, I am sorry for everything. I know you cannot forgive me and I don't expect you to, I just couldn't rest knowing I hadn't told you how I felt."

"I guess you are right about one thing; I would have thought you were lying or crazy. You couldn't rest? You look pretty well rested to me." Tim remarked.

"You know what I mean." Martha said and let out a low laugh, "Anyway, I'll be off. Thank you for being there when I needed someone anyway."

"Don't think about it. Seriously. I must get going anyway I need to sort my paperwork for a meeting at the new office tomorrow with the agent. I've not met her before so I need to have my A game on because it's likely she'll be clueless." Tim said with a shrug. he didn't say anything further and walked past her, opened his door and clicked it shut behind him without so much as a glance back at the woman who a mere few days before had come to feel like a friend.

Martha stood and looked at the door for a moment feeling low and mulling over what she could have said to make that go better, when she had a moment of clarity and realised he had said something that gave them a window of opportunity if they were bold enough to take it. Question was, were they bold enough? Would she be able to get Alicia on board with such a radical, risky idea? It would definitely mean that if they managed to work out a way to execute what she had just envisioned they would be well on their way to their original goal again. Meaning that by tomorrow evening at the latest revenge will have been dealt and they could revert back to living their olds lives again, the fragile balance of karma restored.

She turned on her heel and jogged back home with her heart racing in her chest and breathing quickened, but this time it wasn't anxiety about going to speak to someone she knew was angry with her, it was anxiety about the plan she was formulating. Whether it failed or succeeded there was a huge amount of auric cleansing that would be required for all of them if they had any hope of not being tarnished with a dark soul and potentially earthbound when they passed.

There was nothing worse in Martha's mind than becoming the same thing that Keith was, having to feed off the energy of the living to sustain a pitiful existence trapped to this one plane, she looked forward to the day she could join the spirit realm and see the universe. Gaze upon it in all its glory without the limitations of what tiny amount the human eye could see, she knew in her core the moment would be more than anyone can take in and she could spend her eternity just absorbing it all. The idea that she could be tethered here for the rest of time terrified her and she would do everything in her power to both help her son, and avoid that damnation.

Chapter Forty-Five

He sat in his cruiser cradling his head in his hands. The area was bustling and he had his superior looking over his shoulder at him every couple of minutes presumably to check he was ok. His head was pounding and he wondered why the hell Yeti hadn't just killed him too, he kind of wished he had to be frank, then he wouldn't have to deal with this horrific acidic pit of self-hatred that was bubbling in his core.

He had come around to be faced with paramedics buzzing around and a young female paramedic hanging over the top of him checking to see if his eyes dilated. She had started spieling off questions like if he remembered his name, the date, why he was here. He answered all of them dully and he asked if officer Bridges was ok. He knew he wasn't but on some level he was hoping that the scene he had witnessed before was wrong somehow and he wouldn't have to feel the guilt he was being crushed by. The paramedic had simply looked at him sympathetically and shook her head and moved away. Not long after that two of his colleagues had come and helped him over to his car and sat him down, neither of them looking at him properly or saying anything, something was up and officer Gord could only wait to see what was coming.

It didn't take long, his superior came ambling over with a serious expression. He was a six-foot tall and built like a tank, but his older age and desk job meant he was looking a little softer round the edges of late. He had the thick crop of hair on his head, more salt than pepper and a steely glint in his eye that only hinted at the fierce spirit he possessed that got him into the rank he held.

"Gord." He grunted as he came to a stop in front of him, looking down at Gord's pitiful form and split cheek being held together with medical tape.

"Sir." He replied looking up with a grimace as more pain shot through his face and skull.

"Looks like one of you got a lucky hit to the head and one didn't. We lost a good man today and we need answers, what happened?" he asked.

Gord tried to work out which one got the lucky hit because it didn't feel like it was him right now.

"A robbery sir, officer Bridges came to get lunch and I waited in the cruiser. He radioed me telling me there was a hostage situation and to come over. I did and the scene that greeted me was what you see now."

"Was the culprit still present?" he asked staring him down.

"I didn't see him and thought he wasn't on the scene. I was wrong." Gord lied, internally kicking himself. This was his chance to try and right all his wrongs and still he was protecting himself and for what?

"Why didn't you call it in the moment officer Bridges reported to you?" he pushed.

"I don't know, I just tried to get here as soon as possible." He replied.

"How could it have taken so long that the lives of two young men were lost, if you were simply parked up out here?" he asked gesturing angrily at the car,

"I wasn't parked outside here sir, I was two streets over. I don't know why officer Bridges chose to walk over here instead of using another place." There was silence for a moment as both men looked at each other and eventually Gord spoke again, "Sir?"

"You're suspended effective immediately whilst this case is under investigation officer Gord. Step down. Get yourself checked out and go home. We will contact you when needed."

With that Gord had been dismissed, his heart hung heavy in his chest but with the negligence he had shown his boss he was capable of today, a simple suspension was getting off lightly – for now anyway.

He realised they would likely check the cameras and then his fate would be sealed anyway. There was absolutely nothing he could do now that wouldn't draw suspicion, and thanks to the suspension he couldn't even go into his office or access records without risking immediate dismissal. He stood up on unsteady legs and looked around him once more, aware that everyone in the vicinity was studiously avoiding looking at him and would have undoubtedly heard the interaction he had just had. He knew he deserved it, he deserved far worse in fact. He went and sat in the back of the ambulance and waited for someone to come to him and clean him up again, he could feel the bandage and tape on his cheek was soaked through and wondered if he needed stitches or glue. One of the paramedics came over to fix him up and avoided any eye contact or discussion with him, their only concern was making sure he didn't have concussion so he could drive home.

Chapter Forty-Six

Alicia pulled up round the corner from the offices with Martha in the passenger seat. They hadn't spoken much on the way here, both of them were wrought with nerves for the coming task. It wasn't going to be an easy one and it could go wrong in multiple ways, in fact the chances of pulling this off without a hitch was nigh on impossible. They had called the agents to find out availability for viewing and there were only two slots booked, but not who was booked for which.

They had come here for the one at nine with the hope that this wasn't Tim's, as getting rid of the agent before he arrived would have been a lot harder. Thankfully luck was on their side and it was some middle-aged lady. Grateful that luck was still on their side they called the agency again and pretended to be Tim's receptionist, claiming he was stuck working all day and would call to reschedule. It seemed the plan was running smoothly again, indicating they were in fact doing the right thing.

They'd thought long and hard about how they would incapacitate Tim, in the end they decided to go completely old school, providing she timed it right and held on tight they would be on the home run. The best part of that would be that Steven wouldn't have to take over a drug addled body, but it did require a lot more physical input and risk.

Alicia looked at the time on the clock, it was nearly midday which was the time they needed to be there, she took in a deep breath and readied herself then stepped out of the car and gave a small nod to Martha before turning around and walking round to the entrance. She brushed down the front of her two-piece suit she had chosen to wear today in a bid to look more professional, she had initially been in a pair of slacks and a blouse but the agent they saw this morning was suited up and she didn't want to raise suspicions just because she wore the wrong attire. She went and stood by the door, knowing that Tim would likely be smack bang on time and not a minute late nor early. She tapped her pocket nervously to check she had her weapon of choice handy and then crossed her hands back in front of her, making sure to stand straight backed ready for his arrival. True to expectation he pulled up directly outside the door as the nearby church sounded its bells and he climbed out with a slightly smug expression and looked Alicia up and down.

"You the agent?" he asked with a raised brow.

"That's me, Sally Ower. Pleased to meet you Mr Panel." She said with more confidence than she knew she had and extended her hand, mostly grateful that she remembered the name of the agent he was supposed to be meeting today and didn't stutter.

He bought it, and shook her hand firmly but let go rapidly as though her touch was too much.

"Let us go in, shall we?" Tim said and gestured at the door.

Alicia made a show of smiling and putting her hand in her pocket for the keys, then gasping in surprise when they came out empty handed.

"You have got to be kidding me. The amount of money I'll be giving you lot and you can't even remember a simple key." He scorned.

"I'm so sorry sir, I must have left them in the car or office. I can head back or we can go in the buildings side entrance, your call." She said. He looked at her distastefully and shook his head.

"I don't want to waste my time, the side entrance is fine."

Alicia smiled sweetly and nodded, then turned on her heel and click-clacked to the end of building and stood at the top of the alley that led down to the side entrances of all the offices in the building. She looked back at him and smiled, then looked at the floor and moaned a little,

"Oh dear, hold on there is some glass here let me clean it up, luckily I always carry a bag with me!" she said cheerily, Tim scowled at her as she pulled her bag out of her pocket and shook it out.

"Why the hell would you bother? I'll meet you at the door, I must say this is most unprofessional."

Alicia nodded at him and moved to one side, glad he didn't look down and see there wasn't any glass there at all. Now she could pull the bag out without raising his suspicion there was not far off the grand finale. She quickly looked around the area to make sure there was no-one around and once positive they were alone she followed him and stood about half a metre away. She pulled her phone out of her pocket,

"Just going to get the entry code up one moment." She said as he rolled his eyes impatiently, Alicia realised Martha hadn't been exaggerating about his character. She fumbled the phone and it fell onto the floor, she looked at it in dismay. "Sorry sir, I have a terrible back at the moment and picking up the rubbish back there," she waved the bag for good measure, "has made it flare up. Could you pass me my phone?"

He started muttering under his breath, patience clearly run out and bent down to get her phone. Alicia took her opportunity, thankful that her interaction with him had been so vile that he made this easy. She grabbed a handle of the bag in each hand and brought it up swiftly over his head, quickly twisting her arms as she ran round him and jumped up onto his back, feeling nimbler than she had in years and then held tight.

What ensued reminded her of riding the electric bull at fairgrounds when she was a teenager, she had been pretty good at those and her skill didn't fail her now as Tim flailed around trying to wrench her hands away but the action only tightened the bag. It suctioned to his face as he gasped for air and she felt him weaken very quickly, within moments his knees buckled and he fell unconscious. She released her hold quickly, panting for breath from the exertion but completely exhilarated, then checked his pulse. Good, still breathing. She picked her phone up off the floor and drop called Martha, the plan was for her to bring the car round to the front of the building and they would drag Tim's unconscious form to it. She wasn't sure how long he would stay unconscious for and felt her nerves increase again. Martha must have been waiting anxiously as she pulled up less than thirty seconds later and raced out of the car to her side.

"I don't know if we've given ourselves enough time, I think we may have to do it here. It'll be harder to tune out the outside world but doable, Steven is here and he is ready. Are you?" Martha said at an alarming speed.

"I was thinking something similar. Let's do this and avenge our boys!" she replied, feeling a burning strength in her core.

Martha scrambled back to the car and pulled out her bag, she brought out some sandalwood incense sticks and balanced one between some stones and lit it carefully with some matches from her pocket.

"Ready as we're ever going to be, let's do it." She said and sat down next to Tim's unconscious form whilst hoping the crude manner in which they were carrying out this ritual would be sufficient.

Alicia followed her lead and knelt down next to her waiting for instructions. Martha reached forwards and took one of her hands, and placed her other on Tim's chest. She nodded at Alicia to do the same. Martha then closed her eyes and she copied her, taking deep breaths.

"I call upon all powers above me to protect us from any entity that wishes us harm and guide the soul of Tim as he enters the afterlife. I call upon the spirit of Steven Tawn to come in readiness to accept this vessel being gifted by Tim." Tim's body started to move a little, shifting as the energies began to move around. "I implore the powerful energies above to assist in this transition, grant us the power and remove the undeserving energy from the gift that is a physical vessel. He balances between life and death in this moment and his connection to his form is fragile. Please protect us and give us strength in this moment of need!"

Martha's voice rose as the power within her grew and she could feel the battle of energies happening next to her, Tim was being summoned from his body and Steven was trying to slide in, in his place. Martha could see already they hadn't pushed Tim far enough.

"Alicia! It isn't going to work! We need to push him further away from his body whilst his tether to it is weakened, where is the bag?" Martha cried.

Alicia let go of Martha's hand and immediately she felt the connection weakening but it was a necessity to facilitate the next step. She grabbed the bag and pushed it down over his face again, Tim's already quickened breath made short work of pushing him further into unconsciousness. Alicia waited a touch longer this time whilst Martha waited with baited breath, and sighed with relief when her sister removed the plastic once more and they could see Tim's chest rise and fall. If they'd been bold enough killing him would have made it easier but neither were willing to murder someone, plus the body would have been much weaker for Steven to take over even if the transition took mere seconds.

"Powers above, I take unto myself the cost of this soul transaction, please remove the energy holding on to this vessel and allow the repossession of the form to occur from a new source."

Tim's body jolted violently and suddenly, causing both women to jump. It fell still once more then his fingers started to twitch, Alicia looked at Martha, hardly daring to breathe. Although in a weakened state, if this was still Tim they were in a lot of trouble. His eyes fluttered open and then shut again rapidly, then slowly this time he opened his eyes and squinted.

"Shit that's bright." He muttered.

Martha burst into tears and fell onto his chest unable to hold herself back. Alicia looked on with a mixture of awe and sadness, happy that her sister had her son back but unable to hide her pain that hers could never do the same. She reflected on how terrifyingly easy that was in the end, to have your soul wrenched from your body and have another replace it. Perhaps it was meant to be and the powers above them granted them the means to achieve it, or perhaps Mattie's own spiritual powers were just powerful enough to accomplish the banishment. Either way, it left her with a strong sense of unease and a wondering to what the true cost of what they had just done was.

Chapter Forty-Seven

It had been a day since they'd managed to get Steven into Tim's body and he was now moving around with next to no effort, although he now fully appreciated the amount of energy it took to physically move again. He had mentioned this to his mum and she said that Keith had said something similar and had in fact been quite easy to expel from Tim's body, because he simply didn't want it anymore. He understood in a way, the only real reason he wanted to be in a physical form again was so he could exact revenge on Yeti. Now he had experienced a small taste of the other side and the freedom of not being physically bound to the earth they stood on, he felt almost claustrophobic. He couldn't imagine how restrictive it must have felt to someone like Keith who had been dead for decades.

As soon as they'd got back to his mums he had wanted to get out and hunt Yeti down, but heeded her advice to hold fire for a day until he was steady otherwise he'd likely get himself killed again, she had cried heavily when saying this as though the idea of him dying twice was too much to bear.

Now he was feeling more in control he wanted to get out there and find Yeti before the big bosses did, they would have had to deal with the sudden unexpected passing of Lance for a day or two but the clock was ticking down and Yeti was just about out of time. He left his old room and walked over to speak to his mum who was busying herself in the kitchen with tea, humming an old lullaby like nothing had happened. It was surreal, real life didn't feel real anymore.

"I'm going to go and track him down. I need to swing by my old place, have you got the spare key?" he said. His mums humming stopped and her stance changed.

"I do, what do you need from there?" she asked without turning around.

"What do you think?"

"Maybe I should have cleared it out before and stopped paying your rent." She said, finally turning to look at him. "I have been thinking. Maybe this whole revenge thing isn't the right thing to do, you have a life again and a second chance, something no-one ever gets. What will revenge do?" she implored.

"That was the whole point in us doing this mum! Do you think he should get off free then?"

"No, but he has plenty of other people who are going to do the very same thing you're setting out to do. Let them do it, don't dirty your hands further." She replied with tears in her eyes. "I don't want more death on our hands, I finally got you back and I don't want to lose you. I also don't want to suffer eternal damnation because we got so stuck in the eye for an eye mentality. Your aunt agrees, she wants you to just live your life."

"It isn't an eye for an eye, he killed two members of our family and a friend! He deserves to die by *my* hand." Steven shouted.

Steven stormed out of the door without another word whilst Martha stood in shock, speechless. He allowed his frustration to carry him all the way to his old flat and he picked up some of the junk mail that was sticking out the post box, they weren't fancy flats and their security wasn't expensive, he picked the sturdiest looking envelope in the pile and slid it down the crack between the door and frame until he felt the mechanism pop, then let himself into his old home.

It was musty in here and he didn't plan to stick around long, just long enough to grab his Beretta 9000 pistol and hit the streets to find his foe. Despite what his mum said he knew what he needed to do, he would never feel peace if he didn't. A sound stopped him in his tracks and he paused to listen, someone was here and it sounded like they were snoring, he smiled lightly to himself, maybe it was Yeti? That seemed incredibly unlikely though so who the hell was in his place and using it to crash no less?

He crept further in and looked at the sofa surprised to see the sleeping form of Shells slumped in the corner. Making a quick plan he tiptoed into his bedroom and got his gun out of the secret compartment in his wardrobe and tucked it into his belt, then went back out past the sleeping Shells and out the front door. He knocked loudly on the door three times, making sure it would be heard by his snoozing friend. He put his ear to the door and listened, he could hear him stirring and moving around but for obvious reasons not saying anything. Worst case he probably thought Yeti had found him.

"Shells? I know you're in there. I was a friend of Brute's. I need some info mate can you help?"

"How the fuck did you know I was in here?" Shells shouted.

"I came in, saw you. I chose to come back out and knock to show you I am not a threat. If I wanted you dead I'd have killed you ten minutes ago." He said bluntly.

He could practically hear the cogs turning in Shells head as he tried to find out another way this unexpected visitor could have known he was there. He clearly came up blank as the door soon clicked open and Shells stood there bleary eyed and looked Steven up and down with barely concealed contempt.

"Why would Brute be friends with someone like you?"

"Old neighbours. He probably didn't mention me."

"No. He didn't." came the flat reply. "What do you want?"

"Let me in and I'll talk to you." Steven said and Shells begrudgingly moved aside and closed the door behind him.

"What's your name? You called him Brute but say you were old neighbours, explain it." Shells said.

"Tim. We were neighbours, I also knew him as Steven. He was my supplier so I got used to using his street name." Steven replied, feeling some amusement watching Shells try to work out what was happening.

"What do you want?"

"I want to kill Yeti." He replied bluntly.

"Yeah well, don't we all." Came the bitter reply of Shells.

"I will. I just need to know where he is, I will go right now if you can tell me."

"Shit, you're serious. Weird Brute never mentioned you, you talk like him too. I do know one way we can track him down. His missus, she was with my buddy Grid on the side, she's scared to leave Yeti in case he does something to her. If we call her she'll probably tell us where he is."

Steven had to suppress his surprised expression, once again he realised how much he had underestimated Grid. He nodded in response and Shells pulled his phone out of his pocket, barely able to conceal his growing excitement at the unfolding events. He scrolled his contacts for a moment before finding the right one, he was smiling darkly as the line connected. Steven had a second of missing being able to connect directly with the soundwaves and listen in but settled for just standing close by.

"Yo girl, you clear?" Shells asked as soon as the line connected.

"Yeah what's up? What do you want?" she asked, her abrasive tone audible from where Steven was standing.

"I've got you an out, where's your man?"

"You don't. No one does. He is down in his spot for once unlike you, he has been looking for you." She replied.

"Yeah I know, me and Grid messed with him a bit and it looks like he managed to work it out. Cheers for the info love, you might have some good news soon." Shells said and hung up without a goodbye. He looked at Steven.

"You catch that Tim? You know where his spot is?" he asked.

"Yeah I know where it's at. You wanna tag?"

"I wouldn't miss this." Shells said, walked to the sofa and crouched down to pull out a shotgun he had stashed down the side. Steven laughed, some things never changed.

"Dibs first shot between the eyes." He said and Shells shrugged and smirked.

"If you can do it, fine."

They headed out the door together and for a moment it felt like old times to Steven, except his companion had no idea who he was and he knew he would never be able to explain it to him. They decided to go on foot rather than pulling up in Shells' car and giving Yeti the heads up, Shells pulled his neck warmer up and hood down, leaving just his eyes exposed. They were ready.

Chapter Forty-Eight

He determinedly trudged towards his destination and counted each step. He lost track after two hundred or so because he kept getting distracted but he had found it to be some comfort to try to keep track, like a kind of meditation. He knew what he had to do, there was no doubt in his mind because there was no escape now. Thanks to his misplaced confidence in Yeti always being on top he didn't ever bother to cover his tracks too carefully, just the lightest tug on one of the threads that kept his metaphorical bag of lies, theft and cover ups contained and hidden, would cause everything to come pouring out in a sordid mess. If all that he had done to protect this reprobate was found out, he would lose everything he had worked towards, he would have to leave the force he had spent so long in, in shame. He couldn't bear the thought and had to do something to right his wrongs, he wasn't even courageous enough to speak up when his boss was talking to him despite him making it clear he knew something was amiss. He knew he could never go back, it was just a waiting game now to see what they'd dug up on him.

Gord patted his pocket to check his readiness for what lay ahead and ignored the heavy bolt of fear that shot through his heart. He had made his bed now he needed to lay in it, the death of officer Bridges was the nail in the coffin for him, he wouldn't be dead if he had helped him and not tried to dissuade him from doing his job properly. He'd obviously lost faith in Gord, shown by the fact he had gone out of his way to investigate the area solo.

Once again he had lost count of the steps he was taking but it didn't matter, he could see the place he had been aiming for now. He saw a man hunched over on the bench ahead of him and despite the overly baggy clothing the man donned he could see it was who he was looking for, he pushed forwards and came level with him. Yeti, cocky as ever, didn't even bother to look up right away making it clear who he thought was boss, making him wait.

"What do you want?" he eventually said before looking back down to his lap to resume rolling a joint.

"What do you think I want?" Gord said, and Yeti grimaced at him.

"Jeez man you stink, did you bathe in whiskey?" he sneered, looking at the stained and crumpled police uniform his unwanted visitor wore.

"I might have had a drink or two so what? I meant what I said before, you have gone too far and it's over."

"Fuck off." He spat and stood up. "If it wasn't for me you'd still be scrabbling around pathetically trying to skim confiscated goods. You owe me."

"No Yeti. The amount I've done for you and covered for you, you are in my debt now. I don't want a part of this anymore."

"You can't walk away from me." Yeti sneered and advanced.

Gord took two quick steps back and was grateful his inebriated state didn't make him stumble. His training from back in the day kicked in and he whipped out his old Glock 17 and took quick aim. He took a split second of satisfaction from the look of disbelief that crossed Yeti's face before it crunched up in an angry snarl. He didn't get a chance to speak as Gord shot him neatly in the middle of his forehead. He didn't care about the screams that pierced the air because they wouldn't matter in a moment anyway.

He watched Yeti fall to the ground, eyes rolling back in his head and the hole in his head tiny and black, not yet filled with blood. He fell face first in slow motion and the noise of his body crunching into the pavement mixed with the screaming created a strange cacophony of noise and he could feel his ears ringing. Every blink was heavy and made a thudding noise, wasting no time and with his adrenaline pounding through him he put the gun to his own head and pulled the trigger once more, the sudden pain nothing compared to the relief he felt at the blackness that enveloped him.

He didn't see the two men running up to the scene shouting angrily at him, or the black SUV that drove past the scene slowly with tinted windows, the boss behind it looking out at the macabre scene with a satisfied nod that the matter had resolved itself and he didn't have to get his hands dirty. Gord didn't get the life flashing before his eyes like he thought he would. The blackness was absolute and there was no pain but he realised that he could kind of hear things still too and this was confusing, it took a moment to register that he must just not be dead yet and was in fact in the process of dying, and this brought him peace too. Slowly but surely the sounds faded around him and he was welcomed into the other side at last.

Chapter Forty-Nine

Steven emitted an unholy roar of rage as he stood looking down at the mess before him. The police officer was lying dead on the floor with a stream of blood trickling out the exit wound behind his ear and Steven fought the desire to shoot extra bullets into him for taking away his right to kill Yeti. Of all people to do it, it should have been him and not some bent cop. He turned his furious gaze to the second body staining the concrete and his anger became too much to bear, he lunged forwards and kicked the inert figure of Yeti in the side of the head causing the blood that was now steadily oozing from his forehead to spray violently across the pavement and Shells yelped as he jumped out of the way.

"Come on man let's get out of here!" Shells said, and pulled his arm but Steven yanked it away again.

He couldn't leave it like this, he felt hollow like everything was a huge waste of time and he didn't know what to do. Justice had been stolen from him just like his life had been and now he wasn't even able to get the satisfaction of revenge. He glared down at Yeti's sightless face once more and spat at the ground next to him then turned on his heel and walked away just as the sirens could be heard around the corner. Shells was bouncing on the spot eager to move but not wanting to bail without him, Steven took pity on him and they jogged down the street and all the way over to the park not far from his mums place. It was deserted except for the old guy snoozing on the hill and they sat to catch their breath.

"Shit man, I can't believe that. Never would've seen that coming, I guess it saves us getting our hands dirty. You wanna know something weird? I was going to head to my mums place out of town whilst Yeti was looking for me, and something stopped me. I guess it was for this, seeing Yeti get his comeuppance." Shells said with a small smile, but he could tell from the darkened expression on Steven's face the silver lining he pointed out wasn't one he cared for.

They each sat on a less than stable looking swing and listened to the now distant sounds of the sirens, whoever called it in probably said there was a police officer down so they'd have sent all sorts over.

"I wanted to be the one to do it." Steven said simply.

"Come on Tim can't we say revenge has been had, he is dead isn't that all that matters? At least now if any police start sniffing around they won't be coming for you."

"Sure, but I don't care anyway. I've seen what's on the other side of this life and now I'm wondering if Yeti got off too easy." Shells stopped his rocking on the swing and looked at him with a frown, chewed his bottom lip and shook his head to himself. Steven saw it but didn't say anything.

"Grid and Brute can rest in peace now and we can run the streets like we used to. Ever since Yeti came on the scene and joined the crews it has been a mess."

"Yeah, you do that. See you around Shells." Steven said and stood up, clapping his old friend on the back and walking away without looking back.

He walked the few minutes over to his mums and let himself in and found her sat on the sofa nursing a hot drink. She looked up with a sad expression as he came through the door and waited for him to speak.

"He's dead." He said.

"I saw, they're reporting on the scene. You killed a police officer too?" she asked with a strained voice.

"No. I didn't kill either of them." He said unable to keep the anger from his tone, his mum looked confused.

"Officer Gord, the older officer who was supposed to be dealing with my case shot Yeti and then himself. He was the corrupt one, the reason so many have been killed." He shrugged. "He stole my revenge."

"No, I think this happened for a reason. I asked the higher powers to protect you and this was it, they made sure it wasn't you who pulled the trigger and have to live a life knowing you'd killed a man."

"I wouldn't have cared mum. If this was thanks to the protection of the higher powers then I don't want their protection. I don't want any of this to be honest, it was all a mistake. Keith was right, coming back to physically be in the land of the living isn't worth it." He said.

Martha looked like she had been slapped and struggled to control her tears.

"It is worth it. We got you back!"

"Sure, but that sounds very selfish to me mum. Maybe it should be a wake-up call for you that you should stop living through me and make a real life for yourself. I was a grown man running the streets and beating people down in the name of reputation and drugs, and you were proud of me. What does that tell you about yourself apart from the fact you can turn a blind eye when it suits?" he said angrily.

"How dare you! I dedicated my life to you and made so many sacrifices to get you back like you wanted."

"You made so many mistakes. Bringing me back was your idea, not mine." He said coldly, walked down the hallway into his old room and closed the door without another word.

He could hear her walking down the hallway and she stopped outside the door, thought better of it then walked away. He sighed to himself wondering what he was to do, this life held no appeal for him and he didn't want to be here anymore. He saw his own selfishness as well, he had been willing to steal someone's body from them, something that now felt like a huge waste of time and energy, especially as now Yeti was dead, he realised even if he had been the one to kill him he wouldn't have felt the release he had hoped for.

After cooling his heels for a while he would go and speak to his mum properly. He wouldn't apologise for what was said because he knew it to be true and she needed some home truths sometimes, even if they hurt.

Chapter Fifty

She brushed down the front of her woolly jumper and combed her hair quickly, checking her reflection in the small mirror on the side table before leaving. She looked around the room and spoke quietly,

"It's time."

She opened the front door and stepped out into the daylight, despite the ominous nature of her recent dealings they had taken her out of her comfort zone of the church and she was quite grateful to be out and about experiencing more again. She was rediscovering her love for helping those who had passed and it felt like she was being pushed in this direction by unseen forces.

Irene made good time walking to Martha's, she arrived at the door and took in the surroundings. The front was well tended with no weeds and there wasn't a flower out of place, it didn't surprise her in the slightest to see Martha was the type of woman to busy herself with such things. She knocked lightly and waited patiently for the door to open, it was pulled inwards a few moments later by a stressed looking Martha. Her mouth dropped open when she saw who was at her door.

"Irene! Hi, what are you doing here?" she asked and stepped out pulling the door to behind her so Irene couldn't see in.

"Martha, I have to speak with you and it is of the utmost importance that you listen to me. Can I come in?" she asked.

"Not right now I'm afraid, I'm entertaining." Martha replied, eyes darting around.

"I know you're not entertaining anyone Martha. Father Robins doesn't know I am here and I am not here to judge or change anything but you need to be aware that I know what has transpired." She said sternly and Martha's demeanour collapsed inwards slightly as she realised that Irene really did know everything just by looking in her eyes.

"It's over, isn't it?" Martha said in a quiet voice and stepped back to let Irene in.

Once inside they sat down on the sofas in the living area and Martha waited for Irene to speak.

"It is over, yes. You have made some very poor decisions recently as a result of a broken heart. We all know how this is and I don't pass judgement on such things but the powers above us do. Your auric energy and soul are dulled and severely damaged by all that has happened, you will need a lifetime of repentance to even begin to make it better."

"What do I do? Steven doesn't even want the body anymore, I've made grave mistake Irene. How did you know?"

"Tim followed your sister home, the lady he thought was a 'useless'," she said dramatically gesturing with her hands and smiling, "agent. Your mother happened to be there and you're not the only one in the family with the ability to speak with the other side it seems." Irene said and Martha's head shot up in surprise.

"What?" she asked.

"I guess she never told you. Anyway, Tim realised he could reach Jess and told her everything he saw after being evicted from his body. She came and sought advice from the church and luckily it was me who was there, I knew straight away it would be something to do with you. Tim followed her and I connected with him and he is very much at peace currently. You must know, his soul would never have been able to pass directly into the spirit realm under those circumstances, despite you wishing it so." Martha buried her head in her hands, it was all just too much to handle anymore. "Shall I continue?"

"Yes, I guess so. Let me go and get Steven first though." Martha said with a heavy sigh, she went down the hall and knocked lightly before opening the door and asking him to come out. Irene stood when he entered the room and nodded at him in greeting.

"Good, it makes sense that you're both present for this."

"He's here, isn't he?" Martha asked. Irene nodded in response.

"He won't be for long." She replied cryptically and Martha looked at her questioningly, whilst Steven just inclined his head to show he was listening. "He has made the decision that he doesn't want to come back into physical form anymore, he has had a couple of days in the other realm and been gifted with enlightenment. Once this conversation is over he will to transcend into the spirit realm and be free." She explained.

"What does this mean for me? I don't want this body anymore, I've had time to think about it and I think my time was just up and if it hadn't been Yeti who stabbed me something else would have happened. I can feel it deep within myself that this is the truth and whether it be fate or whatever, I don't want to be here anymore." Steven said.

Martha looked at him with a hurt expression but didn't say anything.

"Well, that is up to you. Tim has allowed you to keep his vessel and so you are bound to it as though it is your own. Death or possession is the only way you'll be able to be untethered again."

"Right." Came Steven's short reply as he tried to process everything.

"Don't you hear what she is saying Steven? You can live a new life again, this is your chance, Tim has given you this chance." Martha said, looking at her son hopefully.

"I don't want it mum. There is nothing in me that tells me I belong here anymore. I'm sorry, I'm not trying to hurt you. I hadn't thought past what would happen when Yeti died, I guess I just assumed I would go back to being dead and finally go to this spirit realm you told me about."

"Is that what you really want?" Martha asked tearfully whilst Irene watched on with great interest, sadness in her eyes.

"Yes." Came his simple reply.

"There is one other way and that would be to perform an exorcism on you right now, a fairly simple ritual as you're not the true energy meant for the vessel. It'll be easier than the ritual you carried out to possess Tim's body to start with. Both yourself and Tim will need to refrain from taking over the vessel and we would be left with an instance of sudden death. I would never recommend wasting the gift of a vessel but you know what your soul needs and both myself and Martha would be overstepping our rights to try to steer you. I will warn you, I believe that your tether to this earth has now been severed and once you leave Tim's body you will find you will go straight to the spirit realm so I'd say your goodbyes beforehand." She warned.

"Could I still reach him in a séance?" Martha asked, already certain that she knew what decision Steven was going to make. She didn't even know why she asked such a question when she knew she could, her emotions were threatening to overwhelm her.

"Yes you can, if he is willing to receive the connection, you know this already Martha please let us not lose our senses." Irene said, putting her hand on Martha's leg comfortingly.

"Of course I would mum. You should never question that." Steven said back with a frown reading her unsure expression. "Let's do it, I'm ready."

"OK, Martha do you have any lilac or white candles? Set the room a little bit?"

Martha nodded and went to collect the last white candle, it was almost finished now, as though it was meant for this purpose.

She brought it over but couldn't bring herself to take the next step and light it, seeing this Irene reached forwards and took the matches from her hand and did it for her.

"You'd be better off laying down." Irene said in a matter of fact tone.

"Right. See you on the other side, mum." He said and laid down next to the candle, the light flickering as he moved and disturbed the airflow around it.

Irene placed her hand on his chest and extended the other to Martha who hesitated but did the same. She knew she would never actually be ready for this moment but also knew she had to do the right thing, if he stayed it was clearly only because she was making him.

"Do you want to do this, or me?" Irene asked, and Martha realised she was giving her the option to balance out some of the wrongs. Her heart panged with pain as she spoke her next words,

"I will." She said, her voice cracking.

"Let us proceed then." Irene said quietly.

"I request protection from the powers above us and guidance as we remove the spirit that does not truly belong in this form. Allow us respite from those who wish us harm whilst we lay open the doors between our world and theirs. Steven Tawn, I command you to leave the vessel you inhabit!" she called out.

The air around her whirled strongly and she fought to maintain focus and not break the connection, she tried not to react as she watched the body that contained her son began to twitch and convulse. Tears streamed down her face as she watched the moment her sons spirit fully detached from Tim's body, he stood before her in his old form for a moment, looking down at her before smiling and nodding. He faded away too fast and Martha's heart was breaking all over again, she couldn't hold on anymore and her head fell forwards onto her chest and Irene put her hands out to support her.

"I request the protective powers above us to now close the connection between us and that which we cannot see. Guide the spirits that have come to join you in your planes and see over us as we heal from our journeys." Irene called out, the atmosphere in the room calmed down and she knew that they had finished their task and both Steven and Tim had gone. "Well done Martha, that is one big step towards redeeming yourself."

Martha laid down on the floor, her grief incapacitating her. Tim's body was no longer moving, the open connection was now closed and as Tim had agreed, he didn't take his body back. This meant the vessel would cease to function within a couple of minutes. Irene patted Martha on the shoulder,

"May I use your phone to call the services?" she asked.

Martha nodded dully and pointed up to the kitchen side. Irene went over and dialled 999 and asked for an ambulance to assist with a collapsed friend, knowing full well that the body would be dead by the time they arrived.

Chapter Fifty-One

Six months had passed since Steven had passed on, Martha was still taking it day by day. Every morning she woke she felt the weight of grief and all that had transpired lessen and she knew that the new path she was taking with Irene was vastly helping with that. This journey also meant she befriended someone who wasn't family and was doing as Steven had advised, living her own life. Alongside Irene she was running grief counselling sessions and coming to the assistance of any entities in the region who may wish to be heard, holding regular open séances for them to approach them.

So far they had helped a handful of spirits who had been travelling this plane aimlessly, most of the time it was simply because they wished for their loved ones to hear a message and just couldn't move on peacefully without knowing it'd been heard. It was a rewarding but sad path she had embarked on, but she finally felt she was answering her true calling and was grateful to Irene for her patient and forgiving nature. If she had to spend the rest of her days helping those lost souls to rectify her actions she would, and happily so – it didn't go unnoticed to her that she had got off mostly unscathed and she was ready to repay that kindness forever.

She hadn't contacted Steven yet and was waiting for the day to come when she felt she was ready. Alicia had taken the news well that all their effort to secure the body of Tim was effectively wasted, she took comfort from the fact that they had inadvertently helped Tim escape from a life that would never have truly made him happy. His cause of death had been exactly what Irene said it would be, SADS, otherwise known as sudden adult death syndrome.

Martha still hadn't confronted her mum about knowing she could converse with the other side and wasn't sure how she would broach it. It hurt her deeply that her mum watched her struggle for so many years with guilt and having to out her psychic abilities without saying a word to comfort or help, when she herself could do it and perhaps could have assisted her when needed.

She never heard from the police regarding Steven's murder and she knew they never would, they'd allow it to become a cold case despite knowing that it was Yeti especially as all parties involved were now dead and buried. His death had been all over the news for a week after he was shot by officer Gord, there had been so much speculation and many accusations flying around with that and no-one ever came forwards to clear it up. They found a heavily decomposed body in his flat, but that was hardly publicised despite its graphic nature. The streets had gone back to the way they were from what Martha could see but with newer and younger faces on the corners, being trained up to fill the roles of those who had died.

Ross's funeral finally went ahead and they claimed there was inconclusive evidence to arrest or charge anyone in the prison despite the camera footage. Seth had reported back to them that the guy who they refused to arrest for his murder had been put in isolation though because he kept rambling on about invisible forces haunting him. Martha had smiled at that and believed that may have been Steven's doing from before. Her phone rang and she looked at the screen,

"Martha? I have just had contact from a young teenage girl having trouble passing over and needing to find her family. Would you like to come assist?"

"Absolutely, I'll be right over." Martha said, and headed out the door ready to put her abilities to good use once more.

Printed in Great Britain
by Amazon